T0147561

Black Coffee

Black Coffee

A NOVEL

Jack Wennerstrom

iUniverse, Inc.
New York Bloomington

iUniverse books may be ordered through booksellers or by contacting:

iUniverse
1663 Liberty Drive
Bloomington, IN 47403
www.iuniverse.com
1-800-Authors (1-800-288-4677)

ISBN: 978-1-4401-3877-5 (sc)
ISBN: 978-1-4401-3878-2 (ebook)

Printed in the United States of America

iUniverse rev. date: 04/27/2009

To Donna

The truth is something desperate.
    — Tennessee Williams

Chapter 1

THEY WERE BOTH TALKING to him at once, but Gabriel Dent seemed not to be listening.

"So my friend knows this doctor who says most of these street people are schizophrenics anyway," chattered Heather, staring down at the blue rose tattoo on her wrist, then looking up suddenly and fixing Gabe with her panda gaze, set deep in purple eye-shadow. Erin sat beside her, twisting the crystal pendant at her neck, and chimed in, "Split personality, isn't it? Like in that movie, what was it? 'Sophie's Choice'? With Meryl Streep and that Jewish actor?"

Gabe put down his little cardboard packet of fries with the Burger King logo. He hadn't eaten a single one, and he pushed them over to the women without looking up. What he *had* eaten was the blueberry pie in its plastic container, a half-devoured portion, really, which he'd fished from the trash bin in the park earlier that day. Now he raised the empty container to the window light and examined the plastic closely. Only smears remained, smashed drops of violet jelly arranged like translucent Rorschachs. On the inside, though—dried and twisted against a bottom corner—was a bit of lost crust and berry. It somewhat resembled a fly, with its blackened center for a thorax and its pastry-shaving wings. He lowered the container, tipped his fork lightly, probed deftly like a dentist, caught the crumb on a prong. Then he ate it with lizard quickness, thrusting the fork toward his mouth with such violent suddenness that both women flinched.

Not even blueberry, he thought vaguely, and reached for one of his notebooks.

"Isn't it, Gabe?" persisted Erin, hoisting the crystal on its silver

1

chain and absently rubbing her cheek with it. "Split personality, I mean. Isn't that schizophrenia?"

Gabe lifted his baleful blue eyes from the notebook and stared at Erin deeply. With two fingers of one hand he twirled the end of his reddish mustache, and with two fingers of the other he pinched the bridge of his steel-rim glasses, then removed them with a grip through the lens-less left side of the frames and set them on the table.

"Not at all," he pronounced with measured solemnity. "It's not split personality, or double personality, or multiple, or any of those things." He raised a finger to the side of his head and shook it for dramatic emphasis. "That movie. 'Sophie's Choice.' Complete crap in its portrayal of schizophrenia. Like most popular representations of the illness."

"See, I told you!" snapped Heather, throwing Erin a put-down glance. "Schizophrenia is more complicated than that. Isn't it, Gabe?"

Gabe did not answer. He was studying his notebook, head bent near the table. The women toyed with their food. Finally, after so long a pause that they'd lost hope of an answer, he looked up and again shook his finger. "Yaahh. It's the most complex event in the world."

Erin had grown impatient. "So where's the stuff? The magic potion or whatever."

"The DROP," offered Heather.

"Yeah, the DROP."

Gabe reached down in the deep pocket of his coat and produced a brown A-1 Sauce bottle nicely scrubbed and refitted with a hand-printed label that read: "Defective Reality Oxidation Prophylactic". He presented it to Heather with an exaggerated magician's flourish, and both women frowned as they studied it. Then Heather reached in her jeans and handed him ten dollars.

"Does this stuff really work?" asked Erin in her skeptical whine. "I mean, for stuff like mood swings and depression, stuff like that."

"Of course it does," Heather bubbled defensively. "I told you I can vouch for that."

"Absolutely," Gabe reassured. "You've got to remember what Defective Reality is. I define it as, well... any of the brain's distorted perceptions brought about when the numerous subcellular membranes of the body, which contain a large amount of fatty acids and oils, are attacked by oxidation and therefore rancidity. My Defective Reality formula protects against that oxidation. It's, ah... the pure DROP, you might say."

Heather squinted her purple-ringed eyes. Erin giggled and twirled her crystal girlishly: "So what's in it?"

Re-gripping his glasses through the side with the missing lens, Gabe replaced them on his handsome nose and smiled wryly. "All I can tell you is it's herbal. Made from local Wisconsin plants. My dear,

the secret of my formula is what keeps me in business, isn't it?" He
dropped his gaze to his notebook and fell silent once more. The women
soon took their cue and rose from the table, sucking dry their Cokes
and setting the cups on the table. They swayed toward the front of the
restaurant, chattering blithely.

Erin had twisted and bent her plastic soda straw miserably, but
Heather's was perfectly intact, and Gabe plucked it from its container,
ran two fingers along its length with an appraiser's examining stroke,
then stuck it in one of the big pockets of his worn khaki coat. He saved
also the plastic pie box after giving it a thorough lick, rose abruptly,
swept along the condiment counter to grab up a handful of napkins
and corregated mini-packs of salt and pepper, then glided toward the
doors, half crouched, his pony-tailed chestnut hair bobbing at his back
as he stuffed each pocket of the coat which, oversized on his wiry
frame, flapped behind him like a cape. A table of gray-haired men in
jogging shoes stared at him briefly as he passed, and a lone woman in
cranberry sweatpants turned away in her seat and fixed her eyes on the
wall as the wake of Gabe's coat brought a sudden breeze, lifting the
napkin in front of her.

Gabe left the Burger King, hiked two blocks east and south, turned
the corner onto Williamson and entered the Four Lakes Cafe. The Four
Lakes was one of the last true diners in Madison. The rotating stainless-
steel counter stools, with their red vinyl seats, were original, as were
the parquet tiles and Formica-topped tables with stainless-steel legs
and trim. An aging Bunn-omatic shared space behind the counter with
assorted steel appliances and a mint-green Hamilton Beach milkshake
blender, and even the greasy black fans that turned near the ceiling
with useless langour, twenty times a minute, were of mid-century
vintage.

The owners, Leo and Laura Vigren, were originals too, having
remodeled the place in '57 to state-of-the-art splendor and stayed on
through the changing decades despite attempts to buy them out. It was
Leo—pink-jowled and bald and sporting a deep pot belly—who Gabe
caught sight of now, shouting from behind the counter at a customer
kicking the Coke machine.

Gabe sized up the problem at once and jumped toward the vintage
device. The customer stepped back. In what seemed like all one motion
Gabe slipped off his coat and dropped it to the floor, shoved his shirt
sleeve to the elbow, kneeled before the trough at the old machine's
base and forced his hand up the opening. His whole arm vanished, till
his head jammed against the gaping slot and the lean pod of his face
was transformed by rubbery contortions. The customer—a dough-

faced college boy with pimples freckling his chin—broke out laughing from both embarassment and surprise. There was a twist and jerk in Gabe's shoulder, and a loud "clunk" attended the sudden withdrawal of his arm. Lying at the base of the slot was a dewy can of Coke. The college kid stared in wonder, his amusement gone.

"Is this what you wanted?" Gabe dead-panned, handing him the can.

The kid took it helplessly and made for the door, with Leo shouting after him, "Don't ever try that again! That's an *antique*! My machines aren't defective, just the people who use 'em!"

Gabe retrieved his coat and headed for his table near the back. Leo nodded and poured from the Bunn-omatic. "Thanks," he blurted with a sigh. "Decaf?"

"Black," replied Gabe, settling into a chair and twisting the end of his mustache.

The unlikely hero of many such small encounters, Gabe had gotten on Leo's good side a few years back, showing up near closing once when Leo and Laura were fussing and swearing at what they thought was a busted refrigerator. The fridge had gone warm and both the Freon tubes and the evaporator-fan wires were heavily ice-encrusted. So Leo had spent all morning replacing the defrost timer and melting off the ice.

But the frost problems returned. Gabe, who at first had angered Laura by lingering too long at the counter and emptying most of an A-1 Sauce bottle on his side order of French fries, had offered to help out. Skeptically Leo and Laura looked on as Gabe came back to the kitchen, removed the cover panel from the fridge's old evaporator, then stood there staring and sniffing. Just when Laura was beginning to roll her eyes and sigh deeply Gabe noticed a hole in the upper corner of the defrost chamber. He worked the fridge out from the wall, called to their attention this factory pre-drilled opening designed for the water-tube of an icemaker (which their model didn't have), and asked if anyone had messed with the fridge's back cover of late. Leo said he'd removed it the week before while cleaning.

"*That's* your problem," Gabe had declared. "The extra warm air from the cover being off is feeding straight into your evaporator chamber from the unused water-tube hole."

Whereupon he drew from his pockets some bubble-pack, stuffed it in the hole, covered the lot with duct-tape and replaced the back cover. Before long the icing stopped, the refrigerator cooled, and Gabe and the Vigrens were friends.

It was not the last of Gabe's fixes. He repaired the clock above the counter with nothing more than a thumb tack, stopped the men's room toilet from dripping, which it had done from a time beyond memory, by modifying the gasket in the holding tank, and, most strikingly, fixed the boom-box stereo of little Adam—Leo and Laura's grandson—by taking apart the whole console till it was strewn across the floor in what appeared a random mess. Then he performed some odd ritual with a Bic lighter and paper clip, reassembling the console in half an hour and cranking up the once-lifeless speakers to a volume that annoyed even Adam, who grimaced and covered his ears.

Little Adam, who, perched cross-legged on a nearby chair, had watched the whole process with rapt attention, was later asked by Laura just what Gabe had done.

"He blew on some parts and said some words," was Adam's only reply.

"Well, that doesn't make much sense," said Laura, whose brown pop eyes had a look of perpetual surprise. "He must have done something else. Didn't he use a cigarette lighter or something?"

"He said some words. And he blew on a paper clip," Adam persisted with the stubborn simplicity of an eight-year-old.

Now Gabe sat at his table in back and drank his black decaf, ignoring most of what Leo said, lost in his private thoughts. Leo was used to Gabe's silences. Gabe would twirl his mustache dry, fix his deep blue eyes—corrected by their single lens—on the door jamb or wall, and occasionally mumble a response.

"I've got some more A-1 Sauce bottles if you want 'em," offered Leo. "Two or three empties that Laura stored in back."

Gabe softly blurted his approval.

"Did you sell any mixtures to that girl from American Family?" Leo was wiping Gabe's table now and bending to meet his gaze.

Gabe returned a puzzled stare.

"You know, that secretary from the insurance company who always meets you at the Burger King. One with the heavy eye-shadow."

"Oh, yah, Heather. She and her girlfriend bought a bottle. She's a soft touch."

"You're gonna get in trouble selling that stuff without a vendor's license, ya know. Let alone its not bein' a safe or certified product."

"It's safe. It's even effective. As for certification, they can kiss my sweet sainted ass." He gulped the last of his decaf and rose with awkward energy, stripping his coat off the chair.

"Before you go, there's a letter for you in back." Leo stepped through the kitchen door, pulled a long white envelope from a pigeon-hole marked "Dent", then walked out and handed it to Gabe.

Jamming the letter in a pocket, Gabe headed for the front as if suddenly late, then remembered near the door to turn and give some response, a bizarre wave of hand and arm that vaguely resembled a salute and passed for both thank you and goodbye.

He wended across the park, which was dingy and pink with dusk. In the distance, behind and to his right, loomed the pale lighted dome of the capitol. He passed the dark granite church in whose basement stairwell he'd spent the hard nights of last winter, climbed a grassy slope to the sidewalk beside Williamson, turned left three blocks later onto a concrete drive newly freckled with fallen leaves and moved along a walkway to the white wooden door of a garage. Turning the knob and kicking the swollen base simultaneously, he popped the door open and stepped inside. The damp air within made him sneeze. Cool musks of mildew mingled with the stale smell of blankets, strewn laundry and old cardboard boxes. Dried herbs hung inverted from nails above a work bench and broken cobwebs, like delicate burst balloons, dangled over a shelf crammed with beakers, flasks, and empty dark-glassed bottles. Plastic sheeting was suspended from the ceiling to his right. A disk of glare from the latticed window threw a pale crescent of refracted light on the wall beside a bike pump, and beyond the window itself the fading day linked long purple shadows in the yard. In a corner below the sill Gabe pushed aside some cartons, threw his notebook on others nearby, stepped past his midden of matted clothes and sat down on a mattress.

Usually, if preparing to enter the Tunnel as he was tonight, Gabe saved all distractions till morning. The Tunnel of Time Past took priority in his life, even over fixing machines or concocting his herbal formula. He brought himself to the lotus position and stared hard at a yard-wide section of exposed insulation that appeared below the window. A tag of foil backing, half detached from the cottony fiberglass, was the key to the Tunnel's door. By staring hard at the bright little flap till its brightness filled his mind, he would trip some latch, feel some inner hinge swing free, thrust his thoughts down kinetic paths and journey most of the night.

The Tunnel baffled even Gabe, but the best he could make of its winding visions and voices was that, in all their compressed flux and power, they built up electro-magnetic fields that afforded him movement in time. By carefully noting his position he was able, he believed, to recede through the ages on selective routes, routes whose clues were concealed in Celtic babbles, lost poems and praises, dreamlike glimpses of half-familiar landscapes, keepsakes from genetic niches that his own birth had uncovered. His brain, he became convinced, was the product of a planned hybridization that unleashed a power of memory some twenty centuries old. His deliverance from its plague of insights lay in a counter-twist of the Tunnel, for if he did not lose his way he would one day reach the source of this ancient hereditary axis, then enter another warren twisting parallel to the first like the twin strand of a double helix. This, he hypothesized, was the Tunnel of Time Forward, and the moment—tonight, next month, next year—that he finally mapped a passage both back and forward through the two winding courses and was re-united with the present, then the strands of the helix would join and his powers would extend to the future.

But this evening, before entering, he grew distracted. From his coat he withdrew the envelope, read the return address, stood up, stepped beyond his nest of possessions to the fading light by the window, and tore the letter open.

Chapter 2

JACKIE DENT STARED THROUGH the sliding glass balcony door of her apartment, high above Anaheim. Night was coming on, and two of the local street people, homeless bums whom she'd often watched from the balcony itself while sipping strawberry daiquiris, would be dragging their blankets and parcels into the vacant lot below, just across the street. There, amid the yucca and desert shrubbery that had once adorned a trailer-park, they would bed down, first pissing or crapping in the jojoba bushes, then sprawling beside the car-port slabs and the disused utility hookups that resembled dark stumps of cacti. She had tried to have them evicted, but it turned out they'd worked several years for some truck farmer up in the valley, picking strawberries and melons. Now he owned the trailer-park lot and refused to kick them out.

She avoided the balcony these days, declining even to go out there, though the sunsets were often rewarding. She had blocked the door with her desk, so she could still look out the window, work at her computer and watch the fireworks over Disneyland a half mile away, which went up like clockwork near the park's closing time, just when the bums and darkness had settled down for the night.

Now she was writing a letter on her PC, pursing her lips and pressing at her cow-lick:

> Dear Eric,
> I am writing to get you off your ass in that City of Brotherly Love. The last time we quarrelled about your fee was I guess the last time we spoke. Seems your phone is still disconnected.

The deal is this. Mother has gotten worse and is now in pretty bad shape. I got a call a few days ago from some lousy doc who speaks like a machine. I'm flying out to Chicago and you damn well better get there yourself right away.

I already wrote to our wayward brother in Madison. Near as I can tell he's still crazy as a shithouse rat—no longer living in stairwells but gets his mail at some greasy spoon, something I found out from his old girlfriend who actually *does* have a telephone. Bro' now lives in a garage somewhere. The little schizo is worse than useless, but I figured I better call in the whole damn litter for this festive occasion. I suppose they don't recognize mail or family crisis on the planet where he's living, but if he doesn't respond I will personally get up there and drag his flaky carcass down to Evanston.

Well, the yuppies are still falling all over each other to buy mail-order coffee, even at inflated prices (make that *especially* at inflated prices) so my bank account is happy. I should get out of this apartment and live richer, but I'm not quite ready.

Are you still living with that cock-tease and doing the reporter thing? When's the big novel due (oops, I'm not supposed to ask, am I). Hey, that last ad copy you wrote for the catalog was first-rate bullshit, they ate it up. Think about doing some more, eh? I won't stiff you this time, honest. I can use your touch with words, even if no one else can!

Anyway, dearest Mum is at St. Joseph Hospital and will be there indefinitely. I need not implore you to take a plane; I know you don't fly. But that jalopy of yours must be rust by now. Don't be a turtle. Make sure it gets you there soon.

Yours, the goose who laid the golden coffee-bean,
Jackie

Fireworks were bursting in the California night as Jackie finished her letter, and she took private pleasure in watching them. She didn't care much for the spectacle; it was more what they represented. Her neighbor, Cecelia, could not stand to watch them at all and said they reminded her of what a soft-headed, grossly sentimental view Walt Disney had of the world. She said he sold everyone short.

Jackie always laughed at this inwardly, and once out loud to Cecelia's face. "He sold them just what they wanted," she told

CeCe with her biggest thin-lipped grin. "People *want* illusion and sentimentality, the grosser the better. Without it they'd dry up. They want happy endings, too. He served them the baloney and they ate it up, made him a king. What could be truer to the reality of what people are? They'll adore you, give you the shirts off their backs, throw their last dollar at you if you'll only tell them a very pleasant lie in a very pleasant way. Until you understand that, my dear CeCe, you can never be truly successful."

Afterward, CeCe didn't speak to her for a week.

Jackie stuffed the letter in an envelope, addressed and stamped it, then moved toward the kitchen to pour herself a drink. She walked barefoot on the plush white carpet, between the welter of beige leather furniture and high-tech lamps that comprised the living room gallery, with its silver-framed modern art hung precisely on egg-shell-white walls, and past a frameless photo of the moon that loomed, huge and pale against the blackness of space, in the passage to the kitchen.

Her refrigerator, except for the freezer compartment, was always near empty. She lived on restaurant carryouts, pizza, and Healthy Choice microwave dinners, the latter stacked neatly to fill the freezer, like manuscripts in an archive. But the refrigerator below it was a desolate cave. She clutched its chrome handle and opened the door part way, releasing a wedge of light across the dark kitchen floor. A single plastic juice jug, half full of ice-blue liquid, sat neatly on the central shelf, clustered round by a lime-juice bottle, a mustard jar, and a small dish of over-ripe strawberries.

"What is *that*?" CeCe had asked one day when she'd watched Jackie pour a drink from the juice jug.

"Sugarless blueberry Kool-Aid," Jackie had replied. "It's the only stuff I drink these days. Other than my daiquiris."

"Jesus, Jackie, it looks like a bottle of windshield fluid."

Jackie's lips had pursed with anger. "I don't care what it looks like. It's blueberry fucking Kool-Aid. I like it."

CeCe was always after Jackie to improve her meager diet. "You're too thin anyway," CeCe would remind her. "Thin as a crane. There's a difference, you know, between food and chemicals."

"That's where you're wrong," countered Jackie. "Food *is* chemicals. It's all the same stuff."

It was true that Jackie was thin. Crane-thin, as CeCe liked to remark. She stood five-foot-ten and seemed to be mostly legs. A long beaky nose and gray-green eyes controlled her face, and the way she wore her coarse reddish hair—closely cropped all around and with the feathery tuft of a cow-lick on top that resisted attempts to subdue it—the suggestion that she looked like a wading-bird was not entirely far-fetched.

As she drank her blue Kool-Aid, Jackie busied her mind with plans. She tried to think through the coming events with her usual control and precision. But certain images eluded her. It had been too long, she realized—six years with both her brothers, and almost four with her mother. Their features were a muddle; her mind's eye failed to recall them. She excelled at visualization, at imagining encounters beforehand, at fixing faces with behaviors and placing people in projected scenes like so many players on a stage. Maybe at 46, she thought, I'm starting to lose my edge. Maybe I should cut back on drinking. She killed the temptation to mix up some strawberry daiquiris and instead gulped the last of her Kool-Aid.

The digital clock on the microwave caught her eye. It was time for the early movie. She set her glass in the sink, padded into the hallway—stopping briefly to inspect the suitcase she had packed and put aside after supper—then turned through the doorway to her bedroom, flicked on the huge TV at the foot of her queen-size bed, and methodically started to undress. The bright images flickered, the sound blared on just an instant before she stabbed MUTE on the remote, and the room, when she'd turned the beige lamps off, was a pulsing cavern of shadows and light, warm electric numina that would hypnotize her into drowsiness and faithfully keep her company through the always difficult night.

Morning found Jackie hurrying to get ready before the bang at her door. Two or three times a week she tolerated visits from CeCe, who would beat the brass knocker before getting in with a key and making her way to the kitchen. Jackie would arrive dressed for work to find her friend settled in a wicker chair, one of several that ringed the table. "My throne," CeCe called it. A huge ceramic coffee mug would be cradled in CeCe's palms, and a napkin-wrapped croissant with one of its twin tails bitten off would be resting beside one elbow. Jackie would move to the fridge and pour a glass of blue Kool-Aid.

Today Jackie heard the knock while in the bedroom adjusting her stockings, then arrived at the kitchen doorway to see CeCe smiling and purring above her coffee. "Mmmmmm...this is that wonderful new flavor of yours, Mauna Loa Magic. Have you tried it?"

"CeCe, you know I hate coffee. It makes me nervous and that makes me quick to compromise."

"Jeez, what's wrong with that?" exclaimed CeCe.

"Once in a while, nothing. But in my business it can be a fatal habit. Besides, the damn stuff gives me gas."

"Well if I stopped eating or drinking everything that gave me gas I'd shrivel up like a prune."

"Cec, I hate the shit, okay? Especially in the morning. The very idea is revolting. This is a tough day for me, all right? Don't push me."

"Okay, okay. Listen, how often should I water your plants?"

"What plants?"

"Your house plants."

"Cec, I don't have any fucking house plants."

"Yes you do. There's that thing by the door. What is it? A croton. And there's a diffenbachia on your balcony."

"Christ, that thing on the balcony is dead as a smelt. Has been since Easter. And that other thing by the door in the hallway, Cec. It's artificial."

"It is? Well I'll be darned. I pass it all the time. I *thought* it seemed awfully hardy."

Jackie often wondered why she put up with CeCe, who could be pretty dense. For the first six months as neighbors they didn't even speak. Then CeCe found out Jackie owned the company that produced her favorite coffee. "Karmic convergence," CeCe had called their meeting. They started talking more often and CeCe told Jackie about her divorce, how she'd dumped her doctor husband when he started playing around, and how she'd taken him for a bundle. CeCe began to grow on her. She was above all easy to be with. And she was really rather clever in her spaced-out way, cherishing too much liberal claptrap for Jackie's conservative tastes, but somehow filling a need, relieving a certain vacuum, making some far-fetched connection. She wore her black hair long and straight like a Sixties hippie, had inky, startled-doe eyes, and claimed to be a witch. "A white witch," CeCe insisted. "You know, one of the good ones." It was laughable, really, but it gave Jackie something to gauge herself by, gave her some far view out along the shattered rainbow of human behavior to the opposite end of the spectrum.

"Forget the plants," said Jackie, glancing anxiously at her watch. "Listen, Cec, what I *do* need is for you to mail this letter right away." She gulped the rest of her Kool-Aid, handed CeCe the envelope and charged out of the kitchen. "I haven't got the time."

CeCe stared hard at the address on the envelope. "Oh, it's for your brother. Which is he, the nut-case or the wimp?"

"The wimp," said Jackie, grabbing her suitcase from the hallway and striding for the door."I'll call you from Chicago when I find out what's what. Just mail the letter."

Jackie's drive to the office was her least favorite time of day. It was not just the traffic that upset her. Her normally thick psychic skin seemed then at its most porous, and the reality of her location attacked her from every side. Mornings in LA, with their sense of a mechanical hive having just been laid bare—as if the gauzy cover on a giant lab experiment had been lifted overnight to reveal a swarm of metallic beetles amid hideous scaffoldings, pink gaseous suffusions, and unnatural arrangements of flora—were occasions to be stoically endured. By noon her crust had hardened, she relished once more the rhythm and reassurance of petty confrontation and was already plotting the afternoon campaigns, when she'd corner her advertising staff in the cool plush inner office, watch them toady to her suggestions, and examine the slick catalog layouts with their color dreams of vigor and fulfillment, their promise of productive excitement, their suggestion that coffee was beauty and truth or at least the fast track to them. By evening it would all become one: the unreal sense of command and engagement cemented by a furious busyness, the immersing welter of messages and billings and contracts on her desk, her abrasive or cajoling responses to phone calls from salesmen and suppliers, managers and foremen, and, beyond the privet hedges outside her picture window, the amphetamine-dream of the LA dusk, thrumming with smoggy warmth, spreading its phony gold-dust out from the far-away Malibu hills.

But at present she was mired in gridlock on the Santa Ana Freeway. What was worse was that just to her right, not one hundred yards away, was the pink brick wall of her company headquarters, flanked by the eight-foot-tall stainless steel letters "MMC", and with her own office—green privet hedge and picture window just visible at an angle—in an alcove to its left. When she stalled in traffic at this point her frustration became unbearable. She hated being helpless. If it weren't for the high chain-link fence topped by strands of barbed wire she could pull to the shoulder, jump out, and sprint to her building in sixty seconds flat. Instead she would have to crawl two more miles in her car, exit on a long winding ramp, backtrack another two miles east, then enter the big corporate drive with its bordering palms and yuccas, still a half mile north of her office. So the rest of the trip from this point might take half an hour or longer. Sometimes she dreamt at night of a ramp that veered off the freeway, climbed above this fence and descended in front of her office, in the little cement driveway next to her personally labelled parking space.

This morning, already anxious about the trip ahead, she pumped up her nerve and ripped her red Lexus to the shoulder, charged up its pitted length toward the exit—barely missing a pickup truck which squeezed right with a similar agenda—and shot up the serpentine ramp, lips pursed with anger and determination. When she finally got to her office she ignored Jesus, the Latino vestibule guard in his scarlet vest and bow tie who always wished her good morning, was rude to both her secretaries, and almost knocked down the rubber-tree that quavered in its pot by her doorway.

At her desk Jackie pushed aside her pink stack of phone messages. Her kindest secretary, Maria, puttered in shortly in spongy Reeboks and placed her boss's blue Kool-Aid, disguised in an insulated coffee pot, wordlessly on her bookshelf. Jackie pulled from her files a batch of catalog back-issues and began paging through them. The images helped to soothe her, especially the outdoor scenes depicted on their covers. "Mellow Mountain Coffee" stood in white-lettered relief against some breathtaking pastoral setting—rarely southern California, which was much too hot to evoke the proper appetites—but generally the Sierras or the Lake Tahoe region, or somewhere near Mount Shasta. Spruce and pine stood out against snow-spotted slopes or peaks, and people in Eddie Bauer clothing were camped along foaming streams with backpacks snuggled beside them. Nearby was a thermos of coffee, and ceramic mugs with the MMC logo, cupped in appreciative hands, were surmounted by pale wisps of steam.

The indoor shots usually framed some fireplace circled by models in Norwegian sweaters and wool-lined boots, all poised on a shaggy rug that was, carefully, not one made of fur. A few covers, like those on the sale catalogs, were devoid of scenes or people but merely arrayed her products: coffee carafes and thermos bottles, cups, glasses, and jars, French presses and drip brewers, espresso sets and electric grinders, even T-shirts, towels, and tote-bags. Her favorite photos were of the coffees themselves, packed neatly in enamel-finished foil, with attractive designs and colors that carefully set off their logo.

The images revived other feelings, other reassurances. More soothing to Jackie than the photos themselves was to see the lie in it all, to roll its sweet plausibility on the tongue of her own clever reason, and to see the lie become truth. There was a multiple pleasure in these subtle commercial deceptions. The triumph of advertising, she appreciated, was not its deployment of illusion but its broad aftershock—the happy reverberant proof that the suckers were satisfied, that they believed they'd struck a fair deal, believed, in fact, that they'd won. Thus they soon converted their families and friends and not only amplified sales but steeped the whole process in acceptance, respect, even a kind of virtue.

Now she pulled from the file a catalog that she cherished. Most of the tempting copy had been written by her brother, Eric. A few years back he'd been strapped for cash so she'd offered to help him out. He had an uncanny way with words, and the style and panache of his copy formed the model for later promotions. The names of her coffees were critical, as were their brief descriptions, and Eric's inventions were unusually creative: Jamaican High Cascade, Gold Djimmah Supremo, Cloud Villa Mocha, Spice River Colombian, Costa Rican Purple Haze, Kona Highland Mild, Mexican Lost Mountain, Deep Rain Forest Java.

Ultimately, MMC's coffees numbered in the dozens and had names based on those of unblended varietal beans such as Java, Mocha, Kona, Colombian, Costa Rican, Jamaica Blue Mountain --renowned coffees specific to certain regions and demanded by connoisseurs— but expensive, and in limited or fickle supply. It was cheaper to offer blended roasts, and cheaper still to blend solely with low-priced beans of modest or inferior origin, while retaining the names of their celebrated betters. A further trick was to sell the idea that blending was an art, not a useful cost-cutting measure. So Jackie's catalogs forever prattled on about the "more complex" taste of her blended offerings, the "multiple delicate sensations" that they induced simultaneously, and the labor involved in the factory "taste-tests" where her experts spent patient hours applying their "discerning palates." And when *flavored* blends became trendy—the endless variations on cinnamon, almond, chocolate, vanilla, raspberry and hazelnut—the task of touting only blends became that much easier. Thus Mellow Mountain Coffee peddled cheap blends at unblended name-bean prices, covering sharp practice with wordplay and the graphic splendor of photographs. It had worked well up to a point, but to really play with the big boys, to expand her operations and make one more stretch in the market...

While Eric had been useful, Jackie still saw his effort as a trifle. His talents were essentially frills, weightless gestures and pirouettes, sky-writings up in the blue. Just to rattle his cage she'd only paid him half the fee that they'd initially agreed on. It would help remind him, she'd reasoned, of just who was in control. Following the pattern of their upbringing, it wouldn't do to let him get too cocky. But she couldn't help admiring his touch as she studied that first revised catalog:

JAMAICAN HIGH CASCADE
> Racy flavor and clean, bouyant smoothness, with richness, floral complexity, and an uplifting spray of briskness, this coffee has the lingering herbiness and

fragrant insouciance of the mist-tipped Caribbean highlands.

SPICE RIVER COLOMBIAN

Rare dark piquancy in a pleasing meander of light-roasted fruitiness and heady aroma, these washed, pebble-bright beans are laced with a berry-like tang and high notes of sweet spice and splashy bouquet.

COSTA RICAN PURPLE HAZE

Our darkest, wildest beans, full of exotic vigor and winey nuance, with a transcendent counterpoint of roastiness that is mellow, evolved, and inscrutably earthy.

⌒

Jackie's appreciation was interrupted by the phone. It was her secretary Carmen, explaining that the limo arrangements to the airport, which Jackie had asked her to make last night, had somehow fallen through. Now no limos were available, anywhere, until some time in the evening. Jackie cursed briefly, but swallowed her anger and disgust and told Carmen to call a cab. Then she suddenly checked herself and told Carmen to give her Maria. When Maria got on the extension Jackie blurted loudly, "For God's sake, Maria, call me a cab for the airport, Carmen screwed up. I need one at eleven." Maria's voice cooed responsively and the matter was soon taken care of.

Maria was young and pretty and coffee-bean brown. There were two things Jackie liked in her: determination and cheerfulness. When barely a teen, Maria had crossed the Mexican border at night with her two little brothers, waiting two days in a storm pipe before splashing across the river with Pablito around her neck and Roberto at her side. They fled the border in the freezer of an ice-cream truck, all three half dead with cold by the time they arrived in the city. At sixteen she was Jackie's first female warehouse worker, lifting coffee bags heavier than she was, all day in the suffocating heat. With her brains and mastery of English she had soon moved up into shipping, and when MMC got prosperous, Jackie put Maria in her office. Maria dressed simply, in colored blouses and soft patterned skirts, and always in comfortable footware. She rarely missed work or complained.

Carmen, on the other hand, who'd failed to reserve the limo, continually tried Jackie's nerves. Only her link with Maria—who had recommended her hiring and to whom she was related—saved her from being fired. She loved strange costume jewelry and flamboyant

Spanish-style dresses that dragged a bit on the floor, full of pleats and ruffles and with billowing arms and shoulders that affronted Jackie's asceticism. Dangling spherical earrings like suspended ping-pong balls, flashy pendulate necklaces and unusual piled hairdos affixed with rapier-like combs completed the excess, and, irrationally fond of spike heels, she was forever twisting her ankles and missing days of work. On the phones she was close to incompetent, and either sullen or strangely loud. Jackie called her "Conchita Bizarro."

Jackie rushed to wrap things up before the arrival of her cab. She bored through her paperwork in less than an hour. She returned most of her phone calls and left detailed instructions for Maria about schedules and unfinished business. Hoping to be back in a week, she explained nonetheless that the thing might run in to two. She would call the office often in case there was some sort of crisis. Finally she cleared her blotter, stacked things neatly in piles at its edges, and packed and snapped shut her briefcase. Jesus called Maria when the cab showed up, and Maria walked in to tell Jackie and to wish her well on the trip. Carmen pretended to be busy as Jackie charged out, and Jesus ignored her in the vestibule while fumbling to make a phone call.

Retrieving her suitcase herself from the small trunk of her Lexis, whose rear end rocked down softly as she closed the hood, Jackie stared briefly at the rubbery distortion of her angular face in the mirror of the car's red enamel. She winced and turned away, then walked toward the waiting taxi.

The cabby drove like a madman. He sped and swerved and braked through a bright jungle of late morning traffic and at last, on the final tricky leg along Imperial Highway—the last place where Jackie wanted trouble—he nearly sideswiped a black man in a sports car, who shouted and gave them the finger. She squinted her eyes, pursed her lips, and endured the last lurching miles.

But somewhere back on the freeway her high gear had kicked in, her adrenalin-fed sense of affinity with life's hurly-burly, her relish of unresolved conflict. When the cabby screeched up to the departure curb at LA International, she calmly got out and followed the driver to the trunk. She took her suitcase silently, searched through her purse with exaggerated poise for the exact amount of her fare, then looked the driver square in the eyes as she handed him the money. He was a short, middle-aged, muscular man—Arab, she guessed, or Greek—with a deeply tanned face whose dark brows and Roman nose were pushed together with his close-set eyes to form a harsh wedge of focus that suggested something canine. She waited for him to count it, then turned and walked away.

It took him a moment to react. "Hey lady, that's a fifty dollar fare. How 'bout a tip?" Then, more frantically as she continued to ignore him: "Hey, lady! Where's the *tip*! Hey!"

She turned her head once, stared at him coldly, then proceeded on her way. "Hey, dammit. Where's my tip? Hey! What's the deal? Hey!"

Finally he ran after her—the sudden violence of his pursuit quickly scattering people by the sliding doors and forcing a muffled bray from a tall blonde in a jump suit.

He crouched as he moved, Groucho Marx-style, and craned his short neck at his shoulder as he caught up from behind. "Hey, I been a cabby 12 years. You can't stiff me like that. Hey!"

Jackie stopped directly on the pressure-plate as the glass door stood open and travellers in front of and behind her slipped sideways to use the next entrance. She turned back at an angle, squinted her gray-green eyes and confronted him one more time.

"I just did," she said with measured calm.

He stepped back for a moment, speechless in his rage. "Hey, bitch, hey you fuckin' bitch," he blurted uncontrollably, but she was already through the doorway, followed by a porter with a cart full of bags who gave the cabby a stare.

Jackie trudged forward, focused her eyes on the long line of monitors banked beside the escalators, and pursed her slender lips. Then she felt her lips quiver, felt their corners tremble faintly, felt her cheeks pinch suddenly upward, felt—with a rising thrill of enjoyment—her whole face break out in a grin.

Chapter 3

WESTWARD ALONG LANCASTER AVENUE, among the stone walls and broad driveways of imposing old houses—their lawns dappled with the shade of ambering maples and dusty, bark-peeled sycamores—the old-gold light of autumn was welcoming Eric Dent home. His Civic puttered smoothly in the late afternoon. As though he had exited a war-zone, junkpiles and trash-strewn lots, abandoned bungalows and warehouses, shattered streetlights, decaying billboards and half-collapsed chainlink fences with their banners of windblown paper, had abruptly disappeared when he crossed City Avenue and entered Montgomery County. Amid the affluent valleys of Philadelphia's Main Line, with their odd Welsh names and worn luster and compressed powdered radiance that suggested a time of solace, a time far removed from the present, he felt himself connected. If it weren't for the traffic and the burgeoning series of corporate pavilions, upscale shopping courts and residential developments that amplified the crowding, he might, he sometimes mused, even find contentment. But contentment seemed a thing of his past.

Eric had interviewed Rosalee Herr with his usual blend of nervousness and reserve. She was the docent at Bartram's Gardens, the restored 18th-century estate of the naturalist John Bartram, which these days was squirreled away behind the failing bungalowed enclaves of Philly's West Side, hard by the Schuylkill River. He had managed to find it amid a post-luncheon daze, sleepily probing the Route 30 corridor, turning south on 52nd, edging across Market and Chestnut and then, near Gray's Ferry, slipping around to Lindbergh Boulevard, off which Bartram's treed estate had emerged like Brigadoon, just when it seemed he was hopelessly lost on a back street of run-down apartments.

As in some incongruous dream he had parked in an alley by a squalid yard, then crossed to a well-kept lawn, walked up a flagstone path between blazes of late season flowers, and knocked on a great wooden door. A woman in floor-length skirt, white apron and linen bonnet had answered, a big ruddy-faced woman with wisps of gray hair at her temples, who smiled and invited him in. The stone house, with its oak and chestnut beams, its odor of char and woodsmoke and its views of the riverside gardens through wavy panes of hand-wrought beveled glazing, had swiftly evoked the past. It was all he could do to maintain his professional demeanor, his air of incisive reporter, as he questioned Ms. Herr about Bartram and his son William, who befriended the elite of their day: Washington, Jefferson, Hamilton, and a host of ground-breaking naturalists such as the birdman, Alexander Wilson.

Ms. Herr was pleasant and cagey in her smiling role as mistress of the manse, sidetracking deftly to favorite topics, politely injecting her expertise, steering a course toward the women, not the men, whom she felt had been just as important. The secret highlight of his visit was a glimpse at Wilson's portfolios, the original volumes of his *American Ornithology*, locked in a case at the top of the stairs but opened for his perusal. Here were the mildew-spotted folio pages bound in their rotting leather, showing ibis and flamingo poised against placid bays and sunlit cumulus, or the profiles of ivory-billed woodpeckers in their pre-extinction vigor, beating the pith out of scaly trees, their red crests inflamed with doomed and ferocious pride.

He revealed none of his excitement, smiled and nodded and politely asked if perhaps these should not be handled. Ms. Herr was ever gracious, whispering "Only for special visitors," and the interview ended on an awkward note when he tripped at the bottom of the staircase and banged his Nikon on the bannister. Outside he photographed the house and grounds, and Ms. Herr posed with a barrow and spade in a clump of asters by the walkway, while out across the Schuylkill, faintly vignetted in a gap among the hardwoods, was a cameo portrait of downtown Philly and its Oz-like skyscraper pinnacles. His editor, he knew, would use only the face, cropped and enlarged to display the grin that anchored Ms. Herr's countenance. "Community newspapers," Eric's editor was fond of saying, "should be about people. Show me faces, not artsy spaces and places."

Now Eric turned off Lancaster Avenue and headed in to Pennwood to get his story on paper. He eased past the Pennwood station and its first commuters bustling toward their cars, turned under the railroad viaduct with its bank of rhododendron deeply shaded by lines of maples, sputtered into the parking lot across from DeLalo's Pizza, and quick-stepped up to the squat glassy building that housed the *Main Line Times*. The paper had gone to press that morning and the only ones left at their desks when he entered were Stacy, the Bryn Mawr intern, and her mentor Cynthia Blott, whose beat was police, fire, and seniors. Out of long-standing dislike, Cynthia ignored Eric and Eric ignored Cynthia. He went wordlessly to his station where the morning's black coffee still half-filled its Styrofoam cup, flicked on his monitor and gathered his notes, then sat down to beat out a rough draft in just under half an hour. As the story noisily printed he unpacked his Nikon, popped out the roll of Tri-X, labeled it, and placed it in the bin by the photo-room door. Then he sat back down at his desk and penned out the following note:

> Neil,
>   Here's a very rough draft of the Bartram piece.
>   I checked and Ms. Herr *does* live in Pennwood, over off Hungerford Avenue. The rest of my stuff is with Susan, who'll be covering my beat. I should be back a week from Monday, at the latest. Dale said you're killing the JayCee story, so I've scratched the Monday rewrite deadline.
>
> Eric

He suddenly felt tired, and after locking his desk and leaving the office he stopped in the nearby shopping court, anchored by its boxy Hechts, formerly a Wanamaker's, and went in to Woolworth's for coffee. Though the food there was often greasy or bland he liked its intimate cheapness and simplicity, its working-class unpretension, and especially he liked the white-haired waitresses—either fat or skinny and none a day under sixty—in their pale gray uniform dresses with red-banded sleeves and collars, red deep-pocket aprons, and white high-top tennis shoes. They were touchingly steadfast and efficient, rarely smiling but quickly refilling his coffee cup at the low Formica counter that was trimmed with ribbed stainless steel and laid out in sweeping curves. They had bright eyes edged by crow's-feet, thin rouged lips, sunken chins and—when they weren't scraping the grill or plopping bleached spuds in the deep-fry—a way of staring out the window, where linden leaves twisted by the sidewalk, that induced him to leave fat tips.

Eric had not done much cooking for himself since Mel had left in August, and he hated the trendy bars and upscale theme restaurants that dotted Lancaster Avenue. Nor could he stomach the bubbling couples in designer apparel or the waiters who recited the "Specials", with nervous and confusing haste, before you were allowed to order. Here, unbothered, he reviewed the guileless menu, ordering the "Fish On A Bun Sandwich" and a small side of onion rings. The deep-fry splashed and slurped while his thoughts broke apart and drifted. Why had Jackie sent a letter when she knew he had a telephone? Why claim it was disconnected? Only when Mel left him the first time had he been forced to cut it off, but that was for just a few weeks. She was up to something, he knew damn well, and he might be too late already.

Helen, his favorite waitress, now refilled his cup, and the tender image of her frail wrist and blue-veined, liver-spotted hand made him look up and smile blandly. As she moved away, Eric's face in the mirror above the grill loomed back with surreal sharpness. His sandy red hair needed trimming, and he noted that his ginger eyebrows, suspended above pale lashes, had grown hoary with middle-age. The once-smooth cheeks were lined and jowly and the long freckled neck on his boyish shoulders now suggested too easily a turtle, with its slender crease and pull. He fingered his right elbow, which was swollen with fluid from a knock he'd given it, and he pushed up his shirt-sleeve and exposed it to the mirror, then quickly rolled the sleeve down. "Pop-eye elbow" his doctor had called it, an inflammation of the bursa that he'd said would go away. It made him feel that much older. But mostly, in the Woolworth's mirror, he saw his simian self, his gangly orangoutang features, the monkey that he spied not just in himself but, these days, in most others around him.

By the time he got his meal the coffee kicked in and his mind reviewed a checklist of pre-departure chores. Set out the bait right away. Pack the unfinished manuscript. Pay the rent. Check the oil and tires. Find the address and phone number of Gabe's former girlfriend. Phone the Logans. Phone Mel? The caffeine compressed and caressed him as he munched on food that was not quite there and stared out at the lindens. But the flip side of this buzz, this brief hugging focus, was a jagged ultra-alertness, and before long anxiety seized him. All the things that might go wrong seemed to strengthen in probability and to lie beyond his influence. On the other hand, there was one thing he might do again tonight, a thing requiring some luck but that, if successful, would ease the pain of Chicago. But it needed immediate attention. He gulped the rest of his sandwich and rings and abruptly signaled for the check.

Out on the streets the day had dimmed. Sunset burnished the landscape as he tracked suburban lanes in his white Honda Civic, and the sight of kids on bikes and in grassy yards, where footballs wobbled through the leaf-shattered light with its pumice of autumnal dusk, made him suddenly blue as hell. If things had worked out as they're supposed to he'd have married Mel long ago, and one of these kids would be his kid, chucking loose spirals and sliding on lawns, running colt-like in the fusty pre-dark, arriving flushed and late for supper.

On the other hand, who wanted it? The exhaustion and sacrifice, the too-touching sweetness of their childhoods, the heartache of their adolescence, the rejection that was bound to come. Who wanted to watch close-up the creature you loved more than life, the kid you put all your marbles in, get chewed up bit by bit by a sprawling culture of neurotic apes who had overrun the globe? Who wanted the slow crucifixion?

The Pennwood Garden Apartments were a series of two-story red-brick affairs that encased a labyrinth of courtyards. They'd been built in the late 1940s, and the shrubbery in places had gotten so big that ground-floor units were walled in gloom even on the brightest days. Such a unit was Eric's.

The odor hit him as soon as he opened his door. A thickish, spicy sweetness filled the rooms. He moved to the kitchen and flicked on a light, stubbing his foot as he did so on a bucket of apples he'd left by the stove. A single scarlet Jonathan bumped softly to the linoleum and rolled beneath a chair. The room reeked of rum and too-ripe fruit. He popped the latch on the window by the sink, wound the casement open, then returned to the narrow livingroom and opened the windows there. In the corner nearest the overstuffed couch, with its floral print upholstery, faded and threadbare, he pressed his nose to the screen and sucked in the damp evening air. More ripeness greeted him, of leaf-rot and chilled autumn loam, of curled brown rhododendron leaves settled thickly beside the brick. The moon was clearing the roofs beyond the courtyard, a bruised harvest moon all yellow and puffy with radiance, and, beside an archway opposite, a TV glowed from a darkened room, its blue tones fractured by intervening twigs to form a tiny mosaic abstract.

Eric raised the window screen. A cool draft brushed his arm. He puttered back to the kitchen and grabbed from the counter—amid a welter of jars, bowls of fruit, and solutions in bottles—a cookie sheet mounded with a discolored wad that had sat fermenting all day. Back once more in the livingroom he crouched in the corner by the couch, balanced the sheet on the window sill, grabbed a handful of the wet fruity mixture, and reached out to smear it thickly on a forked scaly branch that extended, nearly to the wall, from the trunk of a big rhododendron. On other reachable branches he repeated this, then flung what was left at the tree trunk itself, where it stuck near the base like soft clay. He scraped the last crumbs from the cookie sheet and deftly pulled it inside. But he didn't lower the screen. Instead he dropped and closed the Venetian blinds, grabbed two big pink and green rose-patterned cushions from the couch, piled them on the floor below the sill, tested their firmness and height with a downward press of his hand, then stood up and walked to the bathroom through the fruity reek all around him.

At eleven o'clock, tired to a pleasant numbness from completing his chores, cleaning up the kitchen and packing his bags and car, Eric killed all the lights and returned to the corner by the window. Very slowly he raised the blinds, sat down on the cushions and let the smell of his well-placed fruit-bait drift in through the open casement. He held a flashlight in one hand and set a net beside him with the other. The moon was now high in the heavens, sentried by a few pale stars, and in the eerie quiet that surrounded him he listened for the slightest sounds. Usually they made a rustling when they came, in the dry and brittle leaves. A quick check with the flashlight showed that so far the bait had failed. But the period from this time onward had always proved best. He braced himself by the sill, rubbed vaguely at his Pop-eye elbow and awaited the telltale clues: a dry tickle, a faint vibration, an odor like freshly ground peanuts. As in a time long ago he enjoyed this listening and dreaming, poised between shelter and the shadowy night, at the ledge between reason and reverie, wakefulness and sleep, moonlight and inner darkness...

They had called her the "Moth Lady." At the University of Pennsylvania, with its dark gothic towers stretched above the Schuylkill and the streets called Locust and Spruce, Walnut, Chestnut and Pine, Eric's mother Glenda had taught in the Forties and Fifties. Biology was her subject but moths were her special passion. Her private collection was the largest in the state, gathered not by her but by her father, Edwin Reese, from whom it had been passed down. Eric recalled seeing remnants of it, stacked in cases in the attic, and a few of the rarer drawers in the old tower of College Hall. Its orderliness had struck him, but especially the exotic names: Rustic Sphinx, Silver-Spotted Ghost Moth, Sweetbay Silkmoth, Faithful Beauty, Exiled Dagger Moth, Sleepy Underwing, Abrupt Brother, Polished Dart, Stormy Arches, Ruby Quaker, Confused Woodgrain, Chosen Sallow, Wanton Pinion, Grateful Midget, Cloaked Marvel. He had nurtured a taste for the drama of words from those dark little beauties under glass.

But Glenda herself disliked killing, even of ephemeral insects. She gave most of the collection to the Franklin Institute and focused instead on life: on collecting and nurturing eggs and cocoons, especially of the giant Saturniids, or silkworm moths, which she drew and painted as adults. For a time when Eric was a toddler she haunted an office in Hayden Hall, where the windows opened on a tree-shaded courtyard. It was there she baited for moths—"sugaring," it was called. The recipe came down from old Edwin Reese, a concoction of rum and stale beer, brown sugar, brewer's yeast and molasses, rotting apples and pears. Her largest capture of Underwings—including a rare Dejected—had responded to this confection, and she drew and colored them with painstaking care on many a night in her office. But for the huge and spectacular Saturniids—the Imperials and Lunas, the Promethea, Cecropia, and Polyphemus Moths—she would simply capture a female who had come to the aged maples or the light she suspended from her window, tie a string around its thorax, let it release its pheromones, and watch the males assemble. In those days they came by the dozens, circling outside in the late summer dark like delicate, smoky bats. Eric, alone among her children in his shared love for these creatures, was allowed to stay up late and watch, seated by the sill or, occasionally, just under the window in the bushes beyond.

It was a time when her husband's drinking had increased, and she spent most evenings on campus though their house was not far away. The drawings she turned out were impressive enough to interest several editors. For a time she gleaned extra income from illustrating articles and books, but the work finally petered out. Then she continued it for fun. Her portraits, in pencil, pastel, even water-color and oil, became more impressionistic; she moved on to birds, butterflies, and flowers and she nurtured a fondness for the pioneers, for the art of the early naturalists like Audubon, Wilson, and Catesby. To Eric it was all pure glory. He stared at her drawings by the hour and, sitting Indian-style on her desk, attempted to fashion his own with crayons and manila paper.

Glenda hatched moth eggs in her office or at home, in terrariums built for the purpose, then feasted the larvae, quite striking in themselves, on appropriate local food plants till they cocooned and overwintered, usually in the Dent's garage. The next year they would emerge, briefly docile and innocent; she drew them from life perched on Eric's wrist or sometimes on the fingers of her free hand, at a big plywood counter by her office desk that was littered with cages and artwork. Then Eric had the privilege of releasing them, of moving to the tall open window in the sultry Philly nights, the glare from the office ceiling light colliding with the blackness outside, the honk of cars and buses hotly echoed in the courtyard beyond. With his mother towering behind him and one or two of her students at times looking on, he launched her moths on the stream of night, where they fluttered and sank and lifted.

Sometimes youths taking shortcuts would witness these scenes—callow scholars from Geology or Physics heading to or from their labs, or bleary-eyed sports and their Drexel dates escaping from Bennett Hall. They laughed or stared from the pathways until the Moth Lady asked them in, where they gaped in amazement at Cecropias on lampshades, the females redolent of peanuts, their wings marbled wildly with chocolate and buff and auroras of cream and red, or Prometheas astride a chair-arm, palm-sized and trembling with freshness, or a great eye-spotted Polyphemus perched, golden and erect, atop Eric's tiny head. No one left unaffected. Whatever they actually said or didn't, their faces had been slapped by beauty, and they departed a little less safe and smug, even the young grinds from Chemistry or Math whose nerdy calm was its own cocoon and at most times spared them from emotion.

In fact Glenda had met her husband in a related way. He was Walker Dent, scion of an old Main Line family, wayward son of Middleton Jackson Dent whose law firm was an institution, defenders of blue blood causes in real estate and zoning. Walker had been kicked out of Yale and Princeton, had bummed around Canada and Mexico until age 24, then made his third stab at the Ivy League and enrolled, without any prodding, in the law program at Penn. Drinking and fishing had seemed his sole interests but a part of him was ambitious and fierce, and by 29, after buckling down with maniacal zeal, he had managed to pass the bar and set up his own small practice.

One evening in September he returned well oiled from Franklin Field, where Penn had just lost to Princeton on a last minute touchdown, tried a shortcut to Spruce Street in the course of retrieving his Hudson, and saw a vision in a window, a willowy red-haired goddess lifting above her, like Lady Liberty, a torch or flame, or so it first appeared in the luminous frame of the casement. Then the torch came to life, was animate and free, and tumbled out on the dusk. He stopped to clear his vision and according to Glenda's remembrance, stumbled and fell, and cried out in her direction. She thought he was hurt and went to his aid; he thought she was an angel who had answered a private prayer, but was unimpressed by her moths when, minutes later, he drank bitter re-heated coffee from a cracked cup in her office. What impressed him was Glenda herself, her face and hair, her green eyes and high cheeks and freckled alabaster skin. They both claimed he first proposed marriage then, and she claimed she told him he was drunk.

The courtship was short and fiery. They did not hide their opinions nor spare each others feelings. Each had Celtic temperaments woven thickly through their sociable masks. Hers was from a line of northern Welsh—sons of Caernarvon tradesmen who were later immigrant masons, slate cutters and quarry foremen, builders of the Main Line estates. The Reeses were mostly good-hearted. "Reese comes from 'ris', which means roughly 'the loving person' in Welsh," Glenda early told her suitor. "Dent means roughly 'close to cracked' in English," Walker had countered dryly, "but my mother's side are all sound-minded Scotch." "Scots," she had corrected him. "Scotch is what you're always drinking."

They were married in Hayden Hall. As a joke someone made Glenda great paper wings which she wore as they ran through the rice to his Hudson, though one caught on a bush and broke off beside the curb. Walker had been tipped off beforehand, and altered a cane with wire and tape to look like a huge insect pin with which to mount his fresh bride. Glenda laughed loudest of all. They honeymooned on the Schuylkill, out beyond Mill Grove where Audubon had lived, and where Walker fished while Glenda painted Sphinxes and Underwings.

She was the artist and instructor fused, affection's gentle translator, often plebian in sympathies and accepting of human foibles. He was the legal predator and stubborn logician, hawk-nosed, exuberant but fiercely watchful, descended from a line of such haughty beak-nosed cynics, railers against the stupidity of men, renders of weaker flesh. Yet his heart was full and his law firm prospered, and the kids came quickly, one, two, three, each two years apart, all red- or sandy-headed but otherwise different as could be. Gabe was the oldest, a strange little phenomenon even as a boy, gifted, oddly focused, wrapped in himself and his intellect, atuned to inner rhythms. Jackie was the middle child, a cool logician and strategist like her dad, but more practical and ambitious, the family achiever and her mother's right hand, especially in times of crisis. Young Eric was a dreamer without special skills, other than a gift for seeing. He expressed himself well, saw patterns in the weave, stored bright reflections, was mesmerized by beauty. "They're like children from separate parents," Glenda liked to remark when they'd spin off on different tangents in the midst of some organized play.

But Walker was possessed by demons. As Glenda was often forced to remark: "There's something evil in him that comes out when he's boozing. Some sleeping monster that suddenly awakes." His drinking worsened and his law practice slipped. Before long he left it and they moved to Chicago, where he joined a large downtown firm and Glenda started teaching at Northwestern. They bought a big house on the lake. He began to be away on trips and Glenda suspected affairs. Then things badly came apart. Walker was deeply depressed and began living with someone else, toward whom he became abusive. He abused Glenda as well, but never with physical violence. Instead there was the pent-up venom she'd come to know so well, an eerie code of sarcasm and vicious addled wit, delivered white-faced and gleeful, husky-throated, evil-edged, and followed, much later, by crushing and exhausted remorse. Walker wished he were dead. Once he confided to Eric: "I like your moths, really. I wish I were one. They spread their wings, they find a mate, they squander their strength, they die. It's all so perfectly simple and brief." Then he went out on a bender.

In an odd sort of parallel the great silkworm moths, like his parents' love, had begun to fade by the Sixties. No one could explain their decline. Car fumes that baffled the searching males? Over-collecting or habitat loss? Sodium and mercury vapor lights that distracted the adults from mating? There were many theories. The fact was their numbers crashed and they all but vanished in the cities.

Thus Eric sat now by a window, on the eve of his departure, recalling details of lost richness, sifting old illusions, waiting for one more Polyphemus—still his mother's favorite moth. He'd caught six in the last five years here, but none since the previous season. When his mother had first become ill he had thought he would paint a Polyphemus and present it to her as a gift. But his best work fell short of Glenda's and the project lost its appeal. Then another idea had struck him when he'd gotten Jackie's letter. He'd been baiting all that week, as it happened, simply for the pleasure of the search. Now that a crisis had come, why not capture the creature alive and bring it to her sick-bed? Drug it with a surfeit of Ed Reese's potion and carry it with him to Chicago. Polyphemus moths briefly travelled well if properly looked after. Though the vigil all week had been fruitless, he had taken moths on this very date during several seasons past. Perhaps if he stayed up extra late and made a final try? He'd even spiked the bait with an added ounce of rum.

A rustling in the leaves now alerted him. He once more flicked on his flashlight. This time two eyes like tiny headlamps glowed in his direction, and the sight of them made him flinch. No Polyphemus this. Rather a sailor from the torrid South, a subtropical migrant that now and then pushes north. It had huge dark wings that converged to a point, each with markings like violent waves or the death-rays portrayed in science-fiction. It was a maverick species—restless and manic—that would not tolerate capture, only batter itself to pieces. Some knew it as the Giant Noctuid but most simply called it Black Witch. His mother had never drawn it and said it gave her "the creeps." It was a phrase she rarely used, especially in relation to moths, whom she otherwise loved uniformly. The one time he recalled her using it was in reference to some nasty mischief that his sister had gotten up to. Jackie had been ten, but his mother had scolded her bitterly as if speaking to an adult. "You're just like your father," she had tensely accused, "You both give me the creeps."

Eric watched the moth spin slowly on the bait and unwind its coiled proboscis. Here was a rare encounter, yet he felt no trace of elation. And the more he stared at the death-ray wings and burning eyes, the less he liked what he saw. The moon had moved beyond sight, the air was cold, and a shiver ran through his body. He thought about the trip ahead. Exhaustion gripped him and he knew further waiting was futile. Stiffly he rose from the cushions, tossed his flashlight on the couch, dropped the window and locked it, lowered the blinds on his visitor and the uneasy stream of night.

Chapter 4

GABRIEL DENT CROUCHED DOWN to the big clump of mugwort and pressed his nose to the gray-green leaves. A faint pungency touched his nostrils. The herb garden behind the garage, which turned the southwest corner and extended up to the driveway, was warm in the bright morning sun. To the left, beyond a broad lawn, loomed a large white frame house. Adam, the only child of its owners, Rod and Lisa Vigren, leaned at Gabe's elbow, small hands clasped at his back, trying to get a whiff of whatever Gabe plucked or cut and placed in the bucket beside them. Still wet with dew, there were hairy leaves of borage redolent of cucumber, sharp-scented sprays of angelica and southernwood, minty lemon-balm and bergamot, all neatly gathered at the stems and arranged in concentric rows.

"The small glass eye-dropper!" Gabe suddenly crowed, frozen with excitement. "Quick, it's in the garage on a tray beside the space-heater!" Adam was off in an instant, soaring around to the white side-door with arms extended, his blond cowlick aflutter, his unzipped Brewers jacket puffed out, bat-like, at his sides. He returned moments later, dropper in hand, to find Gabe still set in a crouch, staring intently at the mugwort. As Gabe took the dropper with a surgeon's vertical flourish of hand and wrist, his voice dropped to a stage-whisper and he proclaimed in a kind of trance: "Dew-honey!"

Adam leaned in closer with growing fascination. "What's dew-honey?"

Gabe did not reply. He lowered the dropper to the largest leaf and drew off a clear, twinkling liquid that had formed at its drooping tip. He pulled a small vial from his coat pocket, removed its cork and squeezed the nectar from the dropper to the vial, the few drops trickling inside. Working rapidly, he repeated this action until he'd cleared all the nectar from the leaves and the vial was close to half full.

"What's dew-honey?" Adam persisted.

Gabe held the vial to the sunlight, sniffed it, twisted his mustache thoughtfully, examined its contents so long and intently that it seemed he would never answer.

"It's an essence," he finally mumbled distractedly, removing his single-lensed glasses to stare and sniff once more. "In this case a mix of morning dewdrops and the fragrant oils of the plant."

"Where do the oils come from?"

"They're exuded."

"What's 'exuded' mean?"

"Squeezed out. Like sweat."

"Plants sweat?"

Gabe lowered the vial, replaced his glasses, rose from his crouch and gazed down solemnly at little Adam. "Your curiosity is, as usual, admirable. But if you're going to be my helper you've got to ask fewer questions. A helper is not a hindrance."

"What's a hindrance?"

Sighing, Gabe looked toward the sun. "Adam, in half an hour your mother is giving me a ride, and I need to preserve this harvest, pack my things, and be ready beside her car. How's that going to happen if you keep asking questions?"

Adam squinted and shrugged, while in sudden haste Gabe pocketed the vial and dropper, grabbed the bucket of cuttings and stalked briskly inside the garage, his pony-tail bobbing at his shoulders. A bluejay screeched from the maple above the drive. Zipping his jacket, Adam dawdled across the lawn, scuffing at errant leaves, then disappeared through the porch door of his large white frame house.

Gabe had parted the plastic sheets that hid the back end of the garage. Within was what passed for his lab, a place he kept relatively tidy. On a big aluminum table stood a goose-neck desk lamp, a hot plate, a Bunson burner, and an old electric coffee pot. A battered microscope held one corner, and beneath the table itself, humming faintly, was a portable refrigerator. Each of these items he had rescued from some basement or junkpile and restored to working order.

But table center was dominated by an immense yet fragile construction from which he distilled his formula, a Rube Goldberg edifice—fully four feet tall—of connected tubes and pipettes, makeshift hoses and siphons, all concocted of soda straws, odd plastic bits, glass viles, catheters and reeds, feeding or draining small flasks and beakers that winked in the glow of the desk lamp, the lot of it held together with homemade clamps and gaskets, cork washers and rubber-bands, assorted tapes and glues, paper-clips, string, and varying tests of fishing line that were wound with exceptional care. The entire apparatus had cost him not a penny, nor had any of the ingredients which it ultimately processed. Water he kept in a five-gallon jug and drew from the bathroom of the Vigrens' finished basement.

For all its aesthetic chaos there was a strength in this contraption, an aspect of precision and improbable creativity that suggested not the ridiculous but rather some reasonable madness, some essential craft and symmetry at the core of its deviation. It was Gabe's eccentric triumph and he doted on each detail, making repairs and additions and endlessly fine-tuning.

Now Gabe tied up the herbs with string, passing back through the curtain to hang them above the work bench. He returned to the lab, found a clean glass bottle that once contained India ink, and squeezed some tincture of catmint—three drops in all—into the vial of mugwort essence. After shaking and swirling the vial he poured it in a flask labeled "Base", whose contents were a bright chartreuse, and was placing it in the refrigerator when Adam interrupted.

"Mom says she needs to leave early and can you be ready now?" Adam's blond head was all that appeared through an open slit in the plastic.

Gabe winced but did not turn around. "Oh sure. I can be ready five minutes ago. Jesus. Tell her I'll be out there as soon as I can. Say ten minutes."

The slit in the plastic closed up, footsteps scuffled on the rough cement and the warped white side-door banged and bounced back, while Adam announced at the top of his lungs that Gabe was on his way.

~

"I didn't mean to rush you." Lisa Vigren's voice sounded softly weary as they moved up the street in her Taurus wagon. "I forgot that I'm seeing my dentist." She adjusted her designer sunglasses and pushed back a wisp of brown hair.

"No problem. I travel very light."

Lisa glanced at the small red day-pack cradled between Gabe's knees. In his hand was a square cardboard sign.

"Is that all you're taking?"

"Yah. Pretty much." He saw her grimmace slightly. "A lot of stuff fits in my coat as well."

"Oh. I see."

"I often travel with less than this."

"Really? I didn't know you travelled much at all. I mean, you seem to stay in town mostly."

"Well, I travel, um... a lot, really. Not so much in space, though. That is, conventionally."

"Oh. I see." Lisa thought about whistling a tune but finally decided against it. The keys in the ignition jiggled faintly with a sudden bump in the pavement. She doubled her chin to look down and brush an imaginary crumb from her spotless taupe turtleneck, then groped for firmer ground.

"Well, Rod and I were glad we could help you out. With your living situation and all. I hope it's not too much of a hardship. My parents think a lot of you. Especially Dad. He thinks you're very gifted."

Gabe stared straight ahead, absorbed with the way the car ate up space and how sun glinted on the teal-green hood, suffusing one edge to emerald. For a while he forgot his chummy role, expected her chatter to continue, then was suddenly aware of the too-long pause and heard himself quickly blurt: "Leo's been great. And, um...yourselves."

Her lips, tinted faintly with heather-plum lipstick, pursed in a demure smile.

"You know, I'm curious about that potion you make. That stuff you sell to the students."

"They're not all students."

"Well, I mean. The stuff you sell in those old A-1 bottles. Do you mind my asking what's in it? Basically, I mean. I know there's the herb garden and all, but I see you and my son collect things in the yard and, well, frankly, it sometimes just looks like lawn grass. Part of it, I mean."

A very long silence convinced Lisa she'd offended him. She fiddled with the fit of her sunglasses.

"The ingredients are no great mystery, really," Gabe finally offered gently. "All the plants I use are common in Wisconsin, either wild or as cultivars. Your back yard is not all grass."

"Uh, yes, we're well aware. It's rather spotty."

"That spottiness is things like ground ivy and violets, plantains and dandelions."

"Dandelions. Yes. Plenty of those. And you find them useful?"

"Oh sure. Dandelion is a staple with me. I practically survived on the stuff when, ah, when I was living rougher. Cooked big messes of it. But it's an ancient medicinal herb. Was once known as 'heart-fever grass' and was a cardiovascular tonic. Violets are another one. Venerated of old. Both leaves and flowers."

There was silence as Gabe grew distracted by a lever that controlled the heater, and pushed it back and forth with the thumb of his bony right hand. Then he regained his focus: "An old Eastern proverb says 'The excellence of the violet is as the excellence of El Islam above all other religions.'"

"Oh, I see."

"And ground ivy, that's everywhere, though it's not really an ivy. Also called Alehoof, Cat's Foot, Devil's Candlesticks, Gill-over-the-ground, and Lizzy-run-up-the-hedge. The Saxons used it in their beer and it was sold as tea in the streets of London for centuries."

"Oh."

"But I use other quite common things, too. Sweet-flag from around Lake Monona, Indian grass, plants I find by the railroads or in alleys. The trick is in how I blend and distill it and in the little touches I add. My dew-honeys, for example. I tell most people the ingredients are a secret because it raises their sense of its value. But I'm not likely to be copied."

"No, I see."

"My DROP has a pretty loyal following. There are certain people who swear by it. Especially for hangovers."

"Interesting. Did you learn all this in college?"

"No, I only went for a year."

"Oh, what was your major?"

"Celtic languages."

"I see."

The rest of the ride passed in silence. Lisa turned off Washington Avenue as they neared the ramp to the freeway.

"Is this where you want out?"

"Yes, right there above the cloverleaf."

"Are you sure you'll be all right? I mean, hitch-hiking's not much in vogue these days. Dad says it's kind of risky."

"No problem. I generally take my chances."

"Well, I certainly hope your mother improves." She did not turn to look at him but stared straight ahead as the engine idled smoothly and cars and trucks whizzed by.

Gabe thanked her, grabbed his pack and cardboard sign, and scrambled out the door.

"And thence he travelled onward," was the phrase that played through Gabe's mind as he reached the bottom of the grassy slope and stationed himself by the overpass. "Ac odyna ef kerdassant racdunct," in the Welsh language that haunted his dreams and kinetic trances. He dropped his pack beside him and propped against it the cardboard sign, facing the onrushing traffic. "CHI." it said in bold black letters.

An hour passed without a ride. Gabe stuck his thumb out at intervals but mostly relied on the sign. The day's first clouds climbed the sky to the west, dull smears of smoky gray that soon became edged with charcoal. A chill breeze lifted and was lathered into gusts by the overpass, which drew and sucked like a chimney flue and wafted also with high-speed roars and the echo of eighteen-wheelers. The harsh crescendo disturbed and enthralled him, he stared at the tunnel-like viaduct, voices licked at his brain. The horror of last night's journey flickered on the edge of his awareness.

> It was in that place that the fight was,
> And there was great slaughter on both sides.
> Ac yno y bu y gyfranc ac
> Y llas lladua uawr o bop parth.

Battlefields, torture and death, a night of pain and torment. He did not remember sleeping.

Better to keep moving. Sling on the pack, display the sign, venture down the highway. Down the endless ribbon of the shoulder, littered with trash and oil spots, food wrappers, cups and cans, the strewn contents of ashtrays, blue plastic bags, the wind now punching at his khaki coat, clouds lowering, cars whooshing, trucks wailing, the gritty crunch of his footsteps, the marcher's pace, to battle, crescendos of on-going conflict, today as in the past, a great coiled thread of suffering.

> It was then that the fight, immeasurably great, was
> fought.
> Yna y bu yr aerua diuessur y meint.
> And it was no ending, but a shadow of things yet to
> come.
> For I am here to tell thee.

Gabe marched, in his gangly, coat-flapping glide, to the pulsing highway whoosh. Once or twice he stopped beneath an overpass but the echoes drove him onward. There was drizzle by mid-afternoon. He moved beyond the city and its nexus of close-set rampways. The sign was taped to his backpack but still no vehicle stopped. His habit of forgetting to eat now fed his inner awareness. He feasted instead on the brooding sky, the incessant wail beside him, the ancient rhythms in his brain.

> I have borne a banner before Alexander
> I know the course of the turning stars
> I have traced the galaxy on the throne of he who reigns
> I was in Canaan when Absalom was slain
> I conveyed the Spirit to the level of the vale of Hebron
> I held court for the Don before the birth of Gwdion

I taught Eli and Enoc
I was given wings by the spells of the shining crosier
I was nimble of tongue before the gift of speech
I have been thrice in the foul prison of Arius
I have steered the work of the mighty tower of Nimrod
I am a wonder whose root is not known.
And this I can relate:
That those who will next appear
Are intent on wily schemes
Who by craft and devious means
In pangs of affliction
Will wrong the unprepared.
There is an evil host
From the rampart of Satanas
Which has overcome all
Between the deep and the shallow
Equally wide are its jaws
As the mountains of the Alps
It death will not subdue
Nor hand or blades
It has strength of nine hundred oxen
But cannot be engaged
It has sight of one thousand eyes
Clear as the green bergs of ice
Yet it cannot be blinded.

The march obliterated time. On the highway east of the city, lights crossed and converged, dusk fell, the din became a hissing, loud and rhythmic and constant. Lightening flashed in the west, drizzle thickened to rain, the wind blew cold, he trotted ahead toward shelter.

Beneath a concrete overpass Gabe sat for the first time in hours. His legs ached and his eyes watered and he finally unpacked a banana and took the time to eat it in the echoing cave of the bridgeway. No one had even slowed down, several had honked, a few had given him the finger. His chances would worsen in darkness. No sense continuing tonight, he decided; better to return to Madison and make a fresh start in the morning. His pants and shoes were soaked, his pony-tail hung like a drenched pelt, but the back side of his cardboard sign had remained more or less dry. From his coat he withdrew a marker and abbreviated Madison on the square rear face of the cardboard. "MAD." the bold black letters read. After setting his pack on a loose hunk of concrete he twisted the drops from his mustache and wearily leaned back to rest on the hardened dirt incline. The monolith loomed above him, flared with eerie shadows, trembled with roars and screeches.

Discover thou what is
The beast from before the flood
Without flesh
Without bone
Without head
Without feet
Neither older nor younger
Than at the beginning
There are no hungers
With creatures such as this
Great are its gusts
When it comes from the south
Great are its mists
When it strikes on coasts
It dwells in the fields and woods
Without hand or foot
Without the pall of age
Though it be old as the moon
So too is it wide
As the surface of the earth
And it was never born
Nor was it ever seen.
It has come to steal your wisdom
And ye shall be made its slaves
And lose your ancient power
To those who sit and scratch
With hands that once held blades.

Once more time escaped him. Rain poured down in torrents. He was standing as close to the road as he dared, just at the lip of the overpass, holding his thumb out stiffly. He'd finally discarded the sign when its implication struck him. But trucks and cars still blasted horns and cursed him through their windshields. The highway was now a battlefield so vast and awash with menace that it focused him like a laser, set him firmly to his task, branded him with its mission. He grew calm and steadfast, moving only to clear the misted drops from the single lens of his glasses.

A car with just one headlight, a great dark Cyclops trailing spray and weaving, finally braked to a stop on the shoulder fifty yards ahead. A door swung open, there were shouts and laughs and someone roared, "Hey, champ! We're up here! Yo!", and beckoned with a crooked arm. Gabe lurched from the shelter of the bridgeway and charged out into the storm.

"Give him some room there, Zippo. Give the man some room."

"No problem. He's fuckin' wet." Zippo squeezed over against another dark figure on the Bronco's back seat, spilling his can of Leinenkugel. "Shit-fuck. Look what the fucker made me do."

The passenger next to the silent driver, a hulk of thick shoulders and neck, twisted his baseball cap front to back and exposed to Gabe's gaze a large pale "A" on the crown above its bill. "That right, champ?" he bellowed in a deep hoarse voice while reaching to adjust the rearview mirror. "You make Zippo spill his 'Kugel?"

Gabe sat staring at the bill and large "A" and absorbing the warmth of the car.

"Well don't take it serious, champster. Zippo's a fuckin' spastic when it comes to feedin' his face. Aint that right Zippo? Don't know his mouth from his asshole after he gets a few brewskis in him."

A-cap leaned a bit to his left, flicked on the inside lights, fine-tuned the mirror at a steep reverse angle, and caught Gabe's face in its dark bar of glass. "You *are* a drown' lookin' rat, aint'cha, champ? No doubt about it. Where ya headin'?"

"Madison."

"Madison, no kiddin'? Ya know, I'm glad you said that, champski. 'Cause if you'd a said anyplace else you'd be shit outta luck."

The driver was pouring on speed now and the Bronco swung back and forth on the wet freeway lanes as it passed each vehicle it came to.

"Scoop here's a great driver, but ain't good for shit if I let him get much past Madison. Gets totally fuckin' lost. But I let him drive my Bronco 'cause he exercises caution. That's the key. Exercises caution. An' 'cause he's good at hustlin' pussy. An' still has his fuckin' license. So far." A-cap howled with laughter and sucked at his can of 'Kugel.

By the time they exited west on Washington Avenue and headed downtown the rain had let up and the wipers squeaked as they dragged across the windshield. The Bronco swerved and jolted. At intervals during his monologue, A-cap leaned left and addressed Gabe directly through the tilted bar of the mirror.

"This Bronco's a great truck. Don't ever call it a car, it's a truck. Made in America, which is a great country. Know how I got it, champski? I fuckin' *worked* for it. Every summer, between semesters."

Scoop snorted skeptically. "Shut the fuck up and drive," A-cap snapped in his direction.

"Anyway that's what's great about this country. You work for something and you get it, if you've got any balls at all. 'Less you're a nigger or a spic, or some kinda spineless deadbeat."

The Bronco had gotten hot inside. Zippo dozed beside Gabe with the beer can wedged in his crotch, now and then jolting awake, and the dark figure next to Zippo alternately snored and hiccupped. Scoop lit a cigarette and silently swerved through traffic.

"You listenin' back there, champski?" A-cap belched loudly. "One thing I can't stand is when a fucker won't listen. Now take yourself, for instance. I've talked to you before, ain't that right? Fuck yes. You and me are ol' friends. You're that mother who used to sleep in the park in some kinda bullshit tent."

He adjusted the bar of the mirror and stared back at Gabe. "Ain't that right, champ? Slept in the fuckin' park by the lake. An' had a fuckin' bicycle. Maybe panhandled a little down on State Street, too. Ain't that right?"

Gabe stared at the big pale A. "I don't panhandle."

"But you don't work neither, do ya champ? Fuckin' live on the public streets, like some sorta worm or rodent. Well I'm the mother who took yer fuckin' bike. 'Member that? Me an' ol' Zippo, yer buddy back there. We kicked yer lazy ass and dumped that bike in Lake Mendota. Took it down to the pier and fuckin' rolled it off the deep end. It's still there, champster, if you wanna fuckin' *dive* for it."

Zippo had come alert and drained the last of his 'Kugel. The Bronco swung onto State Street.

"But you won't, will ya? Too fuckin' lazy. Well I got news for ya. I've got a dream. Everyone should have a dream, don't ya think? An' my personal dream is to clean this town up and get all you fuckin' worms and deadbeats off the streets. An' you're at the top of my motherfuckin' list, champ. Ain't that right Zippo?"

The Bronco screeched to the curb in front of a dark-glassed boutique. With a sudden grab from behind Zippo managed to pin Gabe's arms.

"State Street all right for ya, champ?"

A-cap had turned in his seat and in nearly the same motion brought his big right arm around to the back with a violent windmill sweep that caught Gabe flush in the face. The bridge of Gabe's glasses snapped and his nose spurted blood. Zippo released him and Gabe grappled for the door, then was pushed and punched when he opened it until he sprawled out onto the curb. His red pack was jettisoned after him. The rear door slammed shut and A-cap rolled down his window. "That's for spillin' Zippo's beer, motherfucker. An' don't let us catch you fuckin' around in any more city parks, you motherfuckin' maggot. Or you'll end up where your bike did. Hear me, fuck-face?"

A beer can bounced off Gabe's chest as tires squealed and the Bronco charged up State Street. The two halves of Gabe's steel-rim glasses had dropped into his lap, where blood that escaped his cupped hands now dripped on his khaki coat.

A man in a fawn-colored jacket stopped to ask if he needed help. Gabe waved the man away. Instead he searched through a pocket and found some paper napkins which he used to plug his nose and wipe the blood from his clothing. From another pocket came a coil of thin wire that, seated Indian-style by the curb, he used to bind his glasses at the bridge, next wrapping the splice up tightly with a length of white tape that he fished from the day-pack beside him.

He rose shakily, stumbled, then bent to vomit on the sidewalk. An athletic-looking couple in nylon windbreakers, arms linked and hands in pockets, cursed and swerved away, throwing angry, disgusted stares. Gabe asked the time of another pair, who ignored him and quickened their pace. Finally he saw a clock in the window of a closed-up restaurant. Ten-forty-five. The Four Lakes would still be open. He hurried over to Williamson and got there just as Leo was locking the twin glass doors.

"What the hell happened to you?" Leo's squat figure was striped by an Art Deco grid of flat chrome bars and his voice came muffled through the doors as he struggled to re-open them. "I thought you were headin' to Chicago?"

Gabe stared wearily through his battered glasses as Leo shoved one door half-open and propped it with his foot.

"There were one or two slight glitches."

"Jesus, your nose looks like a tomata."

Brushing inside, Gabe made for the nearest red stool.

Leo relocked the door and hustled behind the counter. "Laura went home early 'cause business was slow. Forget the decaf, let me get you some real coffee. So what was it, somebody didn't like your looks?"

Gabe did not reply.

"Hey, look, I told you this hitchhikin' stuff is dangerous these days. You can't trust nobody."

Gabe's eyes were like smoke-blue marbles refracted from the depths of a puddle. He did not speak, nor respond to the cup of black coffee that sloshed into its saucer as Leo pushed it towards him.

"Well that does it." Leo moved to the open cash drawer of the register and snapped out two twenty dollar bills. Then he slid them beside Gabe's cup. "Here. You're takin' the goddamn bus. It's cheaper than a hospital any day."

He thought he heard Gabe mumble.

"What? For chrissake speak up. Can't you see I'm trying to help ya? Drink your damn coffee and tomorrow we're gettin' you on the Greyhound."

"Ryued uu hwyret y mi kerdassant."

"What? What the hell are you mumbling now?"

Gabe looked up and seemed to find fresh focus. He reached out and picked up the coffee cup, sucked off a big hot gulp, then replaced it and dried his mustache.

"Ryued uu hwyret y mi kerdassant," he repeated. "It is strange how slowly I travelled."

Chapter 5

RAIN WAS FLOWING DOWN the thick plate of the lounge window in wavy, shimmering sheets. Out on the avenue below, beside the green hotel entrance canopy whose scalloped edges dashed crystal braids downward onto the flooded sidewalk, a red and white cab disgorged a raincoated businessman—briefcase protecting his head—into a silver, light-splashed puddle. Jackie Dent sat at a bar-stool by the window, watching the street scene beneath her and sipping a strawberry daiquiri.

It was her third night in Evanston. Two days before a Stretch DC-10 had whisked her from LA to O'Hare, where she at once caught a cab to the Loop for a pre-arranged meeting with her lawyer. From the 12th floor of his LaSalle Street office he reviewed for her the three kinds of titles for multiple property ownership, filled her in generally on the agreement he'd had drafted, then had his secretary spread four clean copies of it across a big walnut desk.

He was short and stocky, with curly dark hair that spilled over his high forehead, and smooth ruddy cheeks shaded to lavender by the undertone of a close-shaved but heavy beard.

"As I explained on the phone, Ms. Dent, joint tenancy is similar to tenancy in common, where each individual owner maintains an undivided interest in the property. But joint tenancy differs in offering right of survivorship. If one of the owners passes on, the remaining owners split the property of the deceased."

Jackie had been seated bolt upright in a heavy leatherbacked chair, her stockings and skirt pinching and her tired eyes watering. Her head ached and her stomach was sour, but the discomfort seemed only to aid her focus.

"That's just as I understood it, Mr. Hirschbaum."

He pulled at the knot of his paisley tie and fiddled with the pocket of his blazer.

"Now in the case of your mother's property, I took the liberty, based on your information, of filling in the names of the tenants before your arrival." He picked up one of the copies and handed another to Jackie.

"Good. That's fine," she reassured in a low voice, squaring the paper gently with her long fingers.

"As you instructed, there will be three principles in tenancy: yourself, your mother, Glenda Reese Dent, and your brother, Gabriel Dent. Is that correct?"

"Yes, that's right. Yes."

He next took several minutes to go over each page, reading aloud the paragraphs that he felt were abstruse or ambiguous, and re-phrasing in layman's terms. He focused especially on a clause he had added, at Jackie's request, that qualified the agreement. He read it slowly, word by word, in a throaty monotone.

"Is that what you had in mind?"

"Well, yes, that sounds like what we talked about earlier."

Mr. Hirschbaum sighed pensively. "Are there any other special problems that you'd care to discuss at this time or amendments you wish to suggest?"

"No, not really. None that I can think of."

"Well fine, then, here are your copies, and when you get them properly signed you can return them to my office."

His manner had been so succinct and discreet that she had felt like praising him openly, but checked herself in time. Instead she firmly shook his hand, studied his lavender cheeks and jowls down the long beak of her nose, and told him she'd soon be in touch. Then she hustled down and out of the building and caught a cab north to Evanston.

Her mother was in a private room on the hospital's third floor. The wing looked out on a grassy courtyard flecked with leaves from a lone scaly oak. Two plastic water glasses, each partly full, and a single crumpled Kleenex littered a wheeled table at the left side of her bed, and on her right—toward a gray-curtained window that was streaked with fading sunlight—was a blond-wooded chair upholstered in orange, a tall metal stand with a blinking green light, and the clear bladder of an IV-bag suspended like a transparent ham.

Glenda wore a mustache of thin plastic tubing that extended off her pillow to a contraption behind the bed. Her red hair was now nearly white, her cheeks hollow, and her once fine complexion grown blotchy and stained, its opalescence marred by dark veins and a morbid opaqueness like the flesh of boiled lobster. Her thin mouth drooped, her ears had grown big, her green eyes were weak and teary and rimmed by bloodshot swellings.

Their greeting was a hug and a kiss, rather than any words, with Jackie bending her chest down diagonally onto the bed to meet her mother's, and planting the kiss on her cold dry lips with arms and torso raised slightly to spare her any discomfort. Then pleasantries and small talk were exchanged as Jackie sat back in the blond and orange chair, her mother's voice a whispery croak, her own a hushed string of questions and soothing affirmations.

Presently Jackie's manner grew stern. She pulled her chair closer to the bed, unzipped the briefcase on her lap, leaned close to her mother's side...

As the hard-nosed "achiever" of Glenda's three children, Jackie was looked on by her mother as someone to trust about business. Close as her daughter's temperment was to that of her late husband Walker, and as much as that clashed with Glenda's own, yet she respected Jackie's judgement. She was anxious to forget the terrors of her marriage and had lost touch with dark sides, had blocked out the bitterness and rivalries that had grown up among her offspring, seeing each child in simplified terms. Thus Gabe was her brilliant but eccentric son, who as far as she knew ran a bicycle shop where he plied his talent for repairs, but who, odd-duck that he was, was lax about staying in touch. Eric was her good-hearted nature boy, gentle and perceptive, but with no real head for business and with a need to be private and aloof. Jackie was her hell-bent success tale, with Walker's furious focus. If waters got rough, she had always believed, her daughter could hold things together and keep the family afloat. If only the three would communicate more, if only their father hadn't...

"Mom, there's some business we need to take care of." Jackie patted her blond cowlick nervously and pressed her beaky nose close to Glenda's ear. "We've got to deal with your property and pay some of your bills." Her voice was a soothing whisper; Glenda turned on her pillow and stared with watery eyes.

In the next quarter hour Jackie spelled out the grim situation. Her mother's cash and savings had been all but wiped out by her bills, not just those stemming from her illness, but those from her home improvements. For the last several years, under Jackie's guidance and counsel, Glenda had made renovations to her elegant lakeside house, not only making repairs but adding a glassy conservatory to the wing that faced Lake Michigan, and installing an adjacent "museum room" to house her collection of nature art and pioneer naturalist manuscripts. Her late husband's assets and stocks, which had turned out to be considerable, she had lavished on the property, also expanding the gardens and erecting a sizeable greenhouse. The rationale had been Jackie's, in part; she had argued rather plausibly that the home's prime location encouraged some upscale improvements, that they'd hedge well against inflation, and that outlays would be more than recovered when the house was one day sold.

Glenda blinked at the copy before her. She skimmed the bulk of its content and focused instead on the final page that spelled out the names of the tenants.

"But Eric's name isn't on here," she said weakly, frowning and clearing her throat.

"Mom, Eric wants no part of it. I talked to him on the phone. You know he hates legal matters. But I wanted to make sure, so I told him to contact Gabe and thrash it out with him. Apparently they decided that Gabe's name would be sufficient and they'd work out their interest together. Well, you know how close they were. I think, well, it may draw them together again, so it's probably all for the best. But Eric just hates these hassles. He told me to let you know, and I think he felt sort of guilty but, well... there it is. Mom, he's very anxious that you get things settled, that you pay off the last of these debts."

Glenda was not convinced that she should leave Eric out of anything. She'd done no such thing in her will; why should this be different? But Jackie was persuasive. Joint tenancy would have no bearing on her will; it would save excessive probate costs when the full estate came to be settled; and it would give some control to Jackie at a time she needed to take charge, for both Gabe and Eric were hopeless at handling such details. There was no more time to try changing Eric's mind. If he'd rather be on the sidelines then they had to respect his wishes.

Glenda stared at Jackie, watched her intense gray-green eyes, and finally relented. The room had gone purplish with evening gloom. Jackie was all concern and support as she closed the pale curtains and flicked on another light. She cradled her briefcase and straightened her skirt and pecked her mother on the forehead.

"I'll be back some time tomorrow, Mom, and we'll get things squared away."

With a swizzle-stick shaped like an old-fashioned key, Jackie whipped the pink slush of her third daiquiri into a lumpy little whirlpool and stared out at the rain. Eric might be on the road now, she mused, or maybe he'd leave tomorrow. She had given herself ample time. The letter would have taken two days to reach him, maybe three, or maybe even longer if CeCe had dawdled in mailing it, as Jackie had thought she might. And, knowing him as she did, he'd have tried to leave pretty quickly. He might even drive straight through if he thought she was up to something, which she figured he probably would. She smiled to think of his reaction. It was easy yanking his chain, pathetic and blubbering watchdog that he was. But he was a barker, not a biter. And he was already too late...

A businessman entered the tiny lounge and sat down at the table beside her. The barmaid swished over and took his order for a drink. Jackie thought she knew him. She stared for half a minute.

"Well, you're the fellow with the briefcase on his head," she finally ventured cheerily.

"Sorry?" He had dark eyes and thinning hair and those yuppy tortoise-shell glasses with golden bridge and hinges.

"The one who stepped in the puddle. Out there. No smile for you. Your briefcase was your umbrella."

He laughed. "Oh, yes, from my taxi." He gestured pathetically downward. "I just changed my shoes."

"Poor baby," she said with a teasing smile. "Can I buy you something to ward off the grippe?"

The barmaid arrived with his beer, pushed down, with a practiced swipe of two fingers, a napkin that said "Key-Note Lounge", and set the glass in its center.

"No thanks, it's already here, but you're welcome to come and join me."

She was feeling gay now, magnanimous, flushed with her private victory. How often had she seen his type? The beleaguered middle manager getting squeezed from both sides at once, who lives for a certain freedom that makes up for the grind of travel or the pinch of home and office. Careful, responsible schleppers, modest until you approach them, all anxious to show they're alive...

On her second day in Evanston she'd focused on meeting Gabe. "I don't care how you get down there," she had written in her letter, "but we've got to meet up by Thursday. It's critical. I'll be staying at the Harrington Hotel. Call me when you arrive and if need be I'll pick you up. If I'm not in my room leave a message. If I get no message by Thursday noon, I'm coming up to get you, and that bloody well better not happen."

Gabe took the bus Wednesday morning. Leo and Laura both saw him off and he got to Chicago before noon. He thought about taking the train or El north but it was already too late, and besides he was short of cash. Then he couldn't find Jackie's letter, where she'd written the hotel name down, and somehow the name escaped him. It took him a while to figure it out, making calls to Directory Assistance, and by that time Jackie was seething. The front desk reached her in her room, where she'd mixed herself some Kool-Aid and was nursing a stubborn hangover.

"Damn your eyes anyway, Gabe, where the hell have you been?" she shouted over the phone. "I was ready to call that bloody diner in Madison and find out where you were. I can't spend all day in this place!" She cursed him for being downtown as well and not having made it any closer. "Never mind, just don't move. I'm coming down to get you. Just stay in the damn station."

In the taxi she tried to calm herself; it was crucial that she put Gabe at ease. She labored to ignore the meter, the heavy-footed cabby who reeked of sweat and tobacco, the construction on the Kennedy Expressway that delayed them fifteen minutes. Gabe was where they agreed he'd be, curled bat-like in a seat by the ticket line, wrapped in the cape of his coat and reading a shredded comic book that he'd picked up on the bus.

He stared at her blankly when she quick-stepped up in front of him. "Christ, what did you do to your face? You look like a bloody street-person" she blurted. Then she pursed her lips and calmly spoke as if they'd been together for hours. "Come on, we'll take the train from here. I can't stand another cab ride."

Gabe was tired and out of focus and she led him like a child. First she bought him a decaf standing up at a fast-food counter. Then they walked to the Chicago and Northwestern station through the street noise and stink and mild autumnal sunshafts that sunk down through the shadowed canyons. They caught a two-thirty train and climbed to some upper-deck seats in one of the emptier cars, where Gabe stared at the buildings and bridges as they rocked away from the yards, and Jackie dropped her voice almost to a whisper.

"Gabe, I *am* glad to see you, I really am. I'm just a little tense from all this business with mother. She's got no liquid assets and we're stuck with paying her bills. But she's actually improved and the doctor's are saying, right now at least, that she could hold on for months, even a year."

Gabe kept staring out the window. "So why did you write me she was dying?"

"Well she *is*, and she was. Much worse, I mean. I only found out when I got here myself just what her condition was."

"So what do you need from me?"

"So, well, what we need at this point is to get a second mortgage on that white elephant of a house. Really, it's an albatross, and the thing we need is cash. Mom can't deal with it, as weak as she is. But I looked into joint tenancy and with that we can handle it ourselves."

He turned away from the window and stared into her eyes. "You mean *you* can handle it *yourself*."

"Well, I could, if you agree. I mean, I didn't think that *you'd* want any part of it, really."

"I don't."

"And neither does Eric, by the way. He refuses to get involved, won't even return my calls. So I talked it over with Mom. You and I and Mom will be joint tenants, which gives us each a hand in ownership, plus rights of survivorship and the ability to avoid probate when she dies. But I need to ask your good faith."

"Good faith?"

"Yes, I need you to promise that in good faith you'll share your rights of ownership with Eric, since we can't include him on paper."

"Does Mom agree with this deal?"

"Yes, sure, I saw her just yesterday and we talked it through. You'll get to see her yourself."

The train had crossed the Chicago River and was palpitating swiftly between sprawls of low warehouses cleaved by weedy wastes, tire-littered and trash-tangled and ambered by the sun.

"Trust. That's what you want from me?" Gabe twirled the ends of his mustache and gazed at the passing scene.

She sank back in her seat and seemed genuinely weary. "That's right Gabe."

"You're a fine one to be asking."

The meeting that evening with Glenda went as Jackie had hoped. Gabe was distracted and withdrawn and said hardly a word. The shock of seeing his mother so ill only pushed his mind away, and it was all Glenda could do to get him to speak at all. "You've hurt yourself," was the first thing she'd said, to which Gabe had made no reply. To his mother it mattered little. It was enough to greet him and see his face and make small talk over her supper, which she pecked at more actively than usual.

Jackie passed out the agreement at a well-timed moment and, as she'd expected, there was almost no discussion before the parties signed. A collective embarassment prevailed instead, an unspoken feeling that the family was mangled by a failure of will, but that taking some action might help. Gabe anyway hated hospital scenes, had balked completely when his father was dying and had never paid him a visit. He was anxious to be away.

The farewell was the kind of glib leaving that takes place every day when people exit kitchens or foyers and head off to jobs or school: Jackie stuffing her briefcase once more and spewing casual bromides and cheerful inanities, as if comfortably late for the office, and Gabe planting a hopeless child's kiss on his mother's pale forehead, then flailing aside to grab his coat and mumble as he searched his pockets, like a boy making sure his marbles were secure, or his slingshot or favorite toy soldier. Glenda stared from the upright angle of her raised bed, watching her two strange offspring, treading water in the ocean of her losses.

Jackie played generous sister. She put Gabe up at the Harrington that night, in a room down the hall from her own, walked with him in the morning to the train station four blocks away—after first buying him breakfast—and extended a final present as the big yellow engine was approaching.

"What's this?" Gabe blurted as he opened the little envelope.

"Just something I thought you could use."

He spread the green bills with his fingers. "Five hundred dollars? You don't owe me anything."

The signal bells clanged and the platform shivered and the train brakes hissed and screeched.

"Call it a token of faith. No big deal. Let's just say you're worth it."

Their pale eyes met briefly. Gabe blinked, poked at his single-lensed glasses with their fat white patch at the bridge, slung his red pack to his shoulder, then turned and glided to the train.

When the cars were out of sight Jackie ran one more essential errand. She met with a lawyer at a nearby bank where her mother housed her accounts. He too had drawn up papers, and when she'd checked them and gotten his instructions, she visited Glenda near lunch time, watched her poke at her tray of food, explained the last procedure that was needed before she could help. Her mother seemed improved, almost jolly, and was once more sitting up. She devoured her jello salad, drank her carton of milk, and signed what needed signing.

Thus later that afternoon, when Jackie had repaired to her hotel room, mixed herself some Kool Aid, and flicked on a TV soaper that she swiftly silenced with the MUTE switch, she lifted her glass toward the glowing tube and offered an ironic toast, for she now had power of attorney in all her mother's affairs.

"Amazing, just incredible." Jackie was grinning with amusement as she set down the empty bar glass that had held her fourth daiquiri and gazed at her new friend Peter. "That *you* work with Mike Schuster at Continental Carton! They did all our early packaging."

"*Did* work with him," Peter corrected, smiling and running his index finger down the frosty side of his tumbler. "They had a big shakeup and that's when I went to Global. Now I'm out of Global and back in hospital supply where I started. It's more lucrative."

"But still, I mean, even *then*. It's such a small world!"

For the last five minutes they'd been rubbing ankles under the pedestalled table, like Fifties teens in a malt shop. Jackie had gotten giddy, had reached that goosey threshold where all things seem surprising in the grab-bag of human relations, where the cheap little trinkets that one blindly pulls from one's sack of random contact seem like precious, glittering prizes. She liked this Peter What's-His-Name. He was still a chump, to be sure, but bore certain child-like graces that made her almost wistful: the way he shyly stroked what remained of his hair, lowering his eyes as he did so and briefly looking away; the way he laughed like a naughty urchin at her bursts of cynical wit; the way he whispered when he said something intimate, like a boy telling secrets to his sister, or pouted and held his tongue when she offered some ribald rejoinder, but then rubbed her ankle still harder.

They stayed until closing. The waitress, grown disgusted with their bolder displays of affection, haughtily dropped the check by their drinks as she straightened chairs with exaggerated flair and banged ashtrays around on tables. Jackie's tongue darted one last time between Peter's child-glad lips as they hunched forward elbow to elbow and upset his empty beer glass. The lights went up in the tiny room and the barmaid pulled at the curtains. Jackie rose unsteadily as Peter covered the bill. She balanced herself with the chair-back and stared a final time out the window that had ceased to run with raindrops. Suddenly, obliquely, she glimpsed the last strides of a figure who crossed the street to an alley and disappeared through the gloom. He had that glide in his step, and she thought she'd detected a pony-tail at the back of his cape-like coat. She stifled a wave of nausea.

"Something wrong?" asked Peter, boyishly taking her elbow.

Jackie frowned and looked away.

"C'mon," he whispered by her ear. "I know a place that'll make us both feel better."

"So do I," she countered, and led him toward the door.

Chapter 6

ERIC AWOKE NEAR DAWN. He wanted to sleep longer but the urgency of the trip seized a corner of his dream-numbed brain and refused to let it go. It was easy enough to get started after his last night's preparations but quite another matter to be clear-headed about it. Thus in a kind of robot stupor he dressed and washed and gathered his few things, then quietly slipped out the door. He did not want to think about breakfast until he had his car on the road.

The courtyard was all in shadow and a single sparrow chattered as he headed for the asphalt lot. His Honda was drenched with dew. Opening the tiny trunk in back, he wedged in his light bag and briefcase. The engine came to life quickly, coughed and gently idled. An old Wanamaker's shopping bag, which held a gift for his mother, he set gently on the seat behind him and covered with his jacket.

He took the back way toward the interstate, under the railroad viaduct and out along Hungerford Avenue, where the lawns now pinked with daylight and the sycamore limbs, high up, caught fresh rays and glowed like dappled serpents. The stone or frame houses, flanked by enclosed porches and their white latticed windows, showed the oddly fitted detail, the sandstone turret or half-timbered gable, sentried by dark hemlocks and waxy rhododendrons and striped by the long morning shadows. In Bala-Cynwyd he avoided City Avenue, with its jarring pinball jungle of stoplights and tacky commerce, veering instead down the steep slope of Belmont Avenue to where the on-ramp waited in the hollow and a gas station Quik-Stop beckoned. There he bought his morning provisions: two blueberry muffins, a box of vanilla wafers, and a 20-ounce cup of black coffee.

The expressway made him feel free. He had that sense of flying a few feet off the ground, of migrating like some bird, as he gulped at his jumbo coffee and devoured one of the muffins. The lanes were lightly trafficked. Hilltops loomed to his left and the sad old Schuylkill floodplain, glimpsed at flickering intervals down through the hardwoods to his right, seemed freighted with the valley's past. The Reeses had settled thickly here, on the river's far side, from the working-class byways of Manayunk to the heights beyond Roxborough, and especially back in the Germantown enclaves above the Wissahickon. It was old territory. A yellowed map of the thirteen colonies that had hung in his grandfather's study marked only two towns in the region: Philadelphia and Germantown. There was a ghostliness here, a sepia tone to the light in the hills and vales, a residue of history that colored his view of the countryside.

Once it had seemed very real, this ghostly sheen—once when he was young and the world was a haunting promise full of pale suffusions that stirred his love of the planet. Now he saw it as illusion, fetching but quite unfounded, the flotsam of deceptions that bewitch innocent brains.

On he flew, above the old mills and factories, the ridges of gray rock, the ravines and wooded bluffs. The terraced clutter of Conshohocken soon coalesced off to his right, below and across the river, and was contrasted high on his left by a rising Marriott hotel and glassy office complex. The road curved northward at a junction, then a horrid outpost came on: new woodframe dwellings on a barren crest, outlined against the sky like a string of Monopoly houses.

His old white Civic thrummed smoothly, had opened up, was settling into the long-haul groove that would weave him through four different states. He had never adjusted to flying—the real flying in commercial aircraft that most others took for granted. He'd done it exactly twice, and both times was not only scared but annoyed by the glib charade: the code of false politeness and filtered lies that was broadcast by the crews, the lack—amid a dopey faith and jollity—of any real safety should the plane catch fire or plummet, the utter claustrophobia that was passed off as so much coziness. But, to his mind, worst of all was the sense of violent thrust well disguised by padded cabins but otherwise easily picked up: the irrefutable awareness that one was rocketing through the sky at inhuman height and velocity, beyond the threshold of control, both personal and collective, should anything untoward happen.

Eric favored human scale and understandable movement: a firm grasp, as much as possible, of the speed at which one faced fate. Generally, he believed, in order to stay spiritually intact in the teeth of a mad modern world one had to keep stepping on the brakes, not goosing the accelerator. On the other hand there were crises that required a swift response. It was all relative, he realized, but highway velocity was as far as he cared to proclaim his estrangement from the globe's more modest inhabitants.

Let others think him a fool. He'd made peace with his eccentricities. And his book was his consolation. It had nothing to do with the Reeses or Dents, and it certainly wasn't a novel, as Jackie mockingly insisted. It both steeled and soothed him, helped him see life's strange connections, shed light on human darkness. It was the work of almost a decade. He knew some of it by heart, could quote those lucid sections that had silently nagged and obsessed him through the years of its creation.

He called his expanding manuscript *Notes of a Doomsday Philosopher*. It hadn't found a publisher and probably never would. To his colleagues at the paper, especially Cynthia Blott, it had become a standing joke. "Eric's Opus" they called it, usually in good humor but in Cynthia's case, with scorn. To him it existed as a safety valve more than something that might earn him money. He did not let it run his life and, with a horror of being called "crackpot" or "crank", he pushed its contents on no one.

The main problem, as Eric saw it, was that people don't want bad news. And that, by extension, he theorized, would be the downfall of humanity. This bottom line was so simple that most people laughed in his face if ever he bothered to speak of it. "Doom and gloom philosopher," "Chicken Little", and "nihilistic nay-sayer" were some of the judgements thrown back at him. He would chuckle shyly and suggest they were proving his point.

"If the truth brings unpleasant tidings," he had written, "it is shouted down rather quickly. One is told not to dwell on the negative. This is good advice except when one suffers from a tumor, an infection, or a badly broken leg. Then one must admit the problem and focus on it completely in order to effect a cure. To do otherwise is to invite one's own doom."

His Honda labored up a hill. The Schuylkill Gear Works came in view near the town of King of Prussia, where he linked with the Pennsy Turnpike. Wooded slopes and ravines gave way to grassy sprawl, to commercial camps of shopping malls, warehouse hubs and fortress-like corporate headquarters. He headed west toward the farmlands, toward the chestnut earth that the Amish plowed, toward that region where Germans were "Dutch".

Melanie Kelly had never backed him up when it came to the subject of his book. His girlfriend of almost seven years was perhaps his sternest critic and threw in her lot with the optimists, or, as Eric preferred to call them, the "kill-the-messenger set."

"You think you've got some lock on the truth when all you are is a whiner," Mel liked to declare during arguments. He was not by nature a fighter but could put forth a formidable case, was reasoned in thought and precise in language and especially skilled at rebuttal. His logical bent enraged her. Their battles were fierce at the start: she flushed and sneering in an Irish rage and he shouting back his rejoinders. Then a smoldering phase would set in that might last several hours, with Mel pouting and sniping while Eric held ground grimly. If the fight involved his book or his dark view of human foibles, which it very often did, he stuck ever closer to his vision, his complex grasp of a decline that he felt was as certain as sunrise.

She came to loathe his "pessimism". Thinking it partly his wording she hated, his personal turn of phrase, he would throw the onus on others, quoting H.L. Mencken that "The truth that survives is the lie it is easiest to believe," or Tennessee Williams' assertion that "The truth is something desperate," or even—in his own desperation after she'd played her little trump and accused him of being paranoid—the anonymous pop aphorism that he especially enjoyed, "If you ain't a little paranoid, you ain't payin' attention."

It was sex that held them together. At least that's how Eric saw it and, in the end, when she'd walked out this last time, she'd sarcastically agreed. He couldn't resist her white Celtic flesh, her high Kelly cheekbones and color, her soft blue eyes and perfect peach-shaped behind. She was ballerina graceful as well, moving and stepping with tender twists and supple childlike ease, tossing her dark curly hair, smiling shyly, speaking in flirtatious whispers when wishing to be petted or held.

Inarticulate about what she saw in him, yet she readily expressed her passion, was quick to insert her tongue in his mouth and pull his shirt-front out, then slip her hand down his jeans. In the intimate little apartment they made love in every room, on every rug or floor, upon every plausible platform. Their desire diminished little in the years they were together. They especially liked outdoor trysts, enjoyed driving to isolated places and—after hiking to scrutinize the landscape, with Eric stopping to collect the odd moth or examine some cryptic pupae—rolling on mossy carpets, by a rill or rocky alcove, and fucking sweetly in the leaf mold beneath some shaggy bole. Often he caught her in the shower, or she him, where they stroked each others' seal-wet forms, probed tongue to tongue the sweet spot under each's upper lip, while he kneaded the smooth swollen pocket between her thighs till she guided his ramrod home.

In fact she was much too sexy, or so he had often accused. She'd had many partners before him. Once in a bar off Logan Square he had talked with a St. Joe alum who referred to a group of girlfriends Eric knew included Mel, as "that bunch who love to suck cocks." When he mentioned the guy to Mel she'd gone red as a Santa and slapped him with a wooden spoon. In the argument that followed she'd insisted he was a chauvanist pig for condemning women who had casual sex, and he'd countered by saying he condemned men as well, and that promiscuousness was a shame to *both* the genders, not a hallmark of equal rights.

"You're such a bloody *Victorian*," she had screamed at him from the bathroom where she'd fled to regain her composure. "Victorian" joined "Chicken Little" among her favorite accusatory labels.

"If Victorians didn't love lightly, then I don't mind joining their company," was the best he managed in defense. Except for a brief fling in college she'd been his only sexual partner, a fact which she found more than quaint.

Eric drove under haze-softened skies, the sun a gauzy lemon that squirted the fields with light. There were saffron patches in the stubble beside streams, clots of old machinery, crow flocks that squabbled and dispersed, early October shadows newly thinned by fallen leaves. He rubbed at his Popeye elbow, which had swollen to a ludicrous bulb, and glanced now and then in the rear-view mirror to study his unshaven countenance.

At Harrisburg he crossed the Susquehanna, an islanded sheet of glare gouged with rocks and feathery rapids, then loped up toward the mountains as the pale skies clouded over. When driving he was always hungry. At Bedford he gave up on vanilla wafers and stopped for an early lunch, getting off in the cramped little village and buying a sub at a deli. The old frontier outpost was long sunk in modern claptrap, with fast-food, motels, and gas pumps awash at its winding hub. He swung around through the outskirts before facing the turnpike monotony and then stopped to pick up more coffee. Even teenage boys seemed to work in such towns, in these cash-strapped rural backwaters, though he still caught a glimpse of one idle trio—like the many he noticed in his travels—approaching the 7-Eleven on foot, caps turned bill-backwards and boots scuffing dirt, flailing about in loose clothes and judo-chopping at the air.

The food had made him sleepy. He stroked his elbow, worked out a cramp in his leg, turned up the volume on the radio and tried to find some jazz. Only bluegrass and country answered, or Jesus-tunes and folksy ads about the price of bedding and appliances in the towns around Altoona. The big Appalachian ridges broke most of it into static and he finally turned it off. Tandem trucks came up from behind, jockeyed through the curves and passed him on the downslopes. The frost had worked magic in the mountains: the hardwoods were tallow-gold, blotched with maroon and scarlet among outcrops of hemlock and pine. Eric sipped at his coffee and defeated his craving for a nap.

Neither gods, God, Heaven, Hell, ghosts, reincarnation, space-aliens, angels, Nirvana, or what-have-you, nor perhaps even love and beauty, exist... except in our own minds, as products of imagination. For man has a built-in psychological need to believe (and physiological ability to create) such inspirational abstractions.

This is no doubt an evolutionary survival trait, which developed concurrently with man's complex and sensitive nervous system, for without such a development man could not have faced the myriad pains and fears of his existence that were so greatly amplified by his larger brain.

Thus man's complex brain craves solace, and ingeniously creates God and Heaven and love and beauty—creates these inspiring diversions, illusions, and psychic safety-nets out of his brain's multiple capacities. Myth, dream, chimera, hallucination, illusion, pleasing lie and everyday self-deceit—all are intricate compensations for his cerebral overdevelopment. Saddled with the most seething brain in the animal kingdom, he must also have the most soothing dreams, or find life unbearable.

"Even love and beauty don't exist?" Mel was outraged when she read this section of the book.

"Quite possibly not. Our brains may invent them."

"Ridiculous! You don't really believe that!"

"Yes I do."

"And what's all this 'his' and 'man' business? It's not politically correct at all. You sound like a flaming sexist."

"The use of 'man' to designate 'people' is an old and venerable usage," he had countered calmly. "And 'his' is used by extension. Look, lighten up. I use 'man' sparingly when it's essential, mainly for poetic and rhythmic reasons, to have one single-syllable word describe the human race. Oh, and because of its use in biblical contexts, it has overtones of sacredness and epic scale that I like as well."

"Bullshit."

"Look, Mel, I try to be as politically correct as possible without getting downright silly about it. I mean, the fact that some people might be offended by the inoffensive is not really my problem. Any more than if I should smile and say 'good morning!' and watch someone frown and mumble, 'What did he mean by that?'"

"You're so bloody glib."

Therefore man avoids the chief pitfall of his big brain—that is, a potentially crystal-clear perception of life's complex futility—by engaging that other big brain byproduct: fantasy. Each person survives by spinning a continuous (and unique) protective cocoon of illusion and self-deception.

In short, man literally survives by kidding himself—sometimes wildly, sometimes subtly, but always with baroque complexity and ingenuity. Yet once in a while the dream- machine malfunctions, the private myths and illusions fail, and the knack for deluding oneself is lost. Suicide is then considered. Still, barring physical illness, it is a rare and brief contemplation in most, for the dream mechanisms that evolved simultaneously with the big brain are too firmly in place to allow anything but the swiftest interludes of bare reality.

"This stuff is so damn cynical it makes me sick! How can you live with yourself?"

"Self-deception, I guess."

"Very funny. No wonder we can't get along in any place but the sack. You're a walking doom and depression machine."

"Well, I don't believe in the precepts of the Catholic church, if that's what you mean."

"No it's *not* what I mean, wise guy. And stop making fun of my religious background. Jesus, how do I put up with you? It's a wonder you can face the world every day, with all this crap on your mind."

"Well, all it says is we're animals. Apes, really. At the whim of natural selection and the chemistry of our animal organs. Old stuff, really. You know, in a certain sense it's hopeful. I mean, it's nice to know there are mechanisms in place for our protection. 'Gather life's beautiful illusions,' you might say, 'and discover the glory of your natural insulation against a grim reality.'"

"Oh great. You're really far gone, aren't you?"

It doesn't bode well for we moderns. We have overrun the planet but refuse to see it as a problem. A truly immense one, that is. When any animal species completely swamps its turf, disaster for that species ensues. Yet we propose bandaid solutions. Some even twist the facts and call it a global windfall, a boon of fresh talent, of human genius and know-how, when in fact it means critical depletion of every basic resource. As man is aggressive and territorial, the upshot can only be warfare.

Meanwhile, we have thrown up a house of cards, an elaborate commercial culture that thrives and survives on image, on selling through sweet illusion. Man still gets by on sentiment and dreams, but the stakes have grown much higher. Today, the facts and realities on a planet of six billion greedy and energetic monkeys are too appalling to confront. We play with our marbles like children in the dirt, and ignore the approaching cyclone.

Yet all of this is natural, fated by our genes, too organic for disengagement. We should not expect solutions. Life values itself, alludes to itself, each species to its own, cushions itself incessantly with its myriad sly defenses. And men wrap themselves in dreams, in impenetrable layers of deception, as finely woven as the hairs in a pelt, by the well-evolved eye and brain.

"I don't think I can live with someone who really believes this dog-shit."

"At least I'm using my head."

"Your head? Yeah, but the thing is screwed on backwards."

Eric glanced in his rear-view mirror; the essential ape stared back. Crazy, middle-aged monkey, he thought to himself, what have you managed to get into? Thank goodness for your dream-machine brain.

Near Pittsburgh he stopped for gas. Rain had begun around Somerset and was followed by frigid winds. A cold front had arrived from the west. Gusts whipped at his pants legs in the station while trash—two tissues from someone's glovebox and an empty bag of nacho chips whose plastic glistened with drops—skipped by the vibrating pumps.

He lifted his jacket on the back seat and checked the gift for his mother. Without a live Polyphemus he had settled for a part of his mounted collection: two Marbled Underwings, female and male, rare beauties that he'd captured beside his apartment in the days when Mel was still with him.

He'd hoped to give Glenda his rarest find, a color morph Cynical Quaker that he'd taken the year before: a male with a pure white thorax. He'd captured it outside his office where it came to one of the lights. But, one night when all had gone home except Cynthia Blott and her intern, he'd carelessly left it—unpapered and ready for mounting—on a table beside his desk. Then he'd gone to the photo room and returned to find it missing.

"Have you seen my Cynical Quaker?" he asked Cynthia.

"Your what?"

"It's a moth. A moth I had on this table."

"Dead?"

"Well, yes, dead."

She admitted she'd destroyed it and did not even offer an apology. When he showed his dismay she snapped: "People who kill butterflies and pull the wings off flies deserve whatever they get."

"I don't do either."

"No, but you're a bug-nut. And God knows what else with your hatred for humanity."

"I don't hate humanity, either."

"Look, Eric, let's just drop it, Okay? I found something dead by the copy desk, some insect, and I cleared the thing away."

He had hardly spoken to her since.

The afternoon west of Pittsburgh was a stiff little battle with headwinds. He came down out of the low hills and beat into Ohio, into gusts that rattled and shook him under blue skies trailing cirrus. His 1980 Civic was not a car for the ages. A few years later they'd enlarged them, but when Eric bought his they were go-cart affairs, a white metal box on a low-slung chassis, small and light and without much power, and easily chastened by the wind. He bucked like a bronco past Youngstown and Akron and below the outskirts of Cleveland. His body ached, his joints were stiff, his Popeye elbow throbbed. He thought about stopping for the day in the vast sprawl below Toledo, where a cheap motel might be welcome, but he'd told the Logans he would drive straight through, and his thoughts, too, turned to his mother and what Jackie might be up to. Somewhere west of Cleveland he had gotten his second wind and figured he better not waste it. He ate the last vanilla wafer and swilled at his cold black coffee.

Eric's monkey features in the mirror were now positively vivid. His ape-red hair was disheveled, his simian ears protruded, and his unshaven cheeks bristled chimp-like with whiskers, pale and stiff and scratchy. When he smiled and showed his teeth it was thoroughly grotesque. And the people at the various toll booths could not fool his ape-seeking mind's eye. He easily unmasked each one.

When he took a break near Bryan, Ohio and entered a swarming truck stop, fellow monkeys were all around him. First he noticed their walks, certain slouches and swinging gaits, ways of shuffling along. Hands and feet were indelibly of apes, as was unkempt hair, and grins or gnashing teeth. The blonde kid who served his French fries had downy prominent ear-lobes with rolled chimp-flesh edges. And the general hurly-burly—beside wood and plastic tables and the homespun art on walls—not only didn't distract him but made it seem more real, for the gang-like gregarious neediness, the sidestepping, stooping, and hands-on bumping, seemed the essence of ape sociability.

Nor could makeup and manners and fine-formed genetic selection hide for him their origins. He looked at broad brows above eyes, imagined the flatter noses and fleshier lips of their not-so-distant forebears, and thought about hairy arms and legs undisguised by sanitized clothing. He envisioned them squatting to shit, eating food with their hands, picking and scratching at their noses and mouths, grooming each other's hair. The old folks and babies were especially redolent of monkeys. But he'd reached some point of perspective where even the fair and flaxen, with clean-faced proportions of youth, still struck him as lovely primates.

Indiana was a farmland cliché, flat and fertile and with pumpkin fields a lá James Whitcomb Riley. His weariness turned it to romance, a glittering pastoral, a place without toil or terror. Gold light suffused horsey ridges, there were red barns and white board fences, lank shadows embroidering woodlots, occasional olive cedars wiggling smugly between twisted oaks.

The day began dying past South Bend, and by that time he was wired with exhaustion and far too much caffeine. He sensed a mild delirium, began abstracting the separate sounds and sights as the beats in an unending jazz riff. The car bounced and swayed with the rhythm of the tollway concrete as the wind blew notes off his windshield and the cold metal all around him rang with faint vibrations. The pink sky pulsed with clouds and light, there were transmuted tensions in his guts set down by the coffee and travel, bad food and fatigue. His stomach jumped and his colon contracted in tiny trumpetings of stress. A faint tick came from the heater and a rattle from the door of the glovebox.

Hot and cold drafts frothed about him while the lingering imprint of the journey jarred rhythms from his memory and shook out the notes of his past: the trip out from Philly in '62, in the big green Olds, with all their possessions ahead of them in some house they'd never seen. Feuds in the night by the lakeshore, his father's bitterness and rage, Gabe slinking off to college, a tender gangling kid full of mad intellectual promise, coming home at midterm, lost and about to drop out, up all night in a corner on the porch to escape the fighting within, forgetting to eat for two days, three days more in a psych-ward. Walker moving out, Glenda growing distracted, leaving Northwestern and the classroom, obsessing over naturalist art, collecting Audubon and Wilson, Catesby, Abbott, Lear, Fuertes, but forgetting to pay the mortgage. Jackie confronting their father and raging at everyone else, finally winning a scholarship and enrolling at Northwestern, staying in Evanston to tough things out, being there after the accident. He doing dope in the lakeshore ravines, wishing only to survive his high school, bolting back to Philly when acceptance at Penn came through, freaking out freshman year, finding solace in Fairmount Park, by canal locks and old stone mills, collecting turtles and newts there, fish and frogs, naiads and algae, moths and butterflies, anything wild and living that had no knowledge of men, storing them all in the basement of the rundown house on Spruce Street, his fat preppy roommate objecting and dumping it all in the alley.

He bore down on Chicago. Sunset had left a few colors in the dusk, on the fresco of the western sky. Before him was industrial wilderness: sloughs stuck with gantries and silos, factories and towers, the stink of oxidized minerals, a wasteland of tracks and machines, a steel and concrete tundra full of stray alloyed hulks half-collapsed beside dark lagoons. He climbed quickly on the Skyway below the heel of the lake. Gary, Hammond, Whiting. The whole scene lay spread out below him as in some troubling dream, and the skies all around, still smoking with unearthly shades that bled into the plain, seemed charged with colossal sadness. He pondered the lives below him, afoot in a darkening world. With luck they would find love's charm, its protecting magic ring, see it light a path through the blackness and the streets of tangled lies. Then somewhere down the trail of life they would lose it in the weeds of a byway. Like frightened children they would scream in the dark, and love would stumble off a bridge or die in the frozen woods. Once more they would linger on the wayside of dreams, with a single pair of eyes and ears and half a double soul.

Chicago and its nightmare of freeways riveted him alert. A kind of tunnel vision and his final reserves of strength got him north through the city to Skokie, where he exited on Dempster. Jeff and Judy Logan lived somewhere just west of Evanston, on a street of brick homes called Karlov that was lined with parked cars and topiary yews and walks with identical lampposts. Their house had a driveway and yellow-doored garage. Jeff was an old friend from high-school days whom he hadn't seen in years. It was he, bald-headed and big-bellied, who finally answered the door, all smiles and hearty handshakes. Judy beamed buck-teeth and dimples and bear-hugged him like a brother, though the two had never met.

"C'mon in, good to see you!" Jeff shouted to the room at large. "The kids are doing homework. How in the world are you?"

"Tired."

"Well I bet you are! Come in and take a load off! Gosh you look the same!"

"Older, I would imagine."

"Hey, lemme tell ya, aren't we all!"

Judy took his bags and Jeff stepped down the hallway. "Melissa! You've got till eight-fifteen! Then mommy wants the Internet!"

Chapter 7

"DO YOU READ THE funnies?" Judy slid Eric the marmalade at the same time she lifted some newsprint and threw him a questioning look.

"No, thanks anyway," Eric mumbled, his mouth full of egg.

She dropped the section in front of her and spread it full on the table. "I love 'Sally Forth'."

The microwave beeped four times.

Jeff hurried over in his "Garfield" apron and set down a plate of waffles.

"Check this out," he barked, barely pausing as he slipped some creased paper beside Eric. In an instant he was over at the sink shouting, "Printed that out from the 'Net. Isn't it *bizarre*?"

Eric smoothed it with his palm. "What is it?"

The disposal was grinding, and Jeff screeched over it: "*France*, it's from France!"

"Don't *shout*, dear," chided Judy, smiling broadly and leaning confessionally toward Eric. "It's a list of all the McDonald's restaurants in France! From the Paris Web-Page!" She beamed expectantly.

"Interesting," said Eric. "Your kids retrieved it?"

Judy raised her mug and pointed a finger at her chest. "Moi."

"Ah." He nodded and worked on some waffles.

"It's a revolution, really," Jeff insisted, finally sitting down at the table and stirring at his scrambled eggs. "Bigger than Darwin. Bigger than *Gutenberg*, for God's sake."

"What's that?" Eric blinked sleepily.

"The *Internet*! The world will never be the same. I tell both our kids, I say, 'Kids, if you don't master anything else, master computers and the Internet'."

"They seem to have taken your advice. I don't think I've really seen them since I arrived."

"You haven't met Melissa and Cody?" Judy threw him an appalled look.

"Well, I mean, most of the night I was down in that lovely basement guest room you've fixed up..."

"Jeff, call the kids. Eric, I'm so sorry. You've *got* to meet our *children*!"

"Kids, get in here and meet Mr. Dent!" Jeff had rushed to the head of the hall.

"Oh, don't bother them," Eric said shyly.

Judy whispered, "No, they should meet you," and reached as if to touch him. "Since we bought that second PC they never leave their computers. It's hilarious!"

Several minutes and shouts later two pouting children stared Eric down from beside the refrigerator.

"Melissa, Cody," Jeff announced solemnly, "This is Mr. Dent, one of Daddy's oldest friends."

"Hi," ventured Eric when the silence became awkward.

"Hello," they mumbled in unison.

"Melissa is ten and Cody is nine," said Jeff.

Eric offered them a waffle. They shook their heads side to side in unison.

Melissa's cranberry sweatshirt read: "Becky Home-Techy".

Cody's green one declared: "Surf On: WWW".

"They're nuts about the 'Net, aren't you, kids?" Jeff beamed.

They shook their heads up and down in unison, then bolted back toward the hallway.

"Nothing short of a revolution, I'm tellin' you, Eric," said Jeff, returning to his chair.

"There's some concern that it may undermine the sense of community," offered Eric.

"What community?" frowned Jeff, pouring syrup on his waffles. "Kids don't go outside in their neighborhoods these days anyway."

Judy nodded sternly. "Too much crime."

Glenda was sitting up when Eric arrived. Jackie had brought her the oatmeal-colored shawl that she liked to wear at home, and it was spread across her chest, its salt and pepper fringes just reaching the sides of the bed. He had tried to creep in unnoticed, but she was already smiling and staring with delight by the time he was half way to her.

When the kisses and hugs and small-talk ended, and the tears were blotted from her cheeks, she asked him where he was staying.

"Last night, with some friends in Skokie. Just until I could see you here and borrow your keys to the house."

"Oh but I don't have them," she said weakly, wiping at her nose with a tissue. "Jackie does."

"Where's Jackie?"

"Well, she's been at the Harrington Hotel. Only for a few days, while the house is such a mess. They've been doing some work inside."

"Who's *they*, Mom?"

"Well I don't know, really. Jackie's taking care of it. She's in charge of everything now. I didn't expect to see you at all, really. Jackie says you have no phone and didn't want to be bothered."

"Jackie says a lot of things, doesn't she?"

"Why didn't you call or write?"

"I *did* call. No one answered."

"I was very ill, dear. In bed for days at a time."

"And I wrote twice. Never got an answer."

"*When* did you write?"

"This summer."

"Well, since June, I had all my mail re-directed to Jackie in California. Anymore, I just couldn't handle it. All the bills and what-not."

"Mom, Jackie is a liar."

"Dear, don't say that about your own sister."

"It's the truth. She's a liar and I don't know what else. She's sick."

"Don't Eric. Don't start a feud. I'm too ill to deal with it."

"I *didn't* start. You don't have to start anything with Jackie. She's a self-starter."

"Please, it isn't funny, Eric. I needed someone to take charge. She gets things done. The two of you just need a long talk, that's all. You've been out of touch. I think she's still at the Harrington. Till tomorrow. Go see her. Talk things over."

Eric, who'd been standing since he entered, jacket and bag in hand, sat down in the orange and blond chair. He sighed and fumbled through the shopping bag, then pulled out a small glass case.

"I brought you something."

Glenda raised herself further and smiled with anticipation.

"A couple of rarities I caught outside my apartment one night when I was sugaring." He glanced at them briefly as if to make sure they were there, then handed them to his mother, who had stretched out her hand.

"Oh, they're lovely! Mother Underwings?"

"Marbled. They're unusually vivid, I think."

"Yes, oh yes, they are! Thank you so much, Eric!"

"I felt... I mean, I thought they were better than flowers."

"Oh my yes! Flowers are such a waste. Thanks so very much, dear. They really are lovely."

Eric lowered his head and looked toward the window shyly. "I tried to bring something else. Something living. A Polyphemus, really. But I couldn't quite corner one this year."

"A *Polyphemus*! Oh that would have been fine. They were always my favorites. You *remembered*!"

"Well, they seem to be getting scarcer."

"Yes, that's true. Isn't everything? Oh, I loved to paint them. Remember my office at Penn? They used to show up in that courtyard every year. And we raised them, too, didn't we? Such a spectacle, their emergence! When they were fresh and docile I used to perch them on your head!" She placed the glass case on the table.

"I remember."

A kind of embarassment followed, a painful mutual sense that not only had something been lost, but no attempt at retrieving it had properly been made. They both fell silent. Glenda fought back tears and Eric looked away.

He stayed and made more small-talk or listened to her rambling asides. She refused to discuss her condition and as the doctor would not call on Sunday, he learned very little. Near noon he had lunch in the downstairs cafeteria, drinking chocolate milk from its carton and pecking at a small chef's salad piled neatly in a clear square bubble and slathered with Italian dressing that he'd squeezed from a plastic packet, some of it squirting on his pants. From a pay phone he called the Harrington Hotel and found Jackie had left a message for him to meet her in her room at six. When he got back to Glenda she was dozing, her lunch tray—centered by a pink boat of gelatin afloat on a small porcelain plate—all but untouched.

She slept for several hours, then roused herself in late afternoon when sunrays were slanting at the windows and suffusing the leaves of the courtyard oak—whose topmost branchlet quivered into view whenever the breezes stiffened—to a pomegranate luster. Visible, too, were clots of cloud, in the window's high left quadrant, and the drifting ephemeral shapes became the objects of their scrutiny. Glenda described a frog's leg, and Eric saw a satyr. There were several moths, which, by mutual accord, escaped any species definition, one or two bloated dwarfs, and a single train of amoeboid fish, clarifying slowly and strung out like koi in a Japanese garden, with fan-tails and blunted faces.

But Eric was increasingly restless. "Mom, I've got to go see Jackie," he blurted in the midst of a cloud-focused reverie. He was suddenly up, balancing his jacket in the crook of his arm and folding the Wanamaker's bag that he'd long ago set by his chair. "Do you want this?" he asked, extending the creased white parcel. "They're gone now. Out of business."

"Who?"

"Wanamaker's."

"*Wanamaker's*? Oh, I didn't know. What a shame! Yes, just leave it on the chair. Thank you, Eric."

They kissed and hugged and he promised to return, then headed briskly for the door.

The Evanston autumn Sunday was still full of blue and gold. Eric drove slowly amid the flat grid of avenues. The cold front had lost its bite, there was even some warmth in the amber sheets of sun that toppled through the shade trees and shattered in the streets, and with the windows rolled down in his Civic he heard the jig of the leaves, their dance and scuttle along sidewalks and curbs, their horse-tail whisk in the gutters. Students were about, bisecting parks in two and threes, ignoring signals at the corners or frisking across at mid-block, baggy-clothed and oddly-hatted, heavily-booted like lumberjacks, each saddled with a nylon backpack. It was the same town he had known, with its gothic churches and gabled homes, but with more cars jostling the lanes, more rudeness from the drivers, and more office towers near the downtown hub, which threw whole blocks into shadow where he once remembered sunlight.

He parked on the Northwestern campus and took time to stretch his legs and collect his thoughts for the meeting. It was almost six when he bee-lined for the hotel. A small flock of pigeons, bobbing alertly like wind-up toys, crossed his path near the Harrington entrance, then burst up over the canopy and circled onto a ledge. Jackie was in room 302, and she met him out in the hallway, dressed in slacks and a sweater, her weight on one leg, her lips pursed almost to a pucker. Despite the passage of years they did not bother to embrace.

"Well, the cavalry's finally here," she wise-cracked as she ushered him into the room. "Something to drink maybe?" She gestured toward the dresser where her own refreshment, a half-empty strawberry daiquiri, sat crowded by watery rings.

"Thanks no. Maybe a glass of water."

"*That's* my baby brother!" From the bathroom where she was drawing it she yelled, "Tell me, how's the patient?"

"I guess you know better than I." He stood beside one bed, slightly stooped, reflexively tracing a paisley on the spread with the tip of his index finger.

She came back and handed him the water, grabbed her own glass off the dresser, then pulled up a chair across from him and sat down flashing a grin.

"Me? Do you think I'm so well informed?" Her voice dripped with mocking false innocence.

"Right up to your eyeballs," replied Eric, fidgeting with his collar and examining the flush in her cheeks, the sure sign she'd been drinking.

"Eric, you look tense. You're going to need all the calm you can muster on this trip. Why don't you try and relax?"

"Let's not play games, Jackie. Why don't *you* tell me what's going on and we can make this as brief as possible."

"Oh, you're no fun! Since when are you in hurry? I thought you'd be here yesterday, but I see you're still a turtle when it comes to dealing with a crisis."

"I came as soon as I could."

She sipped her drink and crossed her legs and motioned for Eric to sit down. "For God's sake take a load off. I don't speak to statues."

He set his glass on the dresser and plunked down on the end of the bed. "Look, I'll be talking to her doctor tomorrow, so just cut the crap and tell me what you know. I won't believe it anyway."

"Oh, it's Eric the Boy Cynic, is it? Yes, indeed. The famous unbeliever. Writing a novel about overgrown apes who hallucinate their lives away and slash their hairy wrists."

"Cut the horseshit, Jackie."

"Eric, what makes you think I'm going to tell you *anything*?" She sat back loosely, affecting lavish repose. "You've dropped the ball in this family—you and your half-wit brother—for 20 years, and now you want filling in! I'd laugh if you weren't so pathetic."

"Jackie, do you really want to talk? I thought from your letter and message you might. But otherwise I'll leave."

"Oh, don't go away all bruised and abused! I forgot, you were voted Most Sensitive Man on Campus back in college. Just hold onto your gonads..."

"I'm serious, Jackie..."

"Yes, yes, you're serious. So bloody serious you can't see straight! A regular Socrates. Just what is it you want to know?" Her eyes were popeyed with malice, her cow-lick erect, her beaky nose raised slightly.

"Well, let's see, for starters, why didn't Mom get my letters and what's going on at the house?"

She stared at him coldly and said nothing.

"And if it's not asking too much, I'd like to know where Mom stands, what her situation is financially and otherwise."

"*Otherwise*? Otherwise, dear bro', she stands with one foot in the grave."

"Yes, I put that together already."

"Did you, dear Eric? With your fabled steel-trap wits? Well, maybe you know she's got four weeks to live, four *months*, maybe, at the outside, and there's nothing anyone can do."

"Then the cancer has metasticized or something?"

"Brilliant, baby bro'! You're right on the money. At this rate you can skip your meeting with the doc. Yes indeed. But as for your other questions and so-called concerns..."

"You're not about to tell me."

"Uncanny clairvoyance, sir! Why did you bother to come out here? Your perception transcends the miles!"

"I came out here to see my mother, not to listen to your drunken blather."

"Testy, testy! It doesn't flatter you Eric, to lose your...equanimity? Is that the word? You're the literary hot-shot in this family. Surely that word's in your novel?"

"It's not a novel, as you well know. It's a philosophical exploration of... human shortcomings."

"*Shortcomings*! Oh, I love it! Such euphemisms! You mean its about the evil that lurks in men's hearts!"

"No, I don't mean that. I don't believe in evil, only delusion. And the bitterness that feeds it."

"Oh, and here I thought we had so much in common! You and me, Eric, the world's foremost cynics. And now you're softening your outlook! What's the matter with you, baby brother? Get the damn book finished and published, and if you can't, for chrissake do something else that can turn a decent kopek. This cub reporter stuff, it's pathetic. You're 44 years old and you live in the world's richest country. Don't you want to have any, well...dare I use a dirty word... *money*?"

"The world is full of assholes who have money."

Jackie grinned broadly and showed her teeth, ape-like. "Too true."

"And full of a lot more who want it."

"And you're not one of them?"

"Not for what it would cost me to get it."

"It wouldn't cost you that much. You know how to write. Just change your tactics. For one thing, change your name to a woman's, a female pseudonym. That's your best bet. I mean, at least pay attention to the obvious power shifts in your own goddamn industry!"

"Oh that's brilliant. I'd never do anything so foolish and you know it."

"On the contrary, I don't know it at all! You're a fool's fool, Eric. You're still the soft-headed little chump you've always been. A typical 'nice guy', and I emphasize the 'guy'. The successful women of this world are going to eat your type for breakfast. In fact we're already doing it. Men like you are obsolete in a truly competitive society."

"I don't see it as a man-woman thing. There are lots of womanish men as well as mannish women. Gender is not what makes the difference. It's temperament, really. What's between your legs is the least important thing in forming your personality."

"*My* personality?"

"Anyone's."

"If you mean it gets down to quiverers and non-quiverers, you're right. And you quiverers are as good as dead."

"That's *not* what I mean."

"You're a *worm*, Eric. Face it."

Eric sucked in a breath and looked Jackie full in the eyes. "Gee, Jackie, it's been swell chatting with you. I'm sorry you've developed a drinking problem. On top of everything else."

"What would you know about drinking? As if you care, anyway. You've got an answer to everything, don't you, little brother?"

"No, of course not. But it must seem like it to someone who doesn't have an answer to *anything*."

She grinned. "Before you go, I *will* tell you one thing. Well, three things, in fact."

"I'm all ears."

"Number one, you've just been left out of a joint tenancy agreement that makes Gabe, Mom, and myself sole owners of her real property. And two, I now have full power of attorney regarding Mom's affairs." She finished off her daiquiri with a tipsy flourish.

"And the third?"

"Oh... your crazy brother's in town. I personally shipped him out after his little visit, but it seems he slipped back again. I found this under my door." She lifted an envelope from the dresser and waved it in his direction.

"What is it? Or is that another mystery."

"You know I tell you everything, kiddo. Where's your faith? It's a bribe, more or less. I gave him five hundred bucks to play with back in Madison. For being a such a good boy. It seems he's refused it and extended his visit. Now he's *Evanston's* little problem. Check the outdoor heating grates if you want to know where he's staying."

Eric stood up and turned for the door. "You're a sweetheart, Jackie. Thanks for every little thing."

"I thought you'd appreciate knowing where we stand," she croaked hoarsely, rising, her lips puckered tight. "I'll be out of town till Tuesday, in case Mom asks. And oh, if by chance you've still got your key to the house, don't bother. I've already wrapped things up there. And the locks were changed some time ago."

"I figured that one out," said Eric, moving through to the hallway without once breaking his stride.

Eric resisted the temptation to visit the hotel bar and knock down a double scotch. Instead he hit the streets, drifting down to Clark, then west over to Sherman. Even on a Sunday the autumn twilight was full of engine noise and exhaust stink, of snaking multi-colored metal that slowed or squeezed forward around corners and at junctions in a vibrating peristalsis. Turn-signals pulsed and brake-lights blinked like giant ruby beetles. He stood still at an intersection. The traffic signal turned colors against a far off backdrop of charcoal and faintest pink, where the dusk had bled out behind the El and its cars pushed north with a rhythmic clatter, high on the embankment. Standing by the signal he could hear the click of its inner switches, could feel the throb at his temples, the stutter of his heart in his rib-cage. It was suppertime but he wasn't hungry. He walked south on Sherman and slipped into a coffee bar.

A few middle-aged shoppers sat about, clustered round by logo-printed parcels, but mostly it was lively with collegiates, some attempting study as they sat over open books, most chatting or listening, laughing, cursing hiply or gesturing self-consciously.

He stared at the wall-size menu lit by track-lights behind the counter: house blend, espresso, double espresso, espresso macchiato, cappuccino, latte, café au lait, caffe americano, caffe mocha, caffe mocha mint, caffe almond latte, caffe almond mocha, caffe swiss latte, caffe caramel mocha, caffe mocha breve, caffe vanilla latte, caffe nut cream, café wildcat... it went on and on, and—when you added the decaf and tea listings, the "alternative" drinks like steamed almond moo, Italian soda, or Firenze freeze, and the pastries, breads, and bulk coffee offerings—filled eight lengthy columns.

The thought of it all made his head pound. He got the attention of a sullen teen with burr haircut and golden ring in his especially chimpish earlobe, bought a regular black coffee and sat down at a table in back. It had a circular marble top and wrought-iron legs, and it rocked so badly that he folded his napkin four times and stuffed it under one foot. The caffeine finally focused him. If Gabe had stuck around, he reasoned, then he might have guessed Eric was coming and would linger where they could meet. Without a place to stay he'd hang out in cheap restaurants, then pick some cozy stairwell for the night. Eric would check the eateries first, next work the alleys and churches.

Back on the street, where darkness had fully settled, he shuffled down the block. It was familiar and strange together. He'd once often passed these shop fronts when they were shoe stores, laundromats, record stores, tailors, sub shops. Now they were ethnic restaurants and espresso bars, tape and CD outlets, craft boutiques and t-shirt shops.

Bookstores seemed the only constant, but even they looked alien, transformed, as if ashamed to offer mere books.

He finally turned down an alley that would take him back toward the Harrington. This struck him as slightly reckless for these days he might get mugged, but he really didn't care. He was sick of the whole damn business, sick of living, in fact. Besides, Gabe put up with this nightly, or used to, as he recalled—looked for dark corners to hide in, safety zones and niches in the jungle of decaying streets.

The alley divided behind the hotel. One cindered lane led right and continued for nearly a block. The other moved straight ahead and would soon spill out on the street. He pursued it, his footsteps echoing eerily, trashcans and dumpsters jumbled to his right and two white vans—pale in the darkness like nomad tents—looming off to his left. A yellow diagonal of streetlight glare marked the outlet to the street, linking the curbs of the interrupted sidewalk like the big brassy buckle on a belt. The hotel formed one side of this gateway while the left was the corner of a residence, a red sandstone structure with creamy lintels and window-frames and eccentric bevelings and ledges. A recess was defined just back from its front, the rear side of a chimney-like column that petered out higher up.

The street glare touched this recess at its base, illumined one reddish brick and also, as Eric noticed, a leather shoe, and the dull green fragment of a coat. He broke his stride, took five steps to his left and stared down into the alcove. A figure was folded into it, impossibly rumpled and compressed. It twitched slightly, rustled against its recess, writhed like a restless pupae. Eric leaned closer and the figure began to unfold, its coat expanding with the spread of its arms and the audible intake of its breath. Finally the shoulders came forward, the head lifted alert, and the feet dug into the cinders and began to push it erect in a single emergent thrust. Fully righted, it took a tentative step, and the street-glare lit up a sallow cheek, a mustache point, an eye in a lensless rim. The two creatures stared together, each at the other's face.

Eric managed to speak first. "Count Dracula, I presume?"

Gabe twisted at his mustache and smiled like a just-woken child. "Howdy, brother. I was watching for you. Must have nodded off."

Chapter 8

"FOOD WOULD BE NICE."

Gabe was gliding along the sidewalk, arms out from his sides at an unnatural angle, coat flapping.

"Yes, food," echoed Eric as he quick-stepped to keep up.

A Burger King loomed at the corner.

"No 'Burger Kings'," said Gabe.

"Fine with me. No 'Burger Kings'."

They passed the public library and turned the corner on Davis.

"When was the last time you ate?" asked Eric.

Gabe twirled at his mustache. "Don't remember. Yesterday? Yah, that seems right."

The sky had cleared off completely and the night was domed with star-chipped darkness, washed to dull slate by the light-pollution of the town. Faintly, the earth reeked upward, released its accrued daytime ripeness, its bruised autumnal musks. Cars mixed their stink in the coolness and scarred the shadows with light.

They turned up Sherman Avenue. Eric spotted a restaurant and decided it would do. He steered Gabe inside and, obeying the hand-lettered sign, they waited to be seated. The place was white and black and vaguely high-tech, with pedastalled tables and jet enamelled chairs clumped about on a milky tile floor. A cappuccino machine choked and growled by the kitchen, which was stage-lit and open to view. Eric removed his jacket while a waiter showed them to their table, but Gabe kept his khaki coat on even as he dropped in his chair.

"Where's that old pack you used to carry?" Eric asked when they'd settled in.

"The red one? There've been several. Just lost the latest. Left it on the train, I think. After Jackie sent me off."

"Is that when she gave you the money?" The restaurant was almost hot. Eric rolled up his sleeves, propped his arms on the table, studied the tiny menu.

"You heard about that?"

"Yes, Jackie and I have chatted."

"Well, yah. She, ah... she bribed me as I boarded the train. I got off at Howard and walked back north. Stuck the cash under her door, eventually."

"What'd she do, break your glasses, too?"

"No, they've been that way. Some college dirt-balls smashed the bridge. The lens has been missing forever." Gabe adjusted his pony-tail and finally slipped his coat off. "Whadja do to your elbow?"

Lifting his arm, Eric rubbed at the fleshy little bubble. "I don't really know. Probably bumped it once too often. Bursitis. Must be gettin' old."

They both smiled and leaned back comfortably.

"Hi, I'm Janice and I'll be your waitress." The tiny woman all in black was poised between them, pad and pencil ready like a cop preparing to ticket.

"We've got several specials this evening I'd like to let you know about. The Gorgonzola and Apple Quiche is made with a blend of Italian blue cheese and Rome Beauty apples and comes with a walnut-on-mixed-greens salad with raspberry vinaigrette. The Pan Bagna Platter includes mortadella, sopresetta, prosciutto, capiocola, and provolone, with artichoke hearts, cherry peppers, and radicchio on a sourdough baguette, and comes with pasta Florentine. The Sicilian Tuna Surprise is a tuna salad with capers and dried olives and a mixed salad of arugula, mustard and beet greens, and curly endive in a light Balsamic vinaigrette topped with asiago cheese."

"How much are they?" asked Eric.

"The specials?"

"Yes."

"Uh, I think they're all ten-ninety-five. I'll have to check."

"Never mind. I'll have the chicken salad with roasted garlic and a glass of the house burgundy."

Gabe pinched the taped bridge of his glasses and bored a stare into Janice. "I'll have the same. And, ah, bring some bread, please. Lots of it." He twisted his mustache for emphasis.

Janice gave him a quizzical look and turned sharply on her heels.

"You know, I figured you'd be out here," said Gabe when Janice was gone. "I just stayed close to the Harrington. Where've you been staying?"

"With some friends in Skokie, last night. An old high school buddy.

One night was enough. You know, Jackie's got us locked out of Mom's house."

"No I didn't know. But I'm not really anxious to stay there anyway..."

"There's more to it than that. Something about me being cut out of an agreement."

"Cut out? Oh, *that* agreement. Joint tenancy. She said you wanted no part of it."

"Sounds like something Jackie would say. No, I never even *heard* about it. Mom's gotten none of my letters, and no one ever called. Jackie sent me a letter last week, timed so I'd get here late. At least that's how I figure it."

Gabe raised his eyebrows.

"And she's doing something at the house. Mom said they're working inside, but it sounds like bullshit to me."

Gabe whistled softly. "Ooh, yah, this has Jackie written all over it."

"I mean, the joint tenancy thing should be no big deal in itself. I don't think it affects Mom's will. It's part of something else. She's working on something bigger, which is why she got power of attorney."

"She did?"

"Yeah. She made a point of telling me. Even *that* isn't so strange. Mom's helpless and would probably want it. But whatever she's up to, she's awfully damn pleased with herself. Where's your copy of the agreement?"

There was an awkward moment of silence. Gabe looked at him sheepishly. "It was in my red day-pack."

"Oh, great."

Janice swooped in with the wine and bread, asked if they needed something else, then bustled back to the kitchen.

"I think Jackie's nuts," said Eric. "I mean, Mom is doomed, that seems fairly certain. But Jackie has made the thing worse. She's as bitter as she can be and has worked up some strange vendetta."

"She's gotten pretty weird, all right. Tried to hide it with me, but I wasn't buying. The nicer she gets, the more it gives me the creeps."

"Nice? I rarely have that privilege. She's bitchy enough when she's sober. But the drinking, it makes her..." Eric looked away.

"Evil?"

"Well, I don't like that word. I'm not sure evil exists. I see it more as a metaphor for, well... nasty aggression in monkeys. One of the ape brain's illusions."

Gabe removed his glasses and sighed. "Jackie is a 'gwiddon'," he declared softly.

"A what?"

"A 'gwiddon', or a 'gwrach'. A Welsh warrior witch. The great Irish fighter Cu Chulain was trained by woman-warriors. In Welsh they were the 'gwiddonot'. Arthur supposedly fought and killed nine of them. A 'gwrach' would fight with her nails. The 'gwiddonot' wore armor."

Eric was smiling broadly. "I like the image if not the plausibility. 'Jackie the Amazon'. It has a certain fitness."

"I'm serious," said Gabe, leaning forward and flourishing a finger. "She's descended from that line. So was Dad. For a thousand years the druidic Celts of Cymry saw fighting as a sport. It had nothing to do with morality, with warring for righteous causes. And the Welsh bard Rys says there were women warriors till the ninth century, about the same time Welsh kings stopped fighting for sport. By then most were Christians and had been versed in good and evil." Gabe reached for a piece of bread.

"You're really into this, aren't you?"

"I *live* in it, much of the time."

"You *live* in it?"

"I'll explain later," mumbled Gabe, wolfing the bread and gazing off toward the kitchen.

Eric sipped at his wine. "So, really... you'd agree with me, but for different reasons. That evil doesn't exist. I say it's a metaphor for ape-ish aggression, and you say it's a fairly recent invention of Christian morality."

"Sort of." Gabe was losing his focus and staring now at the table, tracing with his fork some pattern or shape that was obvious only to him. The entrées soon arrived and Gabe said nothing more until their meal was finished and a baby began bawling at a table nearby. "Noise pollution," growled Gabe, wincing. Eric signalled for the check.

The brothers walked back to campus in the cool October night. They piled in the Honda Civic and Eric drove west to Skokie Boulevard where they stopped at an upscale motel. Eric had decided to splurge and went into the office, a cramped but fancy room with floral upholstered armchairs, framed prints of barns and orchards, huge ceramic lamps, a plush bold-checked carpet, and, for the desk-clerk, a nook with bullet-proofed glass. He asked for their cheapest double rate.

The room matched motifs with the office. Gabe plopped down on the bed below the barn, and Eric beneath the orchard. For a time they stared at the mirror above the dresser, then kicked their shoes to the carpet and contentedly sighed and belched. Eric took a shower and returned to find Gabe folded down on his haunches, his ass just off the carpet, immobile as a resting bat. He was staring at the bold-checked carpet.

"Ants?" quipped Eric.

Gabe did not answer so Eric knelt beside him. "Counting the threads?" he ventured this time.

"The checks. Per square," was Gabe's belated answer.

"Oh, super. Shall I jot your findings down?"

"Don't bother. It's an easy one to remember. There are six checks per small square, six small squares per large square, and six large squares per row. Six, six, six. It's a magical number."

"I see."

Gabe jumped up from his crouch and smiled like a happy kid who has just solved a tricky puzzle. Eric, still kneeling, looked up.

"Y'know Gabe, I need to ask you...

"What's that?"

"How are you doing with your, ah, your...problem?"

"You mean my schizophrenia?" Gabe descended lotus-style on the bed.

"Yeah."

"No need to shrink from that word. Everyone in Madison knows I'm a so-called schizophrenic. I explain it to anyone who'll listen. Because I'm tired of the misunderstandings."

"And they understand?"

"Some do. Most don't. A lot of people still think schizophrenics are ax-murderers and psychos. Others come on like shrinks, using all the classical jargon—'subverted and scattered thought', 'dis-integrated persona', 'episodically delusional'. All that Kraepelin and Bleuler shit."

"Do you still take medication?"

"No. It's no longer something I want blocked out. I need to let it in. To listen. It informs me."

"By '*it*', you mean the schizophrenia?"

"Forget that word. It's inadequate. What's happening goes beyond science or medicine. I stopped the drugs six years ago, just after I met Pat, and immediately made a connection. The complexity is immense. It's way beyond description."

"Pat...your old girlfriend?"

"Yah. She's a Celtic scholar. We met through that. We're still friends."

Eric stood up. "What's this 'connection' all about?"

Gabe sighed and stared at Eric, who sat down on the bed across from him. "Do you really want to know?"

"Sure. Why not?"

"Because I'm not sure I want to tell you. It's private and it's painful. And it sounds completely nuts."

"Nuts I take for granted. The whole family's that way."

A little smile interrupted Gabe's seriousness. "Okay, I'll give you the short course. None of it really translates, but I'll put it in rational terms, as much as that's possible."

"Shoot."

Adjusting his pony-tail and pressing at the bridge of his glasses, Gabe hesitated. "Well... there's a prelude first. When I stopped the medication—after 15 years—I found I could travel through time. Backwards only. I'm working on going forward, and when I do, well, there'll be a personal breakthrough." He paused to stare at Eric.

"I'm listening."

"Anyway, I'd stare at a certain mark on a wall and the wall would open up. My mind would go in and take off."

"Like Alice and the rabbit hole."

"Well, yah, sort of. These days things will open almost any time, but that's the surest way. Anyway, I'd be on this winding course, like a glassy tunnel with stuff passing right and left. Sounds, images. At first it made no sense and really scared me shitless. It still does at times. But I began to understand, to decipher some of the voices. They started out in Welsh, which I know pretty well, and then recently began to change, to mutate. I ran some fragments past Pat—mostly words and phrases I'd remembered and written down phonetically—and she suggested it might be an archaic form of Welsh called Old Brythonic. Old Brythonic is what modern Welsh sprang from. It's very old."

Eric shifted on the bed. "How old?"

"Well, it pre-dates Christian Wales, so we're talking before A.D. 500. It easily lends itself to sing-song verse and allegory, a kind of chanting and myth-telling—ritualized magic, really. Intended for the praise of kings and to pass down customs and wisdom—there was no written language, so they had to get knowledge into catchy forms and commit the stuff to memory. Like putting all our civil codes in the song lyrics of the Beatles."

Eric smiled. "Go ahead."

"Anyway, to make it short... in this whole Tunnel thing I've connected with our ancestors. And not just of a few hundred years ago, but several thousand. I followed both lines back—Mom's and Dad's. Was led back, really, by a series of, well, bardic revelations. Straight back to a time of druid priests in some violent little kingdom. I haven't quite found the genesis yet, the point where a compact was struck among a picked group of..."

"Whoa, whoa, whoa! First of all, Mom's line is Welsh. But Dad was a Dent. They're English."

"Not really. Three generations back they were Scots: McPhees and McKays, and before that it's all Welsh bastards, Lloyds and Griffiths and such. It's traceable for 400 years."

"But Gabe, that's *hundreds* of people! If you go back further it's thousands. It's like linking yourself to the nation of Spain or something. I mean, it's hopelessly general!"

"No! The names don't really matter. It's not a clan thing. It's an aberrant genetic thread I'm following. Or is following me. I, we... our line...somehow carries a minute strain of cerebral memory-skill that was first cultivated by Cymric druids. The familial names are mere signposts. They're just generalized clues in the stock, like a trail of fish-blood in the ocean that a shark picks up on from afar. A bunch of things came together in an ocean of generations. *My* brain was selected through a random convergence of traits once deliberately nurtured and that periodically erupt in all human stock but are usually ignored." He grabbed his glasses through the lensless frame and slowly pulled them off.

Eric shook his head. "I'm sorry, you're going too fast. Why would the druids give a shit? And what did they know about genetics?"

Gabe took a deep breath and replaced his glasses. "Look, let me start it this way... once there were a people called Cymry whose leader was Hu Cadarn and, ah, they came from Asia Minor and settled on an island called Alban or Albion. Which we know today as Britain. Hu and his successors held the island's best land and prospered for a thousand years. Then came the Romans, who forced them into a corner. A king related to the Cymry, Lles ap Coel, was defeated and confessed faith in Christ. I mean, I'm making this very simple, just stuff based on Roman accounts at the time of Claudius Caesar..."

"No, I understand. Go on."

"So, anyway, druidic orders ruled these Cymry tribes. Orders of priest-poets. The kings were nominally in charge, but druids called the shots, hand picked the successors. Poetry was paramount and had magical origins. The main poet-priest, or 'prifardd', sang the praises of these kings and was in turn protected. The whole syntax of archaic Welsh is, well, a heraldic mumbo-jumbo designed to sustain this king-poet symbiosis. The most gifted young were taught by druid elders, and the best youths committed to memory vast sums of knowledge, often over decades. Basically the elders looked for two things: power of recall and power of prophecy..."

"Gabe..."

"I know, I know. This is sounding like Celtic History 101."

"It's not that."

"Anyway, what happened was—and this is not in the books—the poet-priests saw the writing on the wall, you might say, with the coming of the Romans. Their whole way of life was threatened by this looming monster: *written* language. So they set up an ultra-secret order to sustain their magical dynasty in the face of the onslaught. It was amazing, really. Kingdoms collapsed all around them, there was constant warfare for 500 years, written language prevailed and spread, but the secret oral order survived entirely on its strength of memory and prophecy, which was, well... so potent it could leap the bounds of time..."

"So are you saying the ability to remember and prophesize is the same thing as time-travel?"

"It may turn out to be in this case. I've experienced it as a kind of compressed mental energy, maybe, well... a magnetic field that some brains can generate. As I say, I haven't developed future access yet."

"Mmm."

"Anyway, do you know *how* memory and prophecy were fused so potently by this order?"

Eric's sarcasm surfaced. "I can't guess."

"Genetic selection." Gabe smiled at Eric.

"Gabe..."

"No, the druids knew all about selection. They bred stock—cattle and horses—for centuries. They didn't know *why*, but they knew if you bred a fast horse with a fast horse you'd get a faster horse. So they took their most gifted memorists and prophets and starting interbreeding them—forcing crucial unions and sexual match-ups. I mean, their chieftains sanctioned it. They *had* to. And they did this for 500 years! All through horrible wars with Romans, Scots, Gauls, Saxons—till they came up with a super strain of poet-priests who..."

"Gabe, there are no written records. Jesus, you've no proof whatever that these things were so! You're so steeped in Celtic lore that you've let your mind..."

"My *mind*, yes. The very point, Eric. My mind is one of the genetic carriers they relied on! Today's so-called schizophrenia was nothing of the kind back then. Our 'illness' was considered of old a gift of prophecy and a window into the sacred. The priests of the secret order matched schizophrenics with memorists and built a hybrid race of super-skilled seers!" He flourished his finger in the air. "Do you know what region of the globe has the greatest incidence of schizophrenia? Ireland and the British Isles! Merddin—you know him as Merlin—was a *schiz*! So while the Welsh chiefdoms broke down and were mostly assimilated by the time of the Norman Conquest, well... the hereditary seeds were planted for growing a whole line of genetic memorists—nutsy, dysfunctional personalities who nevertheless had strange powers... time-travelling prophets disguised as simple lunatics who..."

"Gabe! Gabe! Enough already! It's too much... no, I can't buy it. You're spinning wool from your admirable brain, but it's still just so much wool. Science, even history, requires evidence. You're talking to an evolutionist, for God's sake. Someone who believes we're monkeys and only monkeys because we can't just *fantasize* ourselves into angels, or time-travellers, or Tinker Bell fairies. Who believes it so much he's writing a stupid *book* about its iron-clad reality. I admit you combine some elements of evolutionary logic in this genetic thing, but..."

Gabe jumped up from the bed. "We're two different people, Eric. With very different outlooks. I should have known better."

Eric rubbed at his elbow, which was itching wildly. Then he threw out his hands. "Look, Eric. I respect you, your insights, your life. I really do. But don't you see how easy it would be for someone with your grounding in Celtic arcania to mix fact with fantasy and evolve some subconscious memory that..."

"*Subconscious*? Oh, yah, you breathe in that quack Sigmund Freud as easily as bloody *air* but dismiss concepts ages old! A mere hundred or so years ago words like 'subconscious' were *gibberish*. But now we think they're mother's milk. What the hell is the 'subconscious' anyway, Eric? What does it really mean?"

"Gabe..."

"The fact is it doesn't exist. It's the fucking *construct* of some plausible Viennese charlatan! Don't talk to me about real and unreal, Eric."

Eric was up off the bed now, putting his arm around Gabe, who violently pulled away. "I knew I shouldn't have told you. I let you sucker me out."

"Gabe, I've nothing against your insights. We all have our own."

"It's all right. Save the consolation. I'm leaving soon enough. When I break through."

"Leaving Madison?"

"Ooh, yah. Certainly Madison."

Eric flashed a worried frown. "Will you let me know when you do?"

"I'll leave you a message in a bottle."

Groping for a neutral focus, Eric picked the remote off the fake walnut dresser and flicked on the big TV. PBS seemed a good bet, and the voice of George Page droned suddenly into the room, accompanied by scenes of mangrove swamps and a tide flat full of sun glare, rippling puddles, and hundreds of glistening creatures—half fish, half frog, it seemed—scurrying over the mud.

"Oh, *mud skippers*!" enthused Eric, trying to grab Gabe's attention.

Gabe had dropped into a lotus on the bed, facing the other way. Eric tried again: "These things are really bizarre. I mean, they look like something alien. Like something Hollywood invented."

Gabe wasn't buying. He stared intently at the pillow and continued his focus through segments about caterpillars, rare pygmy rhinos, and finally proboscis monkeys—despite Eric's ooh-ing and aah-ing and his wildly comic claim that he'd seen a woman that morning who suggested a proboscis ape.

Eric kept the TV on. Somewhere in the middle of Masterpiece Theatre Gabe began to come out of it. Aunt Betsy was chasing donkeys off the lawn. Gabe turned and scowled at the screen. "That bears about as much resemblance to Dickens as Romper Room does to Tolstoy!"

"I think it's pretty good," countered Eric, encouraging debate. "Mr. Dick is perfect."

"Bah! How can you watch these puffed up English soap operas? The Brits know we'll buy anything that slobbers with their accent."

"Yeah, but this is one of the better ones. A classic."

"It's all a lot of drool," pronounced Gabe, who rose from the bed, retrieved his dark khaki coat and pulled a book from a pocket.

Eric switched off the television.

"Well, if you'd rather read, fine..." He went to his suitcase on the table by the window, drew out his copy of Covell's *Field Guide to the Moths*, and padded back to his bed. "What's yours?" he asked Gabe.

"Louie L'Amour. *The Iron Marshall*. Found it on the bus."

Eric rolled his eyes and sunk himself in Covell, studying the ranges of the Pyralid and Plume moths. Some time later he found himself nodding off.

"I'm turning in," he said to Gabe, who was speeding through L'Amour. Gabe did not respond. "But feel free to keep reading." He flicked off his bed lamp and raised his voice: "Oh, and Gabe..."

Seconds passed before Gabe turned his head. "Yah?"

"We've got to get in there."

"Where?"

"The house. Jackie will be out of town tomorrow." A headlight climbed above the curtains and traced a comet on the ceiling. Gabe set down his book.

"Well, brother. I'm pretty good with a paper clip."

"A paper clip?"

"Yah. Some paper clips and a Bic lighter can get me in most anywhere."

Eric rubbed his elbow and watched the tail of the comet vanish above the mirror. "Jesus Gabe. I sure hope you're right."

"Y gwir yn erbyn y byd," said Gabe, staring at the ceiling.

"Dare I ask for a translation?"

"The truth against the world."

Eric smiled and rolled to his other side. "Goodnight Gabe."

Come morning they had the free buffet that was spread out in a conference room down the hall: wicker baskets of sliced bread, bagels, and sweet rolls, assorted dry cereals, hot coffee and tea and milk in waxy little cartons. Businessfolk clustered around, popping bread in the toaster and grabbing packets of margarine and jam, then huddling at vinyl tables that looked out on a lot full of cars. The toaster was very slow and Gabe almost caused a scene by attempting to fix it right there, moving it out from the wall and turning it upside down before Eric pulled him away.

Eric next went to the hospital. He'd set up a meeting with the doctor, who was due on his rounds at eleven. Then, as tactfully as possible, he recapped for Glenda his hotel meeting with Jackie. She brushed it all aside.

"You caught her in one of her moods," whispered Glenda, who seemed unusually weak and spent much of the morning napping. "Jackie's been under stress, dear. You've got to make some allowance."

Dr. Wurtzburger came by late and spoke to Eric in a vestibule off the hall. He was vigorous, white-haired and stout, and kept tapping at a clipboard impatiently. "I wish the news were better. There's a sizeable tumor on the bile duct at the very top of her pancreas. It's malignant and inoperable and metasticized some time ago. She'll have good days and bad, but I wouldn't say more than three months. It could easily be less."

Gabe had wanted none of it and stayed in the motel. He became completely focused, fashioning lock picks on the tile floor of the bathroom. First he straightened large paper clips, heated them with his lighter and, using two flat stones, slowly beat the hot wires into various shapes, bending and creasing them carefully with the right-angle edge of the soap dish or the different blades of his knife. The picks were then notched or smoothed meticulously and their features finely tuned.

Eric returned in late afternoon, noted the "Do Not Disturb" sign, and found Gabe sunk in his folded crouch, adjusting a pick with his nail file.

"Howdy, brother," Gabe croaked without looking up.

"How's our criminal enterprise?"

"Not bad. I've got three pretty nifty picks."

Gabe swept aside the lighter, knife, file, flat stones, and litter of clips and balled tissues, then took the three wires in his hand. "This one's a half-round feeler, this one's a rake, and this other a half-rake."

Eric gave a puzzled look.

"I'm assuming we'll be dealing with pin-tumbler locks and maybe a standard disc tumbler. Ward locks I can pick with my pocket knife but I doubt if we'll be so lucky."

He twirled the half-round feeler. "This little jewel is essential for getting into the keyway and putting tension on the core. With a feeler pick you can raise each of the pins. You move one pin at a time till you've got them all at the shear line. After that it's fairly easy if you know what you're doing."

"I'll take your word for it. Here, I bought this at the K-Mart." He dropped a new red day-pack on the tile.

Gabe grabbed it and rose from his crouch. "Brilliant, dear brother. I'll break it in tonight."

Gabe furthered his preparations by making one more pick: a wire with a sharpened tip that he simply called a "reader". They had supper nearby and watched the TV news till dark, then headed over to the lake. Their mother's house was in Kenilworth, but to avoid any suspicion they parked on the street in Wilmette and walked down to the beach. Jumping a gate to the parking lot they approached the water and turned north on a sandy ridge, vaulting two low barriers and finally reaching a spot where a snow-fence—with No Trespassing signs and barbed-wire—crossed a dune. The fence was breached in places, but a second fence on the side of a ravine presented greater problems. It was solid and chain-linked and topped with more barbed-wire. Near a heap of leaves and clippings they found its lowest point. Gabe drew from his pack a bath towel he'd borrowed from the room and draped it atop the barbed-wire. Eric climbed over first, nearly catching his foot in the ivy that festooned much of the top, but Gabe got over without a hitch though it took him twice as long.

The greenhouse loomed above the ravine, a bronzy rectangular cage, and then the house itself—set back on a sloping lawn and eerily lit by a floodlight. It was a hodge-podge of fanciful styles: a great Gothic cottage—fronted in tawny fieldstone—with a slate roof steeply pitched, tiny gables, bays, and archways, diamond-latticed windows, and a towering chimney by the dark garage that was half stone and half gray brick.

They checked the back doors first—the one off the new conservatory was heavily bolted from within, while the door with the trellised canopy and flanking wrought-iron carriage lamps had an ornate knob and a pin-tumbler mortise lock. Gabe took his time and tried all four picks and several techniques—including what he called "bouncing"—but could not get the lock to yield.

Warily they moved to the front through the maizes of hemlocks and yews, flagstone paths and arbors. The moon was up; the east breeze stiffened and carried the shush of lapping waves, like a conch-shell held to the ear. They spoke in careful whispers. The main door was too well lit and exposed, so Gabe suggested the garage side-door, which stood at right angles to the street. Leaves crunched underfoot as they crept along the wall. Eric noticed a window that looked like it had no lock. Gabe dropped his pack and with Eric's help pushed upward on the sash. But they saw it was held from inside by a stick wedged tight to the frame.

They slinked down to the side-door. Eric held the flashlight while Gabe studied the lock and probed it with his reader. It was a simple disc tumbler. He fingered his rake pick, steadied his hand with his pinky against the door, and worked away at the pins. Ten minutes passed. Gabe tried bouncing with the half-rake. Then, just as the cylinder trembled and clicked, a car cruised into the cul-de-sac and a searchlight hit the porch. The vehicle eased ahead, the light combed toward the garage, and Eric opened the side-door and wedged his body inside. But Gabe did not follow. He'd noticed his new red pack still sitting below the window. Wildly he bolted back for it. The searchlight touched the yews just six feet to his right. He snatched the pack but had no time left, so stuffed it up his sweater, raised and wrapped tight his coat, folded into a crouch, fell to the leaves at the base of the wall— like some great dark autumn moth—and went completely still.

An instant later the searchlight touched the window, defined a descending arc, and played across his body.

Chapter 9

A SHADOW. A SMEAR of stone. Blurs of hemlock and yew, tangled browns and olives, more lumps of shadow and stone. The cop made another pass, higher this time, checking for broken panes, raised sashes, tools or splintered wood. He pulled into the driveway and his headlights blazed on the garage. Leaving the engine running he slid out of his cruiser. The winding path to the front door was lined by creeping juniper, brassy with ambient glare. His polished brogans swam with the light of the carriage-lamps and clicked on the heavy flagstones. The thick cedar door, set in a Gothic archway, was triple locked: keyed knob and mortised deadbolt, second deadbolt above. He gave the knob a token jiggle, shined his flashlight through the porthole window to the dark hall within, scanned the bushes just off the porch, and swaggered back to his cruiser. The driveway asphalt made a faint tacky hiss—like someone slowly pulling off a bandage—as he backed down into the street.

Eric watched through the corner pane of a window in the garage. He waited an extra minute before peeking out through the door. The cop was gone but Gabe still lay folded in a heap beside the wall, a dark blob of shadow settled among the leaves.

Eric ventured a loud whisper. "Hey Houdini! All clear!"

The blob stirred, stiffened upward, formed crude arms and legs, scuttled toward him along the wall. Holding the side-door open until Gabe was safe inside, Eric locked it after them. His face was tense and ashen.

"Jesus Christ on a bike! What the hell were you doing?"

Smiling like an impish child, Gabe pulled the red pack from his sweater.

"Retrieving your K-Mart Special. Left it under the window."

Eric exhaled wearily. "I thought the man had your ass. Either that's his standard drill or Jackie's got him doing favors."

Gabe pinched at the ends of his mustache. "Yah. Lucky I'm invisible."

"That's not terribly funny."

The garage was cold as a crypt. Glenda's Volvo station-wagon filled the center of its concrete floor. They slipped around it, dodging lawn equipment and cardboard boxes, while Eric swung his flashlight on their last remaining obstacle. The steel inside door to the house was fitted with double locks—a standard key-in-knob topped by a mortised brass deadbolt. Gabe took the flashlight and gave them the appraiser's eye.

"The knob lock is a piece of cake. But the deadbolt is another pin-tumbler." Holding the flashlight, Eric waited while Gabe found his half-round feeler and began to probe the keyway.

Twenty minutes passed and Gabe had gotten nowhere. He paused now and then to blow on his frigid fingers. Each time he thought the pins were in line and went in for the finish, the deadbolt failed to budge. Eric offered encouragement and lame bits of advice, but a quarter hour more brought nothing. At last Gabe pulled away and sat down on his haunches. "Phew, boy, I tell ya. The little bugger is stubborn."

Flicking off the flashlight, Eric sat down on a stack of papers. "Shit. So much for your lighter and paper clips. 'The truth against the world' *indeed.*"

Gabe let out an angry little snort in the darkness. "Just what makes you think I'm through?"

"Oh it's not the end of the world," rasped Eric with forced cheerfulness. "If we fail as housebreakers I'm not going to slit my throat. We made a decent try but it just didn't work."

"Bullshit," said Gabe, flicking at his pony tail and hotly blowing on his fingers. "It just needs a different tack. A more... inspired approach. I should have known earlier..."

"Gabe, look. If we can't get in we can't get in. We'll find out what's going on some other way. She can't keep things secret forever. I should probably contact a lawyer. When Jackie gets back..."

"Shut up!" croaked Gabe, and quickly stood erect. "What I need now is quiet." He lowered his head, stomped his feet, shook his wrists at the floor. Then he went very still and started mumbling to himself. "Gwalch golchiad ei lain. Gweilch gweled ei werin."

"Gabe, don't be nutty. We've gone far enough. I'm not going to sit here in the dark, at my own mother's house, and resort to voodoo ritual just because we're lousy burglars."

Gabe stopped the incantation and turned his head toward Eric. "Brother, you've got no faith. That's your biggest problem." His voice was deeply solemn. "Look, I'll make this as simple as I can. Rituals change moods. And moods change behavior. If I can chant 'Jingle Bells' and it relaxes and inspires me because I *believe* it will relax and inspire me, then it *works*, even if it's silly. Once I'm relaxed and inspired, I'll behave in a *physically different way* than I did before the ritual. And that may alter an outcome that could not be altered before. The spiritual changes the material. Is that clear?" He paused to take a breath. "They used to call it magic. In some places, religion. You squeamish evolutionary rationalists, or whatever the hell you are... can just call it 'auto-suggestion'. If that makes you feel any better."

Eric stood silent in the gloom.

"Now shut up and be ready to hold that light."

Gabe lowered his head again and repeated the words of his mantra. He shook his wrists, mumbled and sighed, went still for a trance-like minute. Then he grasped the little half-rake, eased it into the keyway, and began bouncing the pins.

Five times he probed the keyway, five times he bounced pins to the shear line, five times he turned the pick while holding light tension on the plug. And five times nothing happened. On the sixth he blew on his fingers, dropped into a crouch, worked the rake in slowly and deftly jarred each pin. As he eased the tension on the cylinder core he drove the pick and twisted, the latch lever clicked, and the brass bolt slid away.

Gabe stood and stepped back. "There," he wheezed in weariness. "The shitty little *bugger...*"

"That's it?"

"Yah."

"What about the knob lock?"

Without a word Gabe reached in his coat, withdrew a small plastic ruler, jammed it between the door frame and the latch, then probed for the proper purchase. The ruler bent double, his fingers quivered with strain, he kicked the door with his shoe. It shuddered and fell open.

Gabe threw out his arm with a flourish of mock gallantry. "After you, dear brother. Faith before age and beauty."

For Eric, seeing his mother's house—at night, with a flashlight, for the first time in almost six years—was like probing a kind of dream. Not only did eerie shadows, cast by the wandering beam, trail from every object and palpitate like ghosts, but the objects themselves—framed by dull edges as the beacon formed each cameo—leaked memories, poked heart-sores, summoned corpses, as in a night of haunting sleep. Furniture from his childhood, books and vases and bric-a-brac, corners of rooms and hallways—all were etched with his past, queer domestic gravestones from an old psychic churchyard.

To block out their implications he pumped up his rational self and gave orders to a silent Gabe, who slinked behind him, a sentient shadow, reacting to his movements. For Gabe it was one more foreign latitude, like the dozens he plied each day. The bizarre was his native element, he swam as a fish in strange seas, was adrift in detached Sargassos, each a welter of outlandish threads, of alien interactions. Nostalgia left him alone; he was proto-man with a future cast set loose in modular space, a science-fiction traveller in a world he could not sway.

Together they had picked their way past the remodeled kitchen and laundryroom off the hall, left into the diningroom with its ginger jars, Delftware-dotted hutch, and rosewood table with hand-carved legs, between the study's walls of books and dark Delburgia panels, then out to a parlor of Williamsburg green, Catesby prints in cherry frames, and fireplace dogs—of polished bird's-eye serpentine—set off by a mica fire-screen. The entrance hall had a huge philodendron, Dutch parquet floors, and a bare hardwood staircase that spiralled to the second floor—tightly in its pale plaster silo—like the stepway to a fortress tower. It was here that they reconnoitered.

"Remember we're looking for a document," rasped Eric in the hollow dark. "That means desks and drawers, probably. If she left a copy here it won't be in the open. Let's check the new wing first."

Above them, moonlight defined a pie-wedge of staircase across from the high hall windows. Floorboards creaked like crickets as they padded on a Persian runner to the end of a narrow passage. What was once the doorway to the cellar and afforded a right-hand descent now opened to the left as well, where they spilled through an arch to a low-ceilinged room. One wall was of brick and the other a series of windows, thickly curtained to the floor. This was Glenda's museum room. Track-lights lined the ceiling, and when Eric flicked on the switch, threw purposeful beams on the brick. But the artwork they had illumined was now nowhere to be seen. The brick wall was bare but for its spaced frame-fasteners; the empty frames themselves lay stacked along the carpet in groups of twos and threes.

"Oh Christ," moaned Eric. "She's stripped the whole collection."

Gabe whistled softly and led the way to a cabinet that stood at the room's far end. Its walnut drawers housed manuscripts and outsized folio pages—of Catesby, Abbott, Wilson, Audubon and others—plus drawings from Holland's *Moth Book* and a scarce edition of William Henry Edwards' three-volume opus, *Butterflies of North America*. They slid out the drawers with anxious care and found that each was empty.

Eric beat the flashlight into his palm. "She couldn't have sold them all! There hasn't been time. To get a decent price you need a special buyer. Someone who knows what they're worth."

"She probably set it up long ago," said Gabe . "On the phone from L.A. Maybe a few are still here."

They hustled out of the room. Eric went to a closet and found another flashlight. He took the cellar and first floor while Gabe searched upstairs. There was nothing in the basement, but in a closet off the kitchen Eric found his mother's paintings. Under a bare lightbulb he examined the half-dozen watercolors that had once hung in their bedrooms. It was Glenda's series on Saturniids: a pair of pale Lunas in their washed emerald cloaks, ermine-thoraxed and platinum-veined, facing off on a sumac branch entwined with cinnamon leaves; Spicebush and Silkworm moths, Cecropias and Cynthias, each with fantastic eyespots and three-toned crenulations, stippled blotches and ribbed bays of cream and buff and gold, of toffee or Venetian red. And the one he considered her masterpiece: a fully-spread Polyphemus clinging to a curled leaf, its forewings streaked with undulate grays like a line of volcanic hills; its hindwings set with black-panther eyes, pearl within maize within pitch.

The closet smelled of dried mud. An assortment of raincoats and jackets were suspended from wooden hangers. Boots, sabots, and bright-colored rubbers lay jumbled on the floor, and a card table, neatly folded, leaned on the opposite wall. Eric tilted it out and found another painting—of woodpeckers hard at work, the largest a brilliant ivory-billed with scarlet crest erect. One of Wilson's early prints, it had hung off the upstairs hall in an alcove that led to the attic. It was Eric's favorite work. He slid it away from the plaster and grabbed the frame beside it, then went upstairs to find Gabe.

He found him sunk in his folded crouch, up in the tiny guest room that, near the end of their parents' marriage, had been occupied by Walker. Gabe had found artwork too: three original sketches by William Hart and Edward Lear that he'd spread in an arc on the bare oak floor, beneath the beam of his flashlight. "They were over by the desk," Gabe muttered. "Covered with a bath towel. About all that's left up here. The hallway and other bedrooms are picked clean as a turkey's tooth."

Eric set down the Wilson print and Gabe ran his beam across it in a neat little Zorro zigzag. "I was wondering where that was..."

"Yeah. Down in the mud closet. Only thing I could find. Other than Mom's watercolors, which I guess Jackie couldn't sell."

"This room is full of goodies," said Gabe. "Look what I found in the basket." He pulled two items from his pocket: a flat cardboard box that had once held "Life-Choice" condoms, and two of the blue foil packets whose bold white letters read: "As Gentle As Nothing At All" and "A Case of Condom Sense."

"Oh brilliant," deadpanned Eric. "Very nice. She's been porking some guy here too. In Dad's old bed."

"Yah. So it seems." Gabe couldn't help smiling at the madness of it all and let out a hopeless chuckle.

"So sad it's funny, I admit," sighed Eric, who carefully scooped up the paintings and walked toward the desk. "Any sign of the agreement?"

"The top drawer. There's a copy with all kinds of scribblings."

Eric set the art on the desk, which was littered with lists and receipts. A beige Princess phone filled one corner, a banker's lamp another, and a pair of brass bookends—in the shape of leaping trout— held some works on fish and angling. He slid the top drawer open and focused the beam of his light. It fell on a dog-eared document and another pack of condoms. "She's really made herself at home here, hasn't she? A bloody little command post. Did you look at it?"

"Not really." Gabe was staring at the floorboards and tracing the grain with his finger. "It exceeds my tolerance for bullshit."

"Well, I'm going to check it over," said Eric, plucking the paper from the drawer and heading out to the hall. In the alcove beside the attic stairs he sat down on a cedar chest below a bayed Gothic window, its glass crossed with leaded panes that broke the view into pieces. It looked down on walks and gardens, and a carriage-lamp on an ornate post entwined with English ivy. In the old days this nook was the family "retreat". A troubled one of their number might settle down on the chest, watching the lamp and gardens. It functioned as a kind of safety zone where thinkers were left alone.

Eric remembered the brutal row this window once had triggered. His father hated the medieval theme suggested by pointed arches. "Gothic arches in a private home," he'd railed when they first saw the property. "It's too damn pretentious. What is it, a church? A bloody Norman castle?"

"It's a cottage, Walker," Glenda had countered calmly. "A beautiful stone cottage. It's lovely, for all its pretentions. We simply have to live here."

A month after they moved in, Walker came home very drunk and threw a glass through the bay nook window, which he hated above all others. He ranted most of the night. Glenda had it fixed the next day and installed her favorite Wilson print on the alcove wall beside it. The window became a memorial, the nook an ironic redoubt.

Eric studied the agreement by the yellow gleam of the flashlight. On the last page, just before it concluded with a series of signees and witnesses, he noticed a telling clause:

"Should any joint tenant herein assigned be shown, by medical documentation, to be of unsound mind, then said tenant's rights and holdings herein described shall be forfeited in full."

He read and re-read the paragraph till its meaning could not be confused. Then he pushed the paper aside and flicked the flashlight off. The breeze had died and a mist rolled up from the lake. The carriage-lamp was haloed, the gardens sugared with translucent fog, while a dark moth straifed the halo, buzzed the molten ingot that formed its imprisoned core. He imagined a time before all of it, before the lamp and gardens, the house and its Gothic arches, the shadowed walks and cul-de-sac, the whole spreading fungus of Chicago. A time of unbroken oaks on hills and orchids in ravines, of bats and moths like numina, the dark their only element, the moon their single beacon. A hard but simple time when men led short adventurous lives, when Say probed the upper Midwest, when Wilson tred the Natchez Trace companioned by his bird-gun, his lacquered boxwood flute, and his Carolina Parakeet—a species of brilliant green and gold now dead as the fabled Dodo. A time when all were active and full of faith in a world not doomed by depletion, a world where the living spread their wings and squandered their frantic strength, convinced their line would last.

He gathered up the agreement and took it back to Gabe, who sat now at the littered desk and toyed with slips of paper.

"Ooh, here's a nifty item," he crooned as Eric approached. "An inventory of artwork. Complete with assorted bids." He craned his neck toward Eric. "She got a grand for Wilson's flamingo. One page of the folio. Assuming she followed through."

He punched at the bridge of his glasses. "This is fascinating stuff."

Eric did not share his lightness. "Gabe, I just found something important. In the tenancy agreement."

Gabe remained sunk in figures.

"Gabe," he persisted, "When was the last time you were hospitalized? When and where?"

There was a lengthy pause, then:

"I haven't been in the hatch since way back in college," mumbled Gabe, tossing a list aside. He switched off his flashlight and swiveled in the chair. "Except for once in Madison."

"When was that?"

"When? Jesus, I don't know. Before I hooked up with Pat. Maybe six or seven years ago. Why?"

Eric tossed the paper on the desk. "There's a kind of, well... 'mad clause' in the agreement. Sounds like if there's proof you're weird, then you're cut out of the deal." He thumbed to the final page and pointed to the paragraph.

"That stinking little gwiddon!" Gabe slapped the page with his palm. "She's got more tricks than a twenty dollar whore!"

Eric sat on the bed and threw his flashlight down. "Well, I mean... I'm not sure that would be proof... or even if that's what she's up to..."

"Ooh, that's what she's up to all right! And that's plenty of proof. I was in there five days and there was all kinds of paperwork. Two shrinks had to release me and in order to pay the bills—I had some student insurance—they had to certify an illness. Very damn specifically."

"So it was Madison. Do you think that's where she's gone off to?"

"Ha! Does a bear shit in the woods?"

Eric leaned back and linked his hands behind his head. "So... listen to this scenario. I mean, it's just a guess." He took a deep breath. "Okay, Jackie needs money, for whatever reason. Say her company's in a jam. Mom is dying and won't change her will, but Jackie can squeeze her property with this joint tenancy thing. First she cuts out me, then she cuts out you. When Mom finally dies Jackie controls almost everything because, well... the real property has already been divided to her advantage by the rigged tenancy agreement. The will distributes Mom's money and liquid assets, but they amount to very little since they've all been sunk in the property or used to pay for her illness. The... uh, the art would be worth a lot, but she gets power of attorney and sells it before Mom dies. Maybe uses it as capital for whatever she's trying to leverage. I don't know... some crazy bullshit along those lines. I know it sounds totally weird..."

Gabe jumped up from the desk chair and flourished his bony arm. "Brother, did I ever tell you you're a genius? By the owl's very *bowel*! That knocks it right on the head!"

"Well, I mean... it's kind of beyond belief but..."

"It's not beyond *my* belief. I knew something was coming. I need to get back to Madison."

Eric grabbed his light and rose from the bed. "Before we get out of here I want to do one last thing." He grabbed the Wilson print and frame and headed into the hall. Gabe followed and sat in the nook.

"I'm putting this print back up," said Eric. "And Jackie can be damned."

While Eric fitted the Wilson to its frame, Gabe assumed his lotus and stared out the leaded window. "Y gwir yn erbyn y byd." And the truth was all too clear. The fog had revealed it, something cloaked that is also something bare, something that disguises that also will reveal. It had slipped in at the last, full of watery voice. The old post of the carriage-lamp was coiled with ivy and mist, had formed the double helix, produced the magnetic field, stripped the sheath from the wire and bared its simple core. Was baring it now, even as he watched. Watched as he had long ago, watched how the very walkways were paths to a place beyond. A place of his beginning, their beginning, all beginning. Enter the little keyway, work the pins in line, crack the lock to the hot spiral core, the burning snake of life, the neurons smoked with memory, the helix trail of prophecy and ash, rising like a cloud-wisp, the final curl in time. But the curl was not yet finished. The ash-snake still unraveled.

And it was no ending, but a shadow of things to come.

Yna y bu yr aerua diuessur y meint.

It was then that the fight, immeasurably great, was fought.

Eric had pinched the backing on and lifted the print in its frame. He stood beside the alcove wall, reached the picture up, hooked the wire on the bracket, settled the frame in place.

"Let her gaze on that when she comes back on her rounds," he whispered half to himself. "And one more thing." He hustled into the guest room and brought out the agreement. Gabe had stood up from the cedar chest. "In case she doesn't get it." He creased it open to the final page and set it down on the chest.

"That's pretty unsubtle," said Gabe.

"She's a pretty unsubtle person."

They went back the way they had come: out the garage and around in back, down the slope to the chain-link fence, over it into the ravine, down to the snow-fence and the sandy ridge, then south along the beach. The fog was now so thick they could see neither water or trees, just the gritty strip of sand and grass, littered with bottles and paper scraps, herring gull feathers and blue plastic bags half buried or impaled on twigs. With no other focus right or left it seemed this was all there was—a degraded unraveling strand as far as the eye could follow, to a point one could not grasp, perhaps to the ends of the earth.

They were both very tired. When they reached the car they had nothing to say and Eric drove in silence. In their room the silence continued as they finally got into bed. Desperate to break the pall before sleep, Eric offered some advice.

"Gabe, there's no reason for you to rush back. She's done what she's going to do."

To Eric's surprise Gabe answered at once: "That's where you've got it wrong."

"But she's got the documentation."

"That's not what it's all about."

Eric puckered his brows. "I don't follow."

"She's out for something else. A bigger battle than this. Than money."

A door slammed in the hallway and an ice-machine grumbled.

"Like what?"

This time it was Gabe who killed his light and rolled to his other side. "I told you. She's a gwiddon."

The cab rolled into the driveway before noon. Jackie reached in her purse, found the right fare, threw in a hefty tip. The cabby waited till she'd unlocked the door, then wheeled back into the cul-de-sac. She knew right away she'd had visitors. One of Gabe's plastic straws had been dropped on the parquet floor. She set down her bag and briefcase and went straight upstairs. The agreement was centered on the cedar chest like a speech laid out on a podium. She pursed her lips and sat down.

Down in the gardens was the neighbor's cat—a cream and caramel tabby with a tail like a flute-charmed cobra—rubbing its cheek in the catmint. She smiled as it moved to the lamp-post and tried out its claws on the base.

"So the little shits broke in here," she whispered to herself. "What a pathetic show. Pathetic crawling worms." Her thin lips congealed in a grin. "And they think they know the truth! The truth..." The cat now rose to its fullest height, stretched its legs to their limit, raked the post with its fore-claws.

"I'll give them the fucking truth."

Chapter 10

THE SOUND OF A hallway vacuum-cleaner woke them in the morning. Bright light framed the curtains. They'd missed the free breakfast but Gabe said he wasn't hungry. Instead, before they left for the train, he made a tour of the room, stuffing his pockets and day-pack with extraneous items: the pencil, pad and matchbook on the dresser with their aqua motel imprints, the wrapped bars of bathroom soap and the color-matched shampoo and lotion in their ball-capped miniature bottles, the bright foil packets of coffee, the disposable shower cap in its compact folded carton, even the unused plastic cups, a spare roll of toilet paper and a handful of Kleenex tissues.

A wind had come up overnight and the trees along Lake Avenue shivered in their yards, rattled their massed tawny foliage, as the brothers headed for the station. The sky was a clean cerulean. When the Civic turned in to the lot, which was packed tight with cars, leaves swirled up from the pavement in brief little whirlwinds, and rope brackets under a rippling flag clanged on the metal pole.

The next train wasn't due for half an hour, so Eric parked on a sidestreet and they strolled around the block. He zipped his jacket against the wind while Gabe raised the collar of his coat like a Hollywood detective.

Eric took out his wallet. "Here, take some cash. And buy yourself lunch when you get downtown. I don't want you..."

"Fishing in the trash?"

"Well, no..."

"It's all right. I, ah... do it anyway. If I'm hungry and see things I like. Look, I'd rather pick and choose from a trashcan than settle for that junkfood you like."

"Me? Well, it's *good*. Some of it."

"Yah, well... I've a weakness for pastries myself." He flicked at his bouncing pony-tail. "Maybe just lend me the train and bus fare, if you want. That's plenty. I'll pay you back."

"No, never mind that." Eric pushed him some bills and reached for another twenty. "How about something extra. To get those glasses fixed."

Fingering the bridge and half-lensed frame, Gabe smiled, then threw up the palms of his hands. "I've actually gotten used to them. Save your money."

A gust stiffened Eric's red hair and he rubbed at his arm through his jacket. "About this business with Jackie..."

"It's really okay. I meant to tell you last night. I'll be, ah...past all that fairly soon."

"Gabe..."

"No, she *does* have me in her sights. But I've got a plan to deal with it. You're far more at risk than I am."

"*I'm* at risk?"

"Oh, yah. She hates me but knows I'm not a factor. It's mainly for revenge. For the sport of the fight. You're the one who worries her."

A twig tangled Eric's ankle and he shook his leg to free it. "Why should *I* worry her?"

"You've got the power of written words. She fears that. As any good gwiddon would."

"Gabe, I'm sorry, but I totally reject this gwiddon thing and all these other constructs..."

"I know you do, brother. You don't have to explain. And I don't really hold it against you. You're the family's, ah... chosen one, and the chosen one is always blind. To everything but beauty."

"Oh, so now I'm some kind of 'chosen one'?"

Gabe sighed and pressed his mustache to his cheek as the wind tried to bend it in half. "Just a theory. I won't know till I find the last curl in the Tunnel before..."

A huge gust bumped them together and almost knocked Gabe down.

"Before what?"

Catching his balance, Gabe turned away and filled his lungs with the brisk fall air. "Look, I'm very close. To the start, the first compact. All hell was breaking loose and they had to, well... save the jewels. The oak tree was sacred to the druids but we've never known quite why. Transformation, sky-gods, lightening, different theories. But I think I know. Something becomes something else, and then there's a kind of union. It may have been a ruse, to keep them off the scent. But the joining itself was real. I'm hearing mostly Old Brythonic now, getting way back, and if it jives with the rest then I'll know what parts of the poetry and legend are really just a code, a vault for storing treasures while this holocaust occurred..."

"Gabe, you're making no sense." Eric turned on his heels at the corner and looked down to the station. "I think we should catch your train."

They embraced as the massive engine squealed to a stop past the platform.

"Promise you'll call the motel if there's trouble," said Eric.

Gabe shouldered his day-pack. "Promise," he blurted, and turned toward the car behind him, double-timing his steps.

The platform was a foment of colliding gusts, of buffeting drafts and currents, warm and cool together, fresh and stinking, all of it roofed by blue. Fighting off his sadness Eric focused on Gabe's odd gait, saw the monkey splay and pitch of it, its loose-appendaged ape-ishness. Suddenly it ceased. Gabe stiffened and jammed a hand in his coat, then turned and ran back toward Eric.

"Almost forgot this," he panted as he reached him, extending a slip of paper. "It's Pat's address and number."

"Your old girlfriend."

"Yah."

"I think I've got it somewhere."

"Now you've got it again." He flashed a grin, then wheeled and raced for the car. The conductor was hanging, chimp-style, off the vestibule stairway, left hand clutching the vertical rail, left foot balanced on the lowest step, the right in mid-air, his pants legs plastered to his shins by the squalls of platform wind. With his free hand he held his cap on. Gabe approached him running, tipped an imaginary hat and bolted up the steps. A twisted end of his cape-like coat was the last thing Eric saw, whisking like a tail.

When Eric got to her room, Glenda was once more asleep. He had another lunch in the hospital cafeteria, then bought a *Chicago Tribune* to kill some time with the crossword.

His mother awoke about two. She was groggy and incoherent and seemed hardly to listen when he explained what they'd found at the house. He figured she was sedated, but an hour later, when her eyes cleared and her speech improved, she still didn't grasp his meaning.

"Heart? What heart, dear?"

"*Art,* Mom. Art. You know, paintings in frames. Pictures."

"Eric, they're all in the house. I've got them hung on the walls. In your room, too."

"Yes, I know, Mom. That's what I'm trying to tell you. They *were* in the house on the walls. Now they're not. Jackie took them down. We think she may have sold them."

Her lobster-flesh cheeks rose and fell. "Wheh... well, she *should* look after my paintings. They're irreplaceable treasures..."

He moved in closer to the bed. "Yes, Mom, that's what I'm saying. She *hasn't* looked after them. She's removed them. Almost the whole collection as far as I can tell."

"Yes, the whole collection is there. She protected them from those workmen."

"Mom, there were no workmen. Nothing else has been touched. Only Jackie has been there."

Glenda tried to sit up but winced with the effort and settled back weakly. "Eric, dear. It was sweet of you to check. Very thoughtful. I'm glad you found your key. I'm not well today. But Jackie's been so good. You saw the new addition?"

A nurse came barging in.

"Yes, Mom. Very nice," he cooed hopelessly.

While the nurse replaced the IV bag and drew a vial of blood, Eric stared out the window. The oak leaves shimmied like a tight school of fish with every burst of wind. When the nurse left Glenda nodded and he didn't pursue the subject.

Around five he was ready to go. Glenda was sound asleep. There was no sense trying again today. If she somehow did understand, or just toyed with the possibility, it would probably make her worse. He had risen from the orange and blond chair when footsteps sounded in the hall and a figure burst through the doorway.

"Well, look who's here," Jackie whispered with a smile. "My brother the burglar."

Glenda did not stir. Eric stepped toward the hall and motioned for Jackie to follow. They halted around the corner.

"You sneaky little shit." She tried to stare him down. "Are you proud of your adventures?"

"We're proud we found out the truth."

"Hah! Oh, *you* are a stitch! But you still haven't got a clue!"

"We do all right."

"You're a couple of bloody children!"

"I'll take that as a compliment."

Her green eyes narrowed. "I've no intention of thrashing this out right here."

"Nor do I."

"Good." She lowered her voice. "Then meet me at Mom's house tonight around eight. Use the front door this time."

Eric stroked his stubbly cheeks. "And what makes you think I'll come? I don't parlay with felons."

"Watch who you're calling a felon. My actions are strictly legal." She raised the beak of her nose. "You'll parlay, all right. Because your brother has got big problems. And I'm going to let you in on them."

"Oh, right. Just like you have in the past. Well he's already left town. He got the general idea."

She shot a glance down the hallway and shifted as if to leave. "He didn't get the half of it. But suit yourself. I'm going in to see Mom. If you don't show up tonight his ordeal will be that much worse."

Eric's face flushed. "What ordeal? Don't play fucking games with me Jackie...!"

"Tut, tut! Temper, temper!" She grinned and turned for the corner. "See you at the house?"

Back at the motel room Eric reviewed his options. If he didn't meet with Jackie he'd miss vital information. Not her deliberate pronouncements, which were likely to be lies, but all the peripheral tidbits she was bound to release inadvertently in the course of the night's digressions. On the other hand he'd be walking straight into her lair. She was on a roll, had everything squared away, would be prowling her private turf. She'd be twice as bad as she was before, and maybe far drunker.

He watched himself in the bathroom mirror, fingered his freckled neck, his jowly cheeks and their stubble of reddish beard, toyed with his Pop-eye elbow. Like a kid making faces for fun, he showed his monkey teeth. The thing about Gabe might just be a bluff. What more could she do to hurt him? She'd only been gone a day. Gabe himself had sensed something nasty, but Gabe was pretty far gone. Besides, he hadn't called. She might be inventing a crisis to get both of them out of town. Then once more she'd have Glenda to herself to clinch some further mischief.

He puttered out of the bathroom and sat down at the dresser. His body ached from the wear and tear, the constant emotional strain. He'd only been gone four days yet it felt much longer. He thought about calling Mel but knew it wouldn't help, and that thought tired him further. Grabbing the handle of his briefcase, he pulled it in front of him and popped the latches open. On top was the copy of his manuscript, its black cover dog-eared, its pages scratched with corrections. He picked up a pencil and pulled it out, then flipped the familiar pages. It seemed a hopeless tirade, a misanthrope's voice in the wilderness. Yet somehow it consoled him.

For the diseased and infirm it is often a horrid world, while even the well run a tangled course through daily pain and suffering. If one died calmly in one's sleep it would make not the slightest difference to anyone but the living, and they would soon forget.

Yet every morning we wake to the same crashing battle of fears and regrets, longings and lusts, problems, pains, and disgusts, with illusion our only balm. And still we are brainwashed at every turn into thinking that life at any cost is superior to death. Other animals die with fair ease and acceptance all around us, yet we are expected to fight like fiends against the last release. Our big brain, or a collective social consciousness (the big brains around us), tricks us once again down the path of greatest resistance, suckering us with 'hope', slyest of the illusions.

Eric pushed his book aside and looked in the dresser mirror. He put his hands on his eyes, his ears, his mouth. See no evil. Hear no evil. Speak no evil. It was futile. He wasn't that kind of monkey. Illusion or not, he couldn't abandon hope. He needed, above all, to know. He needed to crash her lair.

Jackie answered promptly when he knocked on the arched wooden door. There was no drink in her hand, and she ushered him into the parlor where they both sat down in armchairs. They were different, he noted, than the chairs he grew up with, which were dark green things with fringes and sturdy walnut legs. On these the legs were carved, the upholstery pale and subtle with a pattern of embroidered birds. Next he observed her glass, half full of strawberry liquid. It sat beside its pitcher, on the lamp-table to her right.

"I see you noticed the armchairs," she began off-handedly. "Part of the renovation."

"Very nice." He thought she looked flushed but not drunk.

"But we're not here to discuss that. Or are we?"

"Beats me. It was your invitation."

She was wearing beige slacks and jogging shoes, and a pale blue pull-over sweater. "Oh, I almost forgot. Would you like something to drink?"

"No thanks."

Crossing her legs with a dip of the toe she leaned all the way back and spread her fingers on the chair-arms. "Eric, I'm not going to rant. There's been too much of that."

"Mmm," he mumbled skeptically, then casually scanned the wall, doting on Catesby's bluejays, the cheap reproductions she had slyly left alone.

"Though I will fill you in some."

"Swell."

"But before I do, I'm confused." She knit her brows, affecting a baffled innocence. "Just why did you two break in here?"

"To get inside. Remember? You changed the locks and wouldn't lend us Mom's keys. Or are they your keys now?"

Smiling, she ignored the question and phrased another of her own. "Did you think there was something to find here?"

"Yep."

"Like what?"

"Like just what we ended up finding. Your copy of the agreement. Gabe lost his. And the bare walls left by your rip-off."

"Rip-off?"

"You stripped Mom's art collection."

Lifting her glass as she stared him down, she took a lingering sip. "Eric, you amaze me. What makes you think I did that?"

"Because it's gone. Almost all of it. And you were the only one here."

She smiled condescendingly. "It's gone, dear Eric, because I'm having the paintings re-framed, as part of the renovation. They were in crummy old frames and most were starting to slip."

"And the manuscripts and folios?"

"They're finally being appraised. We've never known their worth."

"Well that's real nifty, Jackie, but I'm afraid I don't believe you."

"That's your problem, isn't it?"

Eric shifted in his seat and crossed his legs to match hers. "And what about all this other stuff? Like cutting me out of the agreement and including a stipulation that is likely to cut out Gabe?"

"Likely to cut him out?" She squinted. "If you mean the clause about 'unsound mind', it's a very reasonable precaution. Should any of us get loony we don't want it wrecking the estate. What makes you think it applies just to Gabe? We've all got unstable qualities."

"True. But he's the only one with a certified mental illness. 'Unsound mind' is not an easy thing to document. Otherwise the whole human race would be locked up."

She drained her glass, nodded with ironic amusement and poured from the pitcher beside her. "My faithful cynic."

"You've got it all figured out, haven't you, Jackie? A lie for every occasion."

Pretending to groom her sweater, she doubled her chin and looked down, refusing to be rattled.

Eric uncrossed his legs and looked tensely about the room. His gaze fell on the fire-place dogs, which resembled pale gray geese, stippled necks stretched skyward; the mica screen was their algaed pond, ashimmer in summer heat.

"How do you stomach those sweet things," he managed finally, pointing to her drink. "More than one and I'd slip into a diabetic coma."

"I don't *always* drink them," she replied. "Last year it was Absolut in an up glass. With a twist. Before that it was Boodles."

"Boodles?"

"Boodles gin. The one with the Queen on the label. Queen Victoria, that is."

"Oh, yes."

"I have my attachments to style. They make life interesting." A slur had crept into her voice. Her eyes seemed focused not quite on him, but on something just to his side.

"Yes, I noticed. Your boyfriend. Or boyfriends. Is that part of your style?"

She pursed her lips. "My private life is just that. Private."

"Fine. Then find a private motel. Don't use Mom's house."

Jackie went red and took a big swig of daiquiri. He'd finally touched a nerve.

"Look, Eric, if you want to get personal, let's. Style is one thing, but I mainly respect results. And that's where we've got a problem." Her lips quivered and her face broke out in a grin. "Where we've *always* had a problem."

"Always had a problem?"

"Yes. Do you think I'm some lobotomized slob with no feelings or memory? Do you think all the shit that flew in this family was never going to stick?"

Re-crossing his legs, Eric balanced an elbow on his thigh and rested his jaw on his fist. Jackie gulped strawberry slush while her green eyes widened with rage.

"How do you think I got this way? Your hard-ass older sister? I'll tell you how. Sheer determination. To not end up like the rest of you. A couple of mushy losers, a failed lawyer, a soft-headed dreamer like Mom."

"It's nice to be held in esteem."

"Don't be so fucking flip. You and your phony cynicism. Just one more excuse for failure. Where were you when Dad was croaking? You and that schized-out brother of yours? I'll tell you where. Someplace on Planet Bongo. The night of the accident, you know where your brother was? Counting his toes in his bedroom. Locked in his famous lotus. He couldn't even speak, much less act."

"As I remember, he'd just gotten out of the hospital."

"As *you* remember! *I* remember *all* of it, because *I* was here. And Mom was as bad as Gabe. Spent the time painting on the porch or drifting around like Ophelia in a bloody artist's smock. You were back in Philly with your head buried in the sand."

"I was in the middle of exams and I came out as soon as I could."

"You were in the middle of fucking LaLa Land. Snatching moths out of Fairmount Park like a goddamn bat. Living in a basement. No phone, no address."

"They were in my roommate's name. He was a jerk."

"You came out for three lousy days. And your brother split for Madison."

"*You* kicked us out."

She set down her glass and her voice grew eerily quiet. "I don't want your damn excuses. I've heard them for twenty-five years. I lost my scholarship while I straightened that mess out. All Dad's hidden debts. His girlfriend suing the estate. Mom was as useless as a hamster."

"She was grieving."

"She was fair fucking Ophelia, with a paintbrush."

Eric sighed and sat back. "And you were a bloody saint, is that it? Jesus Christ, Jackie. You went totally wild. Or don't you remember that part?"

She sat plastered to the chair-back like an astronaut at liftoff. Once more she ignored his question. Her voice was a weary rasp. "Don't get me wrong, little brother. You made me. You and the whole damn family. By the time I got through dealing with the three of you—four, if you count Dad and his little deathbed dramatics—I knew what I was made of. And I knew what I wanted. You guys were my crucible."

"Yeah, well maybe the metal cracked as it hardened," he said softly.

She ignored him, embraced a brief silence; her features seemed to go limp.

He caught her mood and sunk into the chair, his arms draped over its sides. "What makes you think it wasn't *everyone's* crucible?" he continued. "Gabe's and Mom's and mine? We all changed after that. We all found some sort of focus. Money isn't the only measure of seriousness."

"You all found crap. Failure. Private closets to drool in."

"And you found...what? Anger and vindictiveness?"

Jackie waved her wrist. "Whatever you want to think. Just remember one thing." Her eyes flashed as she uncrossed her legs and sat forward with a thin-lipped, menacing smile. "It's not going to happen again. I'm in charge of this one. All of it. Start to finish. This time *you* can get melted down in a goddamn pot of shit, and see if you come out smelling sweet."

Eric sat forward as well. "Lovely. Is that about it? The story of your brilliant career?"

"You've yet to see how brilliant. As soon as I cut loose the albatross that this family has always been, you're going to see some soaring."

"Albatross? We haven't weighed you down. We've left you nothing but alone."

"Ha! Out from the mouths of babes! Yes, Eric, you've left me nothing but alone! Right from that first crucial moment. That's when I jumped the nest and really learned I could fly."

"Then fly. Don't drop bombs and wreak hell on the ground."

"I still need a place to land, kiddo. And you guys are cluttering the runway."

"So you're about to clear it?"

"Re-arrange it, let's say. Gabe's finally going to end up where he should have been all along. Out of the social flow."

"Out of the social flow?"

"That's right. Locked up."

"You can't lock someone up for schizophrenia these days. At least not very easily."

"Too true, Eric. Unfortunately. So I've taken a different tack."

"Which is?"

"Which is more than I'd like to reveal. I've said enough already. But if you care so bloody much, you'd better get up to Madison."

"Oh, it's mystery time again, is it?"

"That's right."

"I don't believe you. You're trying to get rid of me. So you can pull some other bullshit."

"Suit yourself."

He was rubbing both arms of the chair with his palms, staring at her drink-reddened face. It wasn't a monkey he saw; she was too full of booze to be natural, too full of malice to be animal.

"Jackie, you are truly sick."

"On the contrary, I'm inspired. The cream, dear brother, always rises."

Eric stood up. He straightened his pants and gently stroked his elbow. "Have you ever made soup, Jackie?"

She smiled down the beak of her nose. "No. I always make sure someone else does my cooking."

After taking a step toward the hall he turned and squared his eyes with hers, which were swimming with drunken mockery.

"Well, when you make soup, Jackie, it's not the cream that rises. It's the scum."

She rose and teetered faintly. Reaching for the drawer of the lamp-table, she pulled it out by its tooled brass handle.

"Before you go, kiddo, there's just one more thing." Her right hand gripped an object that she extracted with a flourish. "Don't try breaking in again." The muzzle of a pistol was pointed at his chest. "Some folks shoot burglars on sight."

"Oh, brilliant. What's this?"

"Is that all you can say?"

"Well, gee. How about,'Nice handgun, Jackie. Is it loaded?'"

They traded looks of hatred while she milked the moment slowly.

"Excellent question, bro'. You wouldn't believe me if I answered it, so how 'bout a demonstration?"

She stepped forward and aimed at his heart. After pausing for added drama, she finally pulled the trigger.

The gun clicked like a toy revolver.

His heart raced and his brain reeled. He flushed and wanted to slap her. Instead he summoned his cool. "Wonderful. Is this your new plaything? It looks like it has no hammer."

"Shows what you know, kiddo." She hefted it in her hand. "Called a 'pocket hammer'. Won't snag on your clothes." The nickel plating glowed in the light of the lamp. "A Charter Arms five-shot. Snub-nosed .38 special. Adopted it this year. It fits well in a valise, too." A tipsy, girlish smile crossed her face.

Eric turned for the front hall. "Guess you can never be too sure who you're going home with these days," he said over his shoulder.

"Fuck you, Eric." She pursued him.

His voice echoed loftily as he reached the hall and crossed the parquet tiles: "Once again, Jackie, it's been a pleasure."

Close on his heels, she reeled ahead and clumsily grabbed the door-knob, ushering him out with a mock curtsy of warmth and solicitation. "You boys be careful, now, hear?"

"Careful as thieves," replied Eric, returning the phony smile.

She watched him stride the flagstones to his car, then closed the heavy door and spied through its porthole window, saw his headlights sweep the garden as he backed into the street. The engine whined, diminished. She turned and squinted at the hallway mirror, put the gun to her temple, grinned like an impish child, pulled the trigger three times.

Back at his room, Eric fished out Pat's address. He didn't believe Jackie but he couldn't take the chance. Gabe's old girlfriend might know something, or at least be able to check.

The number rang five times before a voice came on:

"Hello, you have reached 608-301-1877. I can't come to the phone right now, but if you'll leave a message after the tone, I'll get back to you as soon as I can. Thank you."

The beep sounded, and he rallied his steadiest voice:

"Hi, this is Eric Dent, Gabriel Dent's brother. I need to speak with you about something rather important. Please call me back at 847-410-7275. Thanks."

In the room next door a TV droned loudly. He flicked on his own and found PBS, but the program was all about whales and their "songs", about listening to their "language", groping for its meaning. He really couldn't stomach it. The dopey anthropomorphism, with scientists writing books and cashing in on "whale-speak." Why were these not simply grazers of the sea who bellowed like bison or elk to crudely keep in touch? Did we make such a fuss over moose? To imply that such bleatings would evolve like speech, along lines much like our own—along those of bipedal omnivores who began on hot savannahs, exploited supple digits, honed binocular vision in their role as alpha-predators—was to scrap evolutionary sense.

He quickly turned it off. He would sooner tape the lowings of cows and search them for human logic than claim dolphins were trapped cuddly anthropoids, twitching with lost ape messages. Misguided sentiment and romance. To compensate for our sins. Now that we'd fucked up the planet we wanted to make atonement, to hear the wild things forgive us and explain they are just like us, though naturally not quite as smart.

He'd never felt so tired. The very air oppressed him. He stripped off his clothes, grabbed his book off the dresser, crawled beneath the covers under the oak-framed print of the orchard. Jackie could be damned. He refused to let her trip him up, to lure him out of town. Gabe still hadn't called. Tomorrow he'd piece things together; tonight he needed sleep. His own words would console him:

Scientists believe that man is descended from shrews, the smallest and fiercest mammals. They attack and kill prey much larger than themselves, and must eat many times their weight each day or perish in the effort. From this rapacious branch of mammals, it is said, humans slowly evolved. One looks at the history of man—and indeed views man in the present—and finds little cause to doubt it.

As these shrew-like apes overrun the globe, their lusts strengthen and spread. They rub against their fellows and their taste for conflict sharpens. Take five billion giant monkeys —seething with bottomless hungers—toss them about on a shriveling sphere, and behold our world, the Inferno.

On today's planet Earth, Henry David Thoreau, could he transcend the years, would be a certain suicide. The man who savored the sound of falling twigs or the changing colors on a pond, the man who studied subtlety and doted on detail, who was pledged to reasoned thought and open senses, would find scant escape from torture in our mobbed and vulgarized world. He barely found it in his own, an age now looked on with nostalgia by those who cherish the simple.

Transplanted to the present, he would first walk out to the road and look in all directions, sniff the air, watch the sky, listen with both ears, kick the earth, view his neighbors, eat some food, taste the water. Perhaps he would linger for a year or two, to absorb our media circus, our random or focused violence, our spreading collective neurosis. Then he would get a gun, point it at his temple, pull the trigger firmly.

Chapter 11

GABE DID NOT REMEMBER the train ride to downtown Chicago. He did recall the station—mostly its pulse and bustle, its drafts of air and tunnel-like echoes, and the upscale little coffee bar that was somewhere off the concourse. There he'd stopped for a decaf, which was served in a double paper cup (to protect his hands from scalding, the clerk had explained when he asked) and cost him almost two dollars. And he remembered he'd splurged even further: on a blueberry pastry in the thick-glassed case that caught his eye while he waited. It was real blueberry, too; he wolfed it down like a starving man as he sat on a nearby stool.

He'd saved the plastic fork after thoroughly licking it clean, and also the second coffee cup that had insulated the first. When he searched the open trash can, though, on the odd chance there might be more pie, two guys in three-piece suits starting giving him the stare, and the clerk leaned over the counter—a Latina girl with butternut arms locked down tight in front of her—and asked if he needed help. He'd mumbled something that no one caught and ambled on his way.

The rest had been a blur: the wind-blown streets, the skyscraper canyon shadows pierced through by knives of light, the bus station smelling like a washroom. There'd been a bit of a hassle. He couldn't find his money and fumbled through all his pockets while customers fumed behind him, then failed to find the ticket itself when his turn came to board. The bus had pulled out after noon—a lurching crawl toward the freeway scored by the endless belch of air-brakes.

By that time he had departed. He'd found a tiny keyway—the bright metal corner of a window-frame—and tripped his inner latch.

He slipped past familiar guideposts, dark bends in the Tunnel, smoky curls of the helix.

> Great are its gusts
> When it comes from the south
> Great are its mists
> When it strikes on coasts...
> And it is no ending
> But a shadow of things to come...
> Ac yna kychwynnu a wnaeth ef a dechreu rodyaw racdaw.
> And then he set out and began to travel forth.
> Ac sef kyrch a doeth.
> And this was the attack that came.

Somewhere west of Elgin the bus stopped to pay a toll, and the woman sitting next to him, whose young son just behind kept fiercely kicking her seat, offered him a mint. She had to offer twice. He somehow caught her meaning—the disembodied voice was a byway in the curl—and accepted the small white pellet before slipping back on course.

> From the south he was cut off
> And also from the north
> The west was a quagmire deep as night
> The east a den of demons
> It was then that they sent their she-king
> To lay the terms before him
> And he did meet this gwiddon
> And to her start to speak
> "Dioer ny henbydy well di o vot yn dwrc wrthyf i."
> "Truly thou shalt not profit by being evil to me."
> "Ny buum drwc i ettwa wrthyt ti."
> "I have not been evil to thee yet."
> "Trin elyn, dygnaf, nyt hawd fy llad i."
> "Enemy in battle, most dire, it is not easy to kill me."
> "Ny ladaf i di, mi a wnaf yssyd waeth itt."
> "I will not kill thee, I will do thee a worse evil."
> Then this gwiddon left
> But kept her host nearby
> And he did stop his travels
> To draw his tribe around
> For they would be in peril
> And all their way of life
> Unless by force of magic

They formed a perfect match
To keep their line alive
Forever down the years.

The bus had droned in the autumn sun past Rockford and Beloit,
but Gabe remembered none of it. His seat-mate did some knitting,
her brown nimble fingers like a spider wrapping prey. Her young son
fell asleep. Gabe kept close to his inside course and only came around
when a landscape south of Madison intruded on his trance. The viaduct
looked strange in the old-gold light, yet somehow it was the same. Had
he been there in a rainstorm? A loose hunk of concrete marked the
slope where he'd rested. This he remembered well. It resembled the
thorax of a fly, or was it a nubby oak bud? The bus was past it in an
instant. It lay in the echoing cave, the shadowed canyon pierced with
light, the darkened spiral core. He felt the sense of closure, the circle
coming full, the ancient curl of cloud-wisp. Voices he'd traced all day,
barely audible babbles—on the train, in the streets and stations—were
now becoming clear.

Ac yna y aethant yn y geluydodeu, ac y dechreuant
dangos y hut.
And then they went to their magic arts, and began to
work their enchantments.

Gabe straightened in his seat and snatched up his pack from the
floor. He prized out the motel pencil and the little logo-ed pad. The
words in his head were a mantra:

Dar a dyf y rwng deu lenn
Gorduwrych awyr a glenn
Ony dyweda i eu
Oulodeu hi hwnn pan yw hynn.

The woman with the brown spider hands had gradually stopped
knitting. She watched instead her seat-mate's hands which, abruptly,
had grown busy. The left held down the notebook and the right clutched
an aqua pencil that filled up page after page with incomprehensible
jibberish.

Eric was getting dressed when the phone in his room started
ringing. Barefoot and shirtless, he padded over to answer it.
"Eric?"

"Yes?"

"This is Patricia Llewellyn, returning your call." Her voice was quiet and pleasant.

"Oh hi, Patricia. Thanks for calling back. The reason I called was that my brother Gabe gave me your number and I'm, well... sort of worried about him."

"He's in trouble?"

"Ah, no... that is, I *hope* not. That's what I need to find out. I mean, I think it's probably okay, but he was down here on a visit and we found out someone was, well, sort of messing with his private affairs... maybe trying to, I don't know, complicate his life. And you being close to him, or, at least at one time... I thought you might know something more than I do..."

"Is he back in Madison?"

"Well, he *should* be. He went back yesterday on the bus. He said he'd call me if there was a problem, but, well... you know how he is... forgetful and all that."

"Yes, oh yes, he can be. I don't see all that much of him these days. But I can certainly check."

"Could you? Boy, that would be great. I'm staying in a motel, visiting my mother, and I'll probably be here at least one more day. If you could just get back to me, or leave a message at the desk if I'm not here. That would really help."

"Sure. Yes, I'll be working most of the day. But I can slip by some of his haunts later on. Though I can't guarantee I'll find him."

"No, no, I understand. He can be pretty... elusive. No, anything will help. Whatever. It's no big deal. I don't want to trouble you."

"It's no trouble. I've been meaning to contact him anyway. Why don't I give you a call this evening? Say around seven. Not much before, I'm afraid."

"No, that would be great. I'll try to be here. Thanks, I really appreciate it, Patricia."

"You can call me Pat," she said with quiet reassurance. "I'll talk to you this evening, then."

"Thanks Pat. Take care."

She had sounded nice enough, but he hated telephones. They were business machines, really, designed to smooth the greedy rough edges of commerce and consumption. Perfect, too, for con-men and courteous crooks, phonies and cordial liars. Phones made you squirm to express yourself, to present yourself as a transmitter, made you stretch for clues on the other end that were just beyond your reach, made you judge by spoken words alone, which of all things apes produced were the most insubstantial.

Events at the hospital went little better than the day before. Glenda was weak and in pain, and they kept her full of drugs. She slept the entire morning. At least he did not see Jackie, but it wasn't much consolation. The problems with her and Gabe kept him anxious, on edge, and when lunchtime came, though tired, he skipped the cafeteria and instead went out on the streets.

Clouds had moved in and it looked like rain. A few big drops had already fallen, fixing dark seals on the sidewalk. Eric sauntered to the El, feeling blue down to his socks. He'd spent some of his youth here, tramped these streets and alleys, noshed in the pizza and sub-shops, searched the leafy parks. When he wasn't stalking moths in ravines near his home he was off with his buddy Phil, riding the El to Foster, watching films at the Varsity, cruising the Northwestern campus. They hiked along the lakefront, netted Zales by the Noyes Street embankment, smoked dope in the Shakespeare Gardens where he once snatched a Puzzling Dagger.

He decided to take a ride. The station these days looked derelict: white trim all peeling, brick walls sprayed with graffiti, turnstyle rusted and creaking. Up on the platform gusts kicked up and a big break in the clouds let sunlight rouge a spray-painted wall that was screened by brittle leaves, which rattled briefly like clothes-pinned cards in the spokes of a child's bike. The train wobbled down from Wilmette, rocking on its rails, its mechanized heart aflutter. How easy to step off in front of it, to end it all right here and let things come full circle. Like dropping down on a mattress. Embracing the final sleep. Instead he waited with his toes on the ledge till the fat cars slapped him with their breath.

The ride was all too familiar: the rolly-polly pace, the clack that defined each rail-seam, the Marc Chagall vistas. He flew above the town, just at the tops of trees. Nostalgia mixed with numbness. Tension with fatigue. He felt something spent and suspended at his core, like a flapping moth above a flame who cannot come to rest.

At the Main Street stop he got out, walked down the cracked concrete steps and over to a small Greek restaurant that had been around for ages. Once it was open till midnight but now, no doubt because of crime, its hours were much reduced. "7 TO 9, 7 DAYS", said a hand-lettered sign on the smeared glass door. He sat at a booth in the corner, beneath a poster of the Acropolis, and ordered the moussaka and a small Greek salad. It was just as he remembered it: the moussaka gray and spongy, the salad an Iceberg lettuce thing with stingy bits of feta, shriveled peppercini, a trio of oily olives, crackers in cello packets.

Later he walked further south and paused at the head of an alley to glimpse a scene from his past. Down this lane in the shadows had been his first real job. It was after his freshman year at Penn; he'd delivered papers from a truck. In the late afternoons, during record-breaking heat, he'd jumped in and out of a white Ford van, dropping bundles at the Gold Coin and Denny's, White Pantrys and 7-Elevens, mom-and-pop corner groceries. A fat high-school dropout in his twenties, who wore cowboy boots and shades, ran the show from a tiny office, bossing his teenage crew. The yellow-brick corner of the building, still fretted with dusty ivy, was visible from the sidewalk, ringed by its fleet of vans. Eric had lasted eight weeks before retreating to his ravines.

Yet the Evanston alleys appealed to him. Many had yielded lovely moths: Foresters and Sallows, Pinions and Underwings. He especially remembered the Tiger Moths, showiest of the Arctiids. They were rare in the lakeside ravines but from Wilmette down to Evanston they showed up near backyards and alleys. September had been his favorite month, when the alleys bulged with lushness, were walled with shrubs and fruit trees starting to go pale, gnarled willows and maples bandying the dusk, tangles of garden and trellised vine, vivid before the frosts, exhausting the jet of a last tinted petal or burning with fresh flame.

He'd stuff his collapsible net in his pack, with thermos, Snickers, and a single hand-rolled joint, and ride down to catch a matinee, at the Varsity or Valencia, then afterwards buy a gyro-to-go from another Greek place across the street and walk the twilight alleys. There was quiet here, amid garbage cans and waste. Beside discarded armchairs, by the ghost of a crucified kite or the Buddha of a plastic doll, clematis bloomed or hollyhock tilted, and *grammia* was aloft: black, with a hindwing bloodspot and hieroglyphs of cream. Or *placentia*, of carmen body and sun-flared wings, or, loveliest of the family, *Utetheisa bella*, the Bella Moth, with its abdomen like snow and hindwings all afire, all Sonoran desert sunset. He'd make an interesting capture and house it in a jar while—hidden in mock-orange or honeysuckle—he reduced his joint to a roach and admired his winking prisoner, studied its runic markings, released it in the gloaming. His supper tasted best here, improved by the spice of *cannabis*, the oniony grease on his mouth and hands a kind of nomad's incense and he the errant herdsman—his net-crook beside him—briefly leaving his tribe behind, communing at dusk with his numina, tearing at shards of meat.

These days the alleys brought more sinister communions. His moth-haunted lanes were haunted now by corpses. While buying his hospital *Tribune* he'd glanced through the local papers with their grim little buried headlines: "Body Found by Trashbin", or "Homeless Man Found Dead." The first story gave no street address but mentioned that three months before, at roughly the same location, a similar corpse was discovered, wrapped in a piece of carpet. The victims had criminal records. The second blurb gave few details, only that an aging "street person" had been found in an Evanston alley, his skull badly crushed.

Eric stayed on the sidewalks. He wasn't afraid, just no longer felt the connection. These weren't the nomad byways where a dreamer laid down his crook and consulted the trembling seraphs, read the runes of their wings. His old gods were dead; they'd been part of his naive past. He stopped instead at a drugstore, bought a Snickers for old time's sake, drifted on back to the El.

When at last he returned to his mother, who was awake and sitting up, his frustration bubbled over. He assaulted her with the truth, insisted she understand. It mattered little. A blandness clouded her features; she was clear-eyed but witless, cocooned in her own private world where no one was ill-intentioned, no one sneered or lashed out, made war or drowned in bile. All her children were loving, all her children cared, each, in fact, was a child. She smiled a lot when he spoke, a weak smile that faintly pressed her jowls and outlined haunting dimples.

Eric concluded it was hopeless; he would make no more attempts. Perhaps he should never have tried. The whole affair oppressed him, seemed to rob the room of air. He wanted to pick up the orange and blond chair and smash it through the windows. He shredded bits of newsprint, doodled along the margins, rubbed his itching elbow. Staring out at the oak tree he recalled the ad for a film he'd seen posted in the station. When Glenda began to doze he explained he was going out. She managed a dimpled smile.

The Varsity and Valencia had long been out of business but on campus there were revivals, film society offerings, and this was "David Lean Week." The matinée at four was Lean's *Oliver Twist*.

Eric parked along Foster and walked toward the Norris Center. Its big concrete monolith loomed against the lakefront, clashed with the gothic citadels, had all the grace of a prison. He killed some time below it, beside the man-made lake. Goldfish grazed in placid schools like herds of watery heifers. A light rain started; he climbed to the Center, entered the glassy vestibule, mounted a stairway to the theatre. On a bulletin board beside its door—a collage of copied movie bills, reviews and promotional brochures—was the fashionable film esoteria of the last fifty years. Listless students hung about, slung with heavy bags and draped in layers of clothing—outsized sweaters and trousers and bulky leather boots, worn to look casual and cheap, streetwise or working-class, but in fact designer-made and self-consciously correct. He cradled his jacket in the crook of his arm, rubbed the stubble on his chin, examined a photo of Peter O'Toole wincing at Omar Shariff in faded xerox monochromes.

The film started late. Students stared at the ceiling, boots propped on seat-backs. Then the soundtrack blared while the lights were still up, and people scrambled for seats. Black and white images flared. They brought a shock of pleasure; the movie was one of his favorites. Reviewers and promoters had mostly got it wrong. It was not mere

Dickensian fluff adroitly handled by Lean. You took out some soppy scenes and the Hollywood happy ending and it was cynical as hell: an unwed teenage mother dying in a workhouse, the nurses stealing her effects, her identity and that of her baby kept secret by rogues and thieves, the child beaten and exploited, warrens of boy criminals beneath the dome of St. Paul's, rich incompetent do-gooders, kids in league with murderers, blackmail and extortion, a city alive with thugs. Dickens, Eric knew, cast a dark eye under his sentiment. His London was a seething blight; a maelstrom of decay.

Eric's favorite scene took place at the "Three Cripples" tavern and had lost none of its spice. Drunken patrons sing biting songs while men of varied backgrounds plot mayhem in the back. Around the bar the sense of despair, of hopeless suffocation, is palpable: amid choking clouds of tobacco, self-mocking sots push together like sheep in pens, overflowing railings, bleating at the tops of their lungs:

"Look at the drunkards of London!

Lying all over the place!

There isn't a doubt, it's a lovely lookout

For the hu-man race!"

The scene of greatest violence—merely suggested by the frantic whining of a dog—was as chilling now as when the film was made, and really, Eric felt, far better than most things modern with their grossly explicit formulas that cheated imagination.

It ended all too soon. He wanted more of the street scenes, the Gustav Doré backdrops, the songs of Armageddon. Students still snickered in their seats from the corny tear-jerker ending. No doubt they saw it as naive "camp", but it was meaner than anything they knew. He liked Lean's *Oliver Twist* even more than he remembered. Everyone in it plies smallness or desperation, or screws up rather badly. The hero is a dog.

Eric shuffled to his car in the gloomy early evening. His brief refreshment vanished. The rain had stopped but the air was damp and the clouds formed a low dark ceiling. His head ached; the campus seemed a gothic horror. When he got to the Shakespeare Gardens, with their vandalized benches, sodden beds of autumn blooms and sad pretentions to seclusion, he surprised a pair of frat boys who were vomiting by some lilacs. One seemed genuinely ill; the other laughed it off, chuckling between his hiccups and toasting his quart of Coors in Eric's general direction.

Look at the drunkards of London

Lying all over the place...

He quickened his pace. As he turned onto Foster there was

lightening in the west and thunder mixed with the clatter of the El as he sidestepped chocolate puddles. The figure ahead waved an arm; for a moment it looked like Gabe. It was seated against a pylon below the vibrating tracks: a pony-tail tied in back, a khaki coat draped around it, some sort of bundle at its side. Eric swerved to get closer. The mustache now was visible; a bony hand probed a pocket. It was Gabe all right. And he'd finally lost his glasses. Eric jumped a pool of mud and crossed the edge of a lot. Pulling out a bottle, Gabe waved a second time, then leaned against the pylon and knocked the bottle back. "Hey, brother," he croaked as Eric got in closer. "Whad'ya say? Spare ah man ah dollah?"

Eric pulled up short. In the gloom the man still resembled Gabe but the voice exposed his error. He veered back onto the sidewalk and bee-lined for his car. The sky pitched with inky waves and shuddered louder than before. Then it began to pour.

There isn't a doubt it's a lovely lookout
For the hu-man race.

By the time Eric reached his room he'd already gulped the burgers that he'd stopped for on the way. Balling the white paper bag, he dropped it into a basket and took off his rain-spattered jacket. His eyelids seemed made of lead. His elbow throbbed. He pried off his muddy shoes and sprawled across the bed.

The station is shaded by an oak; its leaves are a tight school of fish. He climbs the flight of stairs that rise in a dizzying spiral. No one is on the platform. The train arrives with a single car and whisks him above the rooftops. Night floats in from the lake. It's a city night that can't quite sleep, but is at that point in between where light and dark are a half-closed lid, where perception becomes a flapping moth that cannot come to rest.

All along the high-pitched track the night pursues descent. But only twilight settles. On the ruined plain of vacant lots, beneath curtained windows, through the tunnels of darkened gangways, dusk is altered like twisted thought by the glide and stroke of shadows. Wings pull back, legs lift, a barren branch sits waiting, a child wakes in fear.

He climbs down at an unknown station and enters a vacant house. Another stairway rises; at its top is an open window where he stares out at the moon. Beside the moon are three pale clouds, ranged like lonely tents on a dusky, vast savannah.

Leaves shimmy softly in a tree above the street. Once more the shoal of fish. Their swish becomes a whisper, which becomes a rising voice—first that of a man, then a woman. A babble ascends, a chorus—a great aching wash and winnow that joy and grief together cannot name. He slumps beside the window, sobbing with all his strength.

The tones rippled like a flute. "Tootle-tootle-tootle", in rapid bursts. His eyes opened; he rolled to the edge of the mattress, groping. A voice jarred his ear.

"Eric?"

"Uhn."

"This is Pat Llewellyn."

"Umm, 'ello."

"Did I wake you?"

"No, it's Okay."

"Look, you were right about Gabe. There is some sort of problem."

"You found him?"

"No I didn't. No one has. That's kind of the problem. The police are looking for him. He's under suspicion for something."

"For what?"

"I don't know. The Vigrens wouldn't tell me."

"The Vigrens?"

"They've been sort of his friends. The son is his landlord. Or was. They've locked him out."

"Oh, lovely. So the cops want him and he's got no place to stay? Can I call these Vigrens?"

"Well, the son's number is unlisted. They lease him their garage but always insisted he not use their phone. The father runs a diner where Gabe picks up his mail. But he's not speaking and neither is his wife. I went by both places. They treated me like a leper."

Eric stood up from the bed and shifted the receiver. "So you don't know what it's about? What did the police say?"

"They wouldn't tell me anything. 'The case is being investigated'. That's what some sergeant told me on the phone."

"Okay, Pat. I'm coming up."

"Tomorrow?"

"Tonight. Now."

"Well, I wish I could tell you more. I'm going over to the station now. To see what else I can learn."

"Any chance Gabe will come to your place?"

"No. That's out. We've agreed." She cleared her throat awkwardly.

"Well okay, will you be able to see me if I get there by, say, ten-thirty or eleven?"

"Oh, sure, I can stay up till you get here. I'm not saying I'll learn anything..."

"No, I understand. Just so we can meet and maybe you'll fill me in some."

"Sure. Do you have my address?"

"Yes."

"I'm on the East Side. Turn left off Williamson as you're headed toward the Capitol. There's an Exxon and an Italian carry-out at the corner. It's a frame house, green, with tan shutters."

"I'm on my way."

Chapter 12

JACKIE WAS STARING AT the leaping trout. Their brass finish twinkled, caught the light of the banker's lamp, glowed like twisted ingots. The beige receiver of the Princess phone was clamped by her chin to her shoulder.

"Maria, that's all you have to do. Call this Mr. Ito, Fax him the inventory, and confirm the appointment. Tell him what I've told you. *Do not* let Carmen get involved. No, not even with the Fax. That's right. At the Van Nuys warehouse. The shipment should be there tomorrow. I've already checked things with Ray. Yes, I'll be there in person. Yes. Friday. Great. Then call Jason and set up the Monday meeting. No, Greenberg, Graf, and Diamond. They've already drafted it. Yes, all the managers, too. Yes. Terrific. Super. Just wait till I get there before you do. Okay. And the flight to Honolulu. Did you get the tickets? Perfect. I'll see you soon."

She hung up the phone and fumbled through the papers on the desk. Her glass of blue Kool-Aid had left a ring on the finish; she moved it and wiped the stain. Then she punched out another number on the touch-tone dial.

"CeCe, hi, Jackie. Fine. Great. No, everything's going perfect. Listen, remember that house in the hills that we talked about? Right, Malibu Ridge or whatever. Yes. Right. Look, call that woman back, Rita or Rhonda or whoever. Yes, Rhoda. Call Rhoda and tell her I'm interested. No. I'll put in a bid. Go there yourself then. Yeah. If it comes to that. I'll have Maria draw one. No, you can pick it up. Yes, I know it was just right. Yes, Friday. Great. I am too. Terrific, Cec."

She had just hung up and reached for a sip of Kool-Aid when the phone jangled softly.

"Hello? Well, hel-lo. No. Just taking care of business. Umm. Sure I can come out and play. Ah. Why not? Then let's use *my* sandbox. Hah! I bet you say that to all the girls. That's right. Yeah. Oh, poor baby! Can I kiss it and make it better? Nah. Let's. Aww, my lonesome cowpoke! You can tell me all about it. Nine-ish? Yeah. Oooh. Knock twice. Bye-bye."

Dar a dyf y rwng deu lenn. The tree all hung with cloud wisps, smoky apparitions, breathing through the mists. The lakes smoked with white, their margins silver coils. Marshes beaded with dripping sedge. Strands of dew-honey pearls, entwined like glistening snakes. Dark plumes rising from campfires, smudges of fire and ash, the huts still in gloom, a black helix drawn upward. Gorduwrych awyr a glenn.

Gabe walked from the station, lost to his surroundings. Vaguely he noted the light, the pale pumice of autumn, the quake of amber leaves. No cars were in the driveway and the side-door was locked—not just at the knob, but with a padlock above it. A note was tacked to the panel:

"You are locked out. Leave or you'll be arrested."

He cleaned one point of his mustache. No time to investigate now. Walking back up the drive, he steered for the park by the lake. Ny ladaf i di, mi a wnaf yssyd waeth itt. I will not kill thee, I will do thee a worse evil.

At a place in the park where a stream pushed toward the lake, a wooden footbridge spanned the flow. Under one end of the bridge was a shaded wedge of darkness, a cave-like recess below the planks, laced with trash and weeds. He slipped beneath the boards, dropped his pack on the sloping dirt, coiled into his lotus.

The oak tree has a bud. The bud has a stooping branch. To all the branch seems weak, for it trembles in the breeze. Yet it bows; it does not break. It has weathered fierceness. It waits in the shadow of the valley. Its limbs are those of her swain.

Gabe sat still as a troll while the afternoon aged, lost its luster. The current swirled, coiled with tresses of pondweed. Dusk settled softly.

> Dar y dyf yn ard uaes
> Nys gwlych glaw nys mwytawd
> Naw ugein angerd a borthes
> Yn y blaen hi hwnn.
> Dar a dyf dan hi anwaeret
> Ny bu ohir y ymgael ohonunt
> Ony dywedaf i eu
> Nos honno kyscu y gyt a wnaethant.

Eric left in the drizzle and dark. He took the Tri-State north. Past Lake Cook Road and Half Day, Belvidere and Grand. The road was an endless runway above which he floated but never climbed, flew but never soared nor allowed himself to land. It was slick as a watersnake's back, lit by the bore of his headlights, tunnelled by walls of darkness, streaked by roadside visions. Lakehurst and Great America. Gas, food, lodging. Billboards from his past.

Gabe was there, reluctantly, helping him trap a Leopard Moth on the slope beneath their home. The gangling Gabe of seventeen whose body would never change but whose mind soon changed forever. Gabe staring into a killing-jar. Snow-white wings with hollow spots. Thorax like a lettered tablet. Neatly coiled proboscis. Gabe aflutter in the hay-scented ferns, sweeping his net, sinking on his haunches.

Walker was there, beak-nosed and imperious, drifting down from his lawn-chair perch, sporty in shorts and Weejuns, hair white and thinning, face red with drink, dodging poison-ivy, secure with highball and tweed porkpie hat, flashing his cynic's grin. A stare down the hook of his nose, a jiggle of ice in glass. "Brilliant, boys. What is it this time? Pandora's Sylph or Cynthia's Cherub?"

Glenda was there, catching the flat north light. Smocked and seated on her three-legged stool, on the jalousied porch off the kitchen. Laboring over Robin Moths, the peanut-scented Cecropias, threaded by their thorax to chopsticks in clay, revolving in drunken circles, wings agape, like gaudy Maypole dancers. Her brushes all fouled with color, dripping Venetian red, stiff in jars like candy-sticks, in August heat, in peanutty dampness.

And Jackie was there. Patrolling the grounds in Lolita shades, tanning on the flagstones, white one-piece bathing suit, oil smeared on her heron legs, her cowlick bleached and erect. Jacqueline Susanne splayed open on a cushion, dog-eared, her spine broken, at the base of the pink chaise-lounge.

Wisconsin. The state line a welter of arc-lights and rain, glowing pods of commerce converging through the murk. Kenosha and Racine. The old vacation signposts on the trek to cool Door County, to the trout streams further north, in the swelter of buried summers. Walker taking side trips, fishing the Big Two Hearted, Glenda painting Sister Bay, Gabriel fixing bikes, the search for Bicolored Lichen Moths at a boggy place called The Ridges. Jackie reading Susanne again, tracking Walker down when he lost himself on a junket, driving him back in his pickled state from some camp near Marinette.

Time wounds all heels. So said Glenda. With that she left it to the Fates, let Walker steer his course, his slide on the glassy slopes. Jackie looked at it differently. Dogged him like a Fury, chased him out of dives, shamed him toward the light. Like a moth he preferred the darkness unless some bottle gleamed. Drunk tanks. DWI. Scraping up the bail. His license a slippery fiction.

Eric sped up the wiper blades as he swerved past Milwaukee in a downpour. Their rhythm was a hectic lash. Moisture fogged the windows; he flicked the defrost on high. U.S. 94 West. Waukesha and Oconomowoc. Pewaukee and Menominee. They'd wiped them out but saved their sibilant tongue. Wissahickon, Conshohocken, Kittatinny, Kissamissing. From East to West, a litany of genocide. Europe on the march, leaving only names. Dark tribe, pale tribe. Descended from shrews. The smallest and fiercest mammals. Must eat many times their weight each day or perish in the effort. Jackie the family shrew. Constantly in motion. Evolved a taste for blood. Ate he of the Celtic sounds, ate he of the insect sounds, ate her sibilant siblings.

Or was it something else? A socio-psych phenomenon? Control of chaos and death? More like simple vengeance. For what? For the way they cowered when Walker died? For the way they shrunk from his dying and let her mop the blood? Or did she want the blood to herself? Relish it? Let Walker know where she stood? Let it wake the beast within her? Let the succubus be born? The gwiddon waiting with cat-claws? The beaky gwrach who rends human flesh, the Welsh witch at war with the world?

No. He leaned to genetic imperatives. But not the kind Gabe imagined. Not tribal or druidic. Not a priestly compact. All a rigged game to begin with. The monkey line too strong. Two million years since *habilis*. Not her fault. The blood selects its poisons, its nectars, its lusts. The old shell game of love. Saddled with a seething brain. Must have soothing dreams. Cerebral compensation. Survive by kidding oneself. Sexual illusion. Doting on chest and buttocks, on what waits between the legs. Under which shell is the pea? His conviction of loving Mel. As real as sun and stone. Nobody's fault. Men fall in love with flesh. With peach-shaped bottoms. With kisses sweeter than wine. This last a chemical trick, the one most easily revealed. Probe behind your upper lip. Curl it back. Smell the wetness. Let lip-juice waft to nose. A sweet-spice aromatic. A glandular aphrodisiac as ancient as apes in trees. Kisses older than minds.

Love as the pit-trap of life. Our elephantine senses stumbling in pre-set holes as deep as the helix is old. Charged with negative fancies in search of positive myths. Pawns of primitive attractions, as remote and crude as amphibians, or as neoteny in newts. Mel never believed it. Got furious at the suggestion. "What the hell is neoteny?" "Survival of immature traits into adulthood. Best demonstrated by certain salamanders who retain their gills at maturity. Also shows up in humans." "In humans?" "It's little recognized. Human females show neotenic traits. It's the core of their sexual attraction." "That's the most disgusting thing you've ever said, among the many." "Just think for yourself. Women retain the smooth skin, the hairless face, the high voice, of their girlhoods. It's neotenic, and pretty likely a product of sexual selection." "Oh, so first I'm a monkey and now I'm a salamander? Fuck you."

The rain let up west of Lake Mills. The night was an inky mountain with a chasm through its core, a great black cave of slippery trails, marked by stalactites of light. The heater ticked and the glovebox rattled and his guts trumpeted tensely. The little jazz riffs of stress, the squeaking music of the flesh and brain, of the monkey who flies like a moth, who cannot come to rest. What they all wanted. Rest. Crazy clan of monkey-shrews. Driven by insatiable lusts. Walker had achieved it. Glenda would be next. The others still waiting. Above a barren branch. Of steel? Like the utility pole ahead? Like the one Walker found. Wrapped his Olds around. Snapped a pair of vertebrae. In the cave-dark night. Babbled for days in intensive care. Sneered at the shrews around him. At Jackie in particular. Who shrew-sneered back. Bared her teeth at bedside. He couldn't slap her face. But she slapped Eric's and Glenda's. Spit in Gabriel's face. Raving. Under Wilson's woodpeckers. They left when they were pushed. Gabe heading north. Eric back East. Nomad names by the rivers. Moths by the motel neon. Both late for the funeral. Receiving Jackie's curse. In the garden by the carriage-lamp. Rejecting Glenda's smiles. The barren branch still waiting.

Night beneath the bridge was another glimpse of hell. The current became a torrent that pounded in his ears. The pondweed tresses engulfed his brain, coiled around his thoughts. Battles raged before him. Gabe sheltered in his cave, wrapped his coat around him, abandoned thoughts of sleep. Words of discovery, old clues and phrases which had once seemed near, were drowned by the din of chaos. One voice cried above the rest, beseiged him, beat all night in his head:

Ny buum drwc i ettwa wrthyt ti
Ny ladaf i di
Mi a wnaf yssyd waeth itt
Gwy yn gwanwyf
Gwenwynig fi
Gwyth wastawd dafawd
Nas tyf eli
I have not been evil to thee yet
I will not kill thee
I will do thee a worse evil
I know that wherever I stab

Poisonous is my tongue
Of constant wrath
For which no balm grows.

He lost his bearings. Fear gripped his guts. Perhaps he would drift forever, would find no pathway back. Would be locked away for good, assailed by threats and curses, drooling at those he loved. A single light in the darkness, in the sky beyond the bridge, which was no sky at all but the firmament of his senses, served as a signpost back. He seized its brightness like a drowning man, locked it before his eyes, kept its splinter in view. Time smoldered and flamed, waxed and waned, bulged and withered. The sky light glinted in the stream; the stream cast it back. Comets cracked, and he choked on the dust that rained. He breathed the pumice, drank the slurry, drew it through his veins. He shat black night, piddled burning stars.

Darkness at last drew back; dawn colored in to the east, silent as a bruise. The first thing he grasped was an odor—the subtle reek of the lakeshore, of fishy vegetable muck. The morning then turned gray. He was stiff and sore, his coat and pants caked with dirt. The stream was an opaque gurgle that lapped beside his shoes, sucked bits of flotsam, flecks of foam and paper in clockwise swirls by the bank. He grabbed his pack, dug his heels, rolled from under the planking.

Flat-footed and red-eyed he worked back to the Vigren's. His stomach growled. But what he saw from up the block made him stop and prepare to turn. A police car sat in the driveway. And a cop—only his striped pants visible through a dangling screen of leaves—was facing a stern-faced Lisa, who sheltered Adam behind her as he crouched above the lawn. Her lips moved; she frowned. She reached back for Adam's hand, signalled, with waggling fingers, for her son to grab hold, though he dawdled beyond her reach.

Gabe nipped the impulse to walk up and confront them. Then the trap would close. Whatever snare was waiting, whatever accusation, would pluck him from his goal. To beat them he must withdraw. To beat her. Im a doddes mwyaf addoed. She who delighted to torture. Wished him out of the way. By whatever means. No matter. He would join the fray. But not till he was ready. Not till the course was run. The old tongues linked forever by the last probe of the core. The final curl. The smoke-wisp.

Adrenalin surged through him. He retreated around the corner, glided back, returned to the bridge in the park. A light rain pimpled the water. Current pushed, tresses pointed. He folded under the planking, stared at a glint in the stream, felt the hinge swing free. Now he must find a way.

The rain disappeared near Cottage Grove. Eric barely noticed. Eye-spots were on his mind. Stipples. Freckles. Hind-wings. Bilateral symmetry. Whiteness. Monkey-lust. Stiff as brushes in jars. Snow-white thorax. And bottoms. Freckled and peach-shaped. Peach-bait. Sugaring with love. With juices. Not our fault. The human race. The monkey farce. The shrew-clan, blood-lusty. Eating. Many times their weight. Draining tankards of blood. To the last drop. Drunkards. Of London. Of Conshohocken and Wissahickon. Of sibilant sounds. Of heater ticks. Glovebox rattles. Two-speed wiper pulses. The beat of five billion hearts. Pulsing. Wishing. Kidding. Drinking. To the dregs. To the dream. To the drunken bitter end.

Exit on Route 30. Over to East Wash. White thorax of the Civic. Beating its way through the night. Antennae erect. Rejecting false signals. Suspended. In pinball jungles of commerce. Rainforests of waste. Global consortiums. Subtropical migrants. Noctuids. Witches. Multicorporate mall worlds. Feeding the lust for dreams. For life. For lies. No bad news. Bumper-sticker wisemen. T-shirt Buddhas. Swapping epigrams for truth. Slogans for complexity. To sell the lie. To cover the scent. Of bad news. Of blood. Of lies. Of lust. Of five billion lip-scented monkeys who cannot come to rest.

Look for Italian Exxon. Half-subs soaked in oil. Hold the hots. Spill the oil. Soak the shore. Half-soaked otter cubs. Smooth as salamanders. Look at the pilots of Valdez. Lying all over the place. Soaked to their gills. Like the salmon. The salamander. Smooth. All over. Piloting tankers to hell. Tankards of bloody lies. Drunkards. Five billion half-soaked pilots. To go. Hold the oil.

Italian Valdez sub shop. Soaked in Madison rain. Just as she said. Take a left off Williamson. Find one tan and green. A monkey house. Drunk with wet. In the five-billion-rain-dropped night.

"Are you Pat Llewellyn?"

"Yes, hi. Eric? Come in. What a night!"

"Wet."

"Yes, well, apart from the weather, I'm afraid things aren't too good on another front as well. For Gabe."

"What's it all about?"

"Oh, well, it's a mess, really. I don't know all the details. Or where it started. Someone's accused him. Falsely, of course. But everyone's up in arms."

"Accused him of what?"

"Well, it ought to be a joke but it's not. Anything but. I think it's insane myself. But they think he's some sort of pedophile."

"Oh brilliant. Pedophile? It *is* a joke. Got to be."

"Not to the Madison police. That's why they want to question him. Suspicion of pedophilia. Crazy. Can I get you a drink?"

Chapter 13

PATRICIA LLEWELLYN HAD AN oval face and dark lemur eyes. Maybe a bit marsupial, Eric thought, as he relaxed in a chair by the window and slurped at a scotch on the rocks. Maybe not all monkey. She wore her hair close-cropped, like Jackie, but it was soft and brown and instead of hardening her features it made her seem fresh, boyish. Slim and above mid-height, she was nimble, had a way of surely moving and listening, of seeming ever alert, and her pointed nose and faintly bucked teeth completed the sense of keenness, of direct frontal intelligence. She brought out a plate of oatmeal cookies which Eric quickly devoured, and refilled his glass of scotch before he noticed it was empty. He swirled the ice and whiskey into a slow tinkling vortex, the way Walker used to do, then looked through the half-open casement where a garden was fringed by porch-light.

"You've still got flowers in bloom," he ventured groggily.

"Oh, yes, the Obedience Plants. Aren't they fine? We had a light frost but they're pretty tough. You should see them in the daylight. A lovely ultramarine. And my herbs are still going strong."

Raindrops were smeared through the mesh of the screen like translucent Chinese letters, and a steady drip from the rain-soaked eaves made a metronome beat on drenched leaves. A cool draft touched Eric's elbow.

"Gabe likes herb gardens," he ventured. "I mean, I guess you know."

"Well, yes, he helped me build this one. In fact I gave him a bunch of transplants from here for the one he put in at the Vigrens."

Eric swallowed a big gulp of scotch. "I don't want to belabor it, but tell me again what the Vigren woman said to you."

"Lisa? Oh, she didn't say much. Just that Gabe was no longer welcome there and if I knew where he was, the police would like to speak to him. Her husband's in New York on business. She's Leo and Laura's daughter."

"They're the ones at the diner?"

"That's right. The Four Lakes Cafe. They're not what you might expect from the average diner environment. I mean, they're not just hash-slinging drudges, or whatever the stereotype might be. Not super educated, but they're, well... intellectually curious. I think Laura went to U. of W. for a while. And Leo took some classes there. They put Lisa through school. Ivy League and everything. Mostly on scholarship, I think."

"And they're not talking either?"

"Leo wouldn't comment. He respects Gabe too much to swallow this thing whole. But he was pretty upset. It was like someone had died. I didn't talk to his wife."

"The cops gave you a hard time at the station?"

"Oh, I don't know. I suppose I was pretty tense. I mean, they questioned me more than I questioned them. I wouldn't be surprised if they watch the house. Which is another reason Gabe won't come by."

"They actually said he was a pervert?"

"Well, no, it was Officer Moody who used that term. The heavy-set one. Officer Crouch, the woman cop I spoke to first, she just read from a piece of paper. All about suspect so-and-so, the description of Gabe and so forth, who is wanted for questioning in connection with a sworn complaint about pedophilia filed in this precinct blah, blah, blah. Everything else was confidential. I had to lie and plead just to get what I did. It's like talking to attorneys."

"Did you catch a name?"

"I asked who filed it but they wouldn't say."

Eric sighed and whipped up his scotchy vortex. "Of course I can tell you pretty certainly who's behind it."

Pat was seated across from him in the armchair that matched his own—a big boxy second-hand thing with teal green re-upholstery—and her head twitched alertly, cocked like a clever animal's.

"Please do."

Eric looked at his watch. "Christ, it's already late. I suppose I shouldn't get started..."

"No, go ahead, Eric. We're already into it this far. It's important. I couldn't sleep not knowing." She gave him a toothy smile. "I work for myself. At home. I can get up when I want."

Eric looked down shyly at his glass as if probing the ice-cubes for clues, then launched into a monologue. All about his family, about Glenda and Walker, the way Walker died, Glenda's illness, Jackie's revenge, about what she'd told him at the Harrington and in the parlor of his mother's home. He rambled, digressed, started with the curse by the carriage-lamp, switched to Cecropias on heads, Black Witches on sugar baits, Gabe's schizophrenia, doomed monkey-shrews.

Once in a while he'd stop, stare back into his glass, look around the room. The walls were lined with bookshelves crammed to overflowing, mostly well-thumbed paperbacks that—along with the second-hand furniture, the puffy vintage couch and old pedestal lamps—gave the livingroom a comfortableness, a worn Bohemian air. Pat was drinking ginger ale, looked relaxed in purple corduroy jeans, a beige mock-turtle and canvas pumps, her legs crossed at the ankles. She listened, nodded, frowned with amazement or disbelief, occasionally smiled or laughed. He stopped when he'd finished his third scotch, when his words were slurring badly and he sensed he'd said too much.

"I'm boring you."

"No, not at all. I'm fascinated. Gabe never told me a thing about what went on in his family. I've never had a clue. It makes a lot more sense this way. He does. You do." She set her drink on a table and offered him more scotch.

"No Pat, thanks, really, I've got to get a room. Is there a motel anywhere near?"

"Oh God, don't bother with that. I expected you to stay. There's a guest bedroom in back."

"Well, you're very kind. I shouldn't. I've intruded enough already."

"Not at all. I'm used to odd-hour visits. I lived with your brother for years, remember."

"Yeah, and you finally kicked him out."

Laughing, she picked up the fifth of scotch and poured a shot in her glass. "This stuff goes well with ginger ale. I find." She handed him the bottle.

"Well, jeez, I shouldn't. I almost never... This is really silly. Maybe one more. You must think I'm some sort of drunk."

"Of course not. I think you've been pretty tense. You need a lot of settling down."

He poured out a healthy dollop. "Yes, settling down. I feel more settled already."

Pat started telling stories. About Gabe and their days together. "I mean, we were completely incompatible on so many levels. He's impossible to live with. Complete chaos. It's like living with a chimp or something. Throws everything on the floor. Leaves it where it drops. You end up forging trails through the mess, stepping over mounds, beating things back. Meanwhile he's oblivious."

It was her turn to unburden. Five years of suffering, of negotiating chaos, of making peace with confusion, of suffering silence or lunacy.

Eric flailed his hands in sympathy, guffawed or cringed or moaned. "Five years!" he muttered wildly. "I couldn't stand him five weeks!"

"And yet we had some kind of bond. He was good in the sack of course, when he happened to be paying attention, but apart from that we shared the same fantasy of words, of verbal fascination. He's a gifted linguist, really, and of course we had that in common from the start. He picked up Welsh very quickly. But he brings something extra, a kind of quirky understanding of where it all comes from. Full of little insights that aren't of the present, I mean, I don't want to sound mystical or New Age or anything. I don't believe in genetic memory. But he has a way of seeing the Welsh language and its roots as if he'd sprung from their history, witnessed their development. That's the best I can explain it. I've no patience with his theories, that's another thing. I'll speak frankly and call them delusions. They're not real. That may be what drove us apart, more than anything. Because it got to be all the time, his whole universe really. When I stopped teaching I had to get on with my life, in the real world. I'm trying to run a business."

"He says he moves back in time. And has been hearing this Old Welsh, this Britonic language or something."

"Old Brythonic?" She rolled her eyes. "Oh God, that's another thing he got off on. I mean, Old Brythonic doesn't exist."

"The whole language is a fiction?"

"Well, no, it *was* a language. The basis of not only Welsh, but Cornish and Breton as well. It's sometimes called Proto-Brythonic. But it disappeared about the fifth century and, of course, had never been recorded except on some Roman coins and in a few names and places, because the tradition was all oral. No one quite knows what it consisted of."

"He said you identified it for him at first."

"No, not true. Not really. I mean, he would write these things down in all these notebooks he keeps. Phonetic transcriptions of what he'd heard, even a phonetic alphabet he devised. I explained the *clues* about Old Brythonic that I knew of—apparently the Welsh "d" sounded like a "t" in Old Brythonic times, the "f" like a "b", and there were strange little suffixes, vowels breaking up consonants in compound words, stuff like that. But it's fragmentary evidence. Not a language. Old Brythonic is still one of the greatest mysteries of the archaic Celtic world."

"So he accepted your clues and took it from there?"

"I guess. I mean, he *does* hear things, and he writes it all down and tries to make sense of it. God knows what he's come up with. Look, that's not the half of it, of trying to live with your brother."

Eric sat back and listened. It seemed certain she had loved Gabe, observed the same things in him that Eric did, admired him despite his faults, his great chilling blind spots, his infantile helplessness. She had seen through the frosted glass of his remoteness, found the transparent cracks—those places scratched or cleansed by the persistence of his humanness—and discovered they focused her vision, magnified her tenderness. She learned to love splinters of light, to spy through handsome chinks. Trying to ignore his distractedness, the long silent withdrawals into places he alone knew, she waited instead for the focused re-entry and brilliant little flashes that accompanied his homecomings, like some explorer's lover who greets his miraculous return and abides his Sinbad rantings, his tales of mad encounter that are more than hallucination.

And mostly, she confessed, she admired his courage. He was a marked man in all situations, a magnet for slings and arrows, a stranger in an unstrange land, a land that hated deviance and hunted down its misfits. He took his beatings gracefully, could smile in the face of the onslaught, stood resigned to crucifixion.

But it hadn't been enough. In the end it was all too painful and she had to pull away. Eric sighed and nodded. They regaled each other with candor, with separate stories of woe that began to take on humor and even a kind of hilarity. When they'd had a few more drinks Eric staggered to the couch, laughing uncontrollably, exhausted, red-eyed, barely able to move. Pat had levelled off, was having a fine old time but holding firm to her reason. Gleefully he proposed several toasts, each sillier than the last and concluding with one to his "dear badgered brother, the pedophile of the Badger State." She laughed good-humoredly, punning further off his phrases and stewed pronunciations. Then she gathered the glasses and slipped out to the kitchen, returning a few minutes later to find Eric stretched out and still, his head on a brace of pillows, his breathing close to a snore. She closed the half-open window, covered him with an afghan, flicked out the livingroom lights.

"What's the matter with your elbow?" Pat watched across the table as Eric rubbed away between pecks at his scrambled eggs, occasionally pausing to touch at the bulge that was visible under his shirtsleeve.

"It's hung-over," said Eric, frowning at his own bad joke. "No, actually... it's bursitis. Won't go away."

"You can have that drained," said Pat helpfully. "Drawn off with a needle. I had it done one time."

"Sounds fascinating. I can't wait."

"Sorry. I know you're a bit shaky this morning."

He moaned softly and sat back, watched a cardinal out the window—its breast feathers ruffled to a mousy pink—take a bath in a silver puddle. Sunlight glinted off a clothes-line post; a large oak tree shivered, aproned with fallen leaves. The room smelled of bacon and the cranberry scones she'd turned out before he'd gotten up. "Not really my game. Drinking."

"Well I should hope not. Your family has that one covered."

Pat lifted from her chair, swooped to the kitchen counter to slice some homemade bread. "More toast or scones, Eric? More coffee?"

He tried to rally his spirits. "No, really, it was all great. Super. I'm a little off my feed. Besides I should get organized. Need to talk to this Vigren character."

"Leo?"

"Is that it? Yeah, Leo."

"I wish there was some way I could help more. I have to stay here today and finish a proposal."

"No, you've done a lot already. I'll find my way around."

"I hope you'll be in town for supper. I'm making a stew, with wild mushrooms." She beamed her alert lemur smile.

"Thanks. Until I find Gabe I'm not going anywhere."

He tracked down his jacket in the livingroom and agreed to phone around five, regardless. Pat scribbled directions to the Four Lakes Cafe on a loose scrap of paper and pressed it into his hand.

"Eric," she called as he headed through the door, "It won't stick. It'll blow over."

Leo Vigren was not very happy to see him. In fact when Eric explained who he was, Leo told him to get lost. They stood at the entrance to the kitchen while Laura manned the register, grim and distracted behind her pop-eyed countenance.

"You've got a helluva nerve to come pokin' around my place," Leo blurted in anger. "My family's upset as hell."

"I'm sorry. I'm here to help my brother."

"Hah! You see this pigeon-hole here?" scowled Leo, stepping back through the doorway. "That's where your brother gets his mail. When was the last time you wrote him? Do you ever send him some dough? Hell no. So don't come around here actin' so damned concerned. You're about as concerned as a goddamn toilet-seat."

Eric's head throbbed. He studied Leo's pink jowls. "Gabe's a grown man. I don't run his life and he doesn't want me to. Not every family turns out like 'The Brady Bunch'. The fact is Gabe's in trouble and I'm here."

Leo folded his arms above his belly and dug in deeper. "Damn right he's in trouble. And I'm caught in the middle. My daughter's screamin' like a banshee, her husband's out of town, the police are all over, my wife's sayin' I told ya so..."

"Look, Gabe is no weirdo. Not like that. He's eccentric but..."

"I know all about it. Don't tell me, I grew up with one. My brother Del, he was different like Gabe. They hounded him to death. A genius, wouldn't hurt a fly. They crucified him. My own parents crucified him. I know all about it and it makes me mad as hell. Everyone gets it wrong. It's the same crap all over again."

"Then why did your daughter kick him out?"

"That's her business. Talk to her. She's got a damn kid, that's why. Husband's not there. She asks me to lock up that garage, I lock it up. What kinda note she leaves or what she says to the police, that's her business. The kid's only eight."

"Yeah, and now he's scared to death."

"Kids oughta be scared to death. It's a nasty world. Sooner they learn the better."

Leo had lowered his arms now, and the knots in his voice unlimbered. Rubbing softly at his cheeks Eric tried to deliver his point. "Look, is there some way he can still live there? I mean, it's his home right now."

The arms went back on Leo's chest. "The thing's not up to me. Like I said. And besides he's still wanted by the cops. I know he's no damn pervert. And I'll say my bit for him. But he's got to face the music. Sooner the better. I'd like to know who's behind it."

Eric stared down at the door jamb and bit his tongue. There was an awkward silence before Leo spoke again.

"Maybe Lisa will settle down. Maybe she won't. It's their garage, their property. Their kid. I run a restaurant here, or so my wife tells me."

"And you wouldn't have any idea where Gabe is?"

"Listen, if I did I'd talk to him myself. Whole thing is a crock. Sooner it's cleared up the better. Whole damn country is pervert-crazy these days. A paranoid mess. They're looking for weirdos under every rock. You even look sideways at a kid these days and they call you up for perversion. Didn't use to be so. 'Course now you get put on a talk show so maybe there's a connection."

⌇

Lisa was even less glad to see him than Leo. She stood behind the screen door on the porch of the big white house and talked to Eric from the shadows, wearing designer sunglasses. "Go away," she said softly.

"Listen, I know it's a scary thing. But Gabe is completely innocent. Has your son accused him?"

"No."

"Has he incriminated Gabe at all?"

"No."

He ditched his caution. "Then I think I know where it's coming from. It's coming from a relative of mine who's made the whole thing up."

Lisa frowned skeptically. "According to the police it's a reliable source."

"Reliable my butt. She doesn't even live here. She's one of my nutty relations."

"Then that's another reason. If your family is that nuts. Look, I don't want to talk to you." She started to close the wooden door.

"Hold on. I'm telling you it's a fraud. A false accusation. Even your father thinks so."

"And I'm telling you I'm Adam's mother and I want you out of my face."

"I'm not *in* your face. I've been trying to explain. Why have you locked up the garage?"

"It's always been locked. The big door was chained from the inside to protect my husband's special tools. The windows are nailed shut. We had a break-in a few years back, if you really want to know. Nothing is safe these days. That's why we let Gabe stay there. My dad said he was all right." She smiled ironically.

"He *is* all right. Look, I'm talking about the door where he gets in."

"They're all locked. And they'll stay locked. I'm not going to argue. Go away." The white wooden door slammed shut.

Eric walked through the neighborhood to let off steam. He wandered toward Lake Monona, saw a park and a shining creek, crossed a little planked footbridge. The park had a few nice oaks and willows down by the water. It smelled of soaked grass and vegetable muck, there were puddles along a bike trail, the blue sky rippled in the stream. He sauntered for half an hour till his headache and anger subsided.

Later he drove to the Italian place on Williamson and bought a sub for lunch. It dripped with onions and salad oil; the wrapper became stained with translucence. He splotched his shirt, then spilled his can of Sprite when he tried to fasten his seatbelt.

The police station looked like an old gymnasium, a dark blocky sandstone thing that was built at the turn of the century. He got there just after one and spoke to a woman at a desk behind what looked like a bank-teller's cage. Lunch was still beside her, some Coke and a half-eaten sandwich, and he guessed she was maybe nineteen, chunky and chewing gum while she swiveled in a wheeled captain's chair. Her sweatshirt said "WE WILL ROCK YOU".

"We don't give out information on any of our suspects," she pouted when he asked to see an officer.

"I'm not asking for information, I just want to talk to an officer."

"They're all out on duty right now. I can't say when they'll be back."

"Can I make an appointment to see one?"

"Okay."

"I'd like to see whoever's in charge of the child molestation investigation." It felt wrong even to say it and he wanted to explain, to fill her in on the background, on the obvious mistake.

"Oh the pervert thing?"

"Well, whatever you're calling it."

"The pervert thing. That's what I'm calling it. Okay. I'll let them know."

"Who'll I be speaking to?"

"Does it matter?"

"Well if I'm making an appointment..."

"Okay. Officer Moody. He should be back around three."

"Do you want my name?"

"Don't need it."

"But if I'm making an appointment..."

"Okay. What's your name?"

"Eric Dent."

"Okay Mr. Tent". She chewed her gum busily and glided away in the chair.

"Dent. With a D," he said as she hooked on a set of earphones and turned up a pocket radio.

Eric drove past the capitol, checking out all the parks, then up along Lake Mendota. Finally he parked on campus by the old student coop. Another damn university, he mused. One more vast diploma mill for a world that insists on pass-keys. Skipping the noisy rathskeller and the outside verandas with their plants and striped umbrellas, he strolled down to the water, to the pier where students sailed Sunfish and locals fished with worms. A gaunt old man in a big-billed cap soon pulled up a yellow perch, its orange flanks plated with gem-like scales and scored by vertical bars. Its fins were suffused with deep tangerine and its belly milky white. He sat on the end of the pier for a while, watched the man unhook fish and drop them in a bucket, then took a walk by the shore. Gabe had once fixed bicycles here, and slept one summer behind a hedge where he'd set up a homemade tent.

When he got back to the station just at three the policeman was nowhere around. Nor was he there at four. The clerk shrugged her shoulders, gnashed her gum, said it was okay if he wanted to wait. Eric sat in the dirty hallway with its cracked marble tiles and frosted globes suspended from a lofty ceiling, and stared at a cork-board of wanted posters and advice about CPR. Grabbing a paper off a table he read the local news, did a goofy little crossword. It was past four thirty when he finally approached an officer in one of the square partitions. He'd been hearing his garbled voice on the phone for the last twenty minutes.

"Excuse me, I've been waiting for Officer Moody but he doesn't seem to be here. Maybe you can help me."

"I'm Officer Moody." He was slouched back in his chair and his red face beamed impatience.

"Oh, well, perfect...I didn't know..."

"What's the problem?"

"It's about my brother, Gabriel Dent. Apparently someone filed a complaint accusing him of sexual deviance or something."

"No 'something' about it. I took that complaint. From a pretty heads-up woman. Spelled it right out. We're looking for him now." The cop turned his head away as he reached to close a drawer; his crewcut was pinkish-gray at the back like a hunk of boiled corned-beef.

"Yes, I know," Eric offered meekly. "But it's not true. My sister filed that complaint. As some kind of revenge or something. It's false."

The cop swiveled to face him. "Looked pretty solid to me. A whole written record that the guy's a skitza-freeniak. Hospital files and everything. We've seen him around for years. Seemed pretty harmless but it turns out he's got a split personality. Psychotic and like that."

"Well that's not what schizophrenia is. And it has nothing to do with sexual perversion."

The cop stared at him hard. "I don't suppose *you* know where he is?"

Eric got a lump in his throat. He often felt guilty when innocent, or like a liar when he told the truth. "No I don't. I've been looking for him myself."

Officer Moody was restless. "Look, I'm not even supposed to discuss this. That's as much as I can tell ya. We're busy as hell right now and we don't talk about cases. I've done you a favor to this point but that's all I can say."

It was almost five o'clock. Eric found a pay phone in a nook under the stairs and gave Pat a call.

"Hi, Pat, Eric. It's been a lousy day."

"I figured it might be. No sign of Gabe?"

"Not a trace."

"I'm making supper now. Come on by and we'll talk about it. It's not as dark as it looks."

"I'd like to take your word for it. But I'm not a believer in satisfactory endings."

"I noticed that about you. We'll work on it together."

Pat's supper perfumed the neighborhood. He could smell it from where he parked the car, halfway up the block, and especially through the porch screen as he came up the concrete walk. The door was unlocked, the teal armchairs within streaked with sun, green as the heads of mallards, the bookcases flickering with shadows. The hallway was dark and he glimpsed Pat aflutter in the kitchen like a moth in a sunlit box. He called out before going further and heard her lilting "Hi-i!" There were mushrooms spread on the counter by the sink, spilled around like lumpy seashells on a little shelf of beach. They smelled of forest loam, had the faint spice of beech woods, of tree bark and crumbling boles. Not merely gray or whitish, these were rust and salmon, ochre and chartreuse gold.

"They're boletes," she said as he came close and gave them a sniff. "Delicious when they're prime like this. Got them out at a piece of land that we're saving from development. One of my clients. Everything else is ready. I've just got to add these in."

Pat sliced some into hunks and left others whole, sauteed them in butter till the hot reek filled the kitchen, made his nostrils flair. She swayed along the counter like a lithe sylph, her sweater sleeves pushed to the elbows to reveal slim forearms and wrists, her fingers busy as wings.

He watched for a while in silence. Then he came up very naturally and kissed her, touched her on the shoulder and met her gaze when she turned—the marsupial eyes and forthright mouth—and pressed his lips into hers. There was the sweet spot again, sweeter than he remembered, and he probed it with his tongue. Mushrooms hissed beside them, the rank humid smoke in their hair. He bumped her gently against the sink, got her pants wet at the back where, like a sponge, the denim soaked up some puddle that had pooled along the trim, while a fat yellow bolete rolled in an arc and bumped off onto the floor. His hand moved under her sweater at the same time she reached down his pants; they each found something warm and round and kneaded it with their fingers. Then they both sunk down to their knees on the runner below the sink and licked each other's cheeks, pecked each other's noses, kissed each other's eyelids. She got his pants half way down and tickled the base of his scrotum, stroked the stem of his cock, while he submitted briefly, then gathered her hands, gripped the ends of her sleeves and stretched his arms overhead, stripping off her sweater while she writhed like a Turkish dancer, rippling her pendulate breasts.

The mushrooms sputtered and wheezed and the phone rang in her office. Eric unzipped her jeans, slipped a hand down her belly, below her bikini briefs, and soaked his fingers in her dew. She pushed her pants off her buttocks while he stroked and tweedled till her bush was misted and the fork of her thighs all wet, then let her roll on top of him. Trading off breasts to his mouth, she dangled each like a pippin to be licked and buffed at its tip. She didn't come down on his wobbling prick but clutched it between her legs, played with its stem and cap, teasing it with her fingers till it finally erupted as he gripped at her ribs and twisted to the side.

Yellow smoke rose above them; a fat cap crackled in the butter, popped and sizzled like a June-beetle zapped by a bug-lamp. They laughed, and Eric reached up with a long arm and turned the burner off. Then they were side to side again on the crumpled little runner. "How's that for safe sex," he mumbled through his smile. "Safe as money in a mattress," she whispered in his ear.

They ate the stew an hour or so later, by candle-light, after they'd had some wine. They ate it in Pat's queen-size bed, naked as salamanders, smiling and laughing softly, occasionally licking a morsel off one another's skin. Pat lit more candles later, and they didn't say a word about the problems of their day. She put on some music in her den, something called "Airs from the Hearts of Space", which tinkled in from the hallway like rain in a flooded garden.

The candles threw shadows on the ceiling, smoldering veils that breathed and swayed above them. Eric sat in the center of the bed, borrowed Gabe's lotus and beckoned Pat to straddle him. She mounted his throbbing staff, her thighs around his waist, and he kissed her lemur eyes, chased her tongue with his own. The flames lit her shoulders, her boyish hair goosed the shock of her breasts and made him want to spend, he worked his fingers in her supple back, between the blades of her shoulders, the hollow vales of her symmetry, squeezing her tits to the fore where the nipples caught in his chest hair, burrowed like hot little shrews. At once she was beautifully human—woman and man, girl and boy, heroine and hero, sinner and saint. She was animal, insect, plant—monkey, marsupial, lemur, shrew, soft and nimble moth; bird, fish, amphibian; fruited limb, wet vine, winding rill, carpet of mushrooms and moss, all things supple and dewy. They fucked each other as earth clods, as the twisted pith of forest boles smashed together in brutal storms, as the fragile sap of the planet encased in limber boughs, oozing life at their roots, spilling their essence to the soil. They fucked death out of their minds, beat back chaos, saved themselves for one precious night, settled on the branch of tenderness, exhausted and at peace.

Chapter 14

IT HAD POURED WELL into the night and the sky was an inky slate. There were no beacons in the wedge of heaven seen from below the footbridge. It didn't matter. Gabe was not off course. He had followed the curling word clues and the lilt of rhythmic signposts. He found himself in a circle, and not alone, facing a core of flame. Tongues rolled, words mixed, were repeated as incantations. Patiently he waited, committing all to memory, bit by bit, clue by clue, curl by curl. The fiery core and dark plume before them focused all their energies, drew them up through the dampness, above the ring of smudges to a great crown of oaks.

Tarr a tybas, dar a dyf... here an oak tree... korduawryk hawyras a klennos... gorduwrych awyr a glenn... shadowing sky and valley... rwngos teu lennos... rwng deu lenn... between two lakes... of smoky white... of sedges coiled with dew... entwined as curling snakes... as fog above its shore... ash above its flame... wings above a branch... that bends but does not break... neither heat nor rain... has weathered all their fierceness... the first storm and the last... high in glade... low on slope... waits upon its flower... of springtime oak... of broomsedge and of meadowsweet... of fairest white... of beauty and enchantment... of first match and of last... of all we praise tonight...

The rain came up in the stream and lapped beside his shoes. It dripped through the wooden planks, soaked his hair and face, misted his half-lensed glasses, drenched his coat and pants. Mud oozed beside him, trickled down the slope. The current bulged and roared. For him it had no existence.

Tarr a tybas y rwngos teu lennos

Korduawryk hawyras a klennos
Honyas tywethas i ewo
Houloteu hi hwnnos panos ywa hynnos.
Tarr y tybas ynn hardos huass
Nyos kweloyk klaww nyos mwyodawtt
Naww ukennos hangertt a borodess
Ynn y flaennas hi hwnnos.
Tarr y tybas tan hi hanwaeredd
Ny fua ohirr y ymkaelas hohonundd
Honyas tywethas i ewo
Noss honno chyskud y kydda wnaedoandd.

Pat set her coffee on the night-stand, propped herself on her pillow and read aloud from the dog-eared manuscript:

"I believe in the doomed condition of the human race. It is my one faith. But no one wants to hear it. They want to misunderstand, to twist my words and conclusions and dismiss me as a crank. My evidence makes them furious. They refuse to look in the mirror, probe beyond their own smiles and those of their neighbors, closely study their lives and those that came before them. At times they admit they are greedy or jealous, hateful or selfish. But, surrounded by illusions, the ingenious walls of a lifetime that they've built up stone by stone as a fortress for the blind, a castle for sightless royalty who are none else but themselves, they dare not lower the moat. They block out thoughts of death until it is upon them and won't admit even then that the ramparts and ornate gates—those crucial but temporal hedges against invincible reality by which they became "themselves"—must tumble down to nothing at their passing. Their own brains invented who they were, carved out the chimeras of their intricate personalities, and with those brains shall decay, and simply, sadly, unacceptibly to most, be no more."

"You sure *don't* believe in satisfactory endings, do you?" Pat grabbed a scone off the plate on Eric's stomach and took a delicate bite.

Picking crumbs from the sheet that half covered his chest and rose and fell with his breathing, Eric flicked them on the plate and took a sip of orange juice.

"I suppose I shouldn't have shown it to you."

She reached under the bedclothes and pinched him on the thigh. "I like everything you show me."

"Yeah, well, no one has to worry. It'll never find a publisher."

"Publish it yourself." She closed the manuscript carefully and eased it to the floor.

Eric winced. "Right. COLLECTED RANTINGS OF ERIC DENT by Home Basement Publishers."

Sidling up beside him, she dipped her finger in some jam. "Would you plunk down money to read it?"

"No. I know the contents too well."

She smeared the jam on his nipple and slowly licked it off.

"My point precisely. Most people know the bad stuff. They want to hear the good."

"I don't think they *do* know the bad stuff. Not really. That's *my* point." He rolled toward the edge of the bed. "Pat, I think it's weird the way Gabe has disappeared. Even for him."

"Maybe. But he does this periodically. I used to say he was 'at the office'."

"Guess I'll at least check the churches and shelters. And the area hospitals. What do you know about this time journey he's been piecing together?"

She folded her hands behind her head and sighed. "How much do you want to hear?"

"Well, I've heard some of it already. About magnetic fields in his brain, connecting with our ancestors and going back two thousand years, about genetic selection and a hybrid race of schizophrenic seers that were developed by some druids. How he wants to find the 'beginning'."

"Yes, that's basically the outline."

"But he's drenched in the stuff, from college and years of study and being around you. I mean, why can't he see he's just projected some sort of fantasy off the groundwork of his scholarship, that he's somehow become obsessed to the point where his dreams have become his reality..."

"Because for schizophrenics the dreams are so real that the brain accepts them as fact. How do *any* of us know what's real and what's not? Well, the brain gives us clues, has worked out screening mechanisms for sifting out the fool's gold and obvious deceptions. But for some reason, chemical or cellular or psycho-neurological or whatever the technical terms are, those mechanisms fail to function in so-called schizophrenics."

Eric threw up his hands. "But he *knows* that! He should *know* his screen has holes in it and work to patch them up!"

She smiled ironically. "Well, *you* of all people should understand why he doesn't. It's just what you've been saying, that people prefer their illusions to reality. They make life less painful. In his case they're just more baroque, more all-consuming. He's gone so far as to *replace* this world with another inside his head. He knows he could take the medicine. And he did, for years. But it made life too damn boring."

Eric was up now, getting his pants on, hopping on one leg. "Better boring than completely unviable."

Pat grinned at his little dance, then, without rising, picked her sweater off the floor with an outstretched lanky arm. "But you're forgetting again. To him it's totally *real*. I mean, it's very Celtic, really. The early cultures didn't separate dreams from reality. Two worlds intermingled all the time. People became animals or haystacks or trees, and vice versa, and when you died you really didn't, but became something else. So he's come to appreciate that moving between these realms was natural for thousands of years. It's the way humans interpreted the world, for far longer than the way we've interpreted it since Christ and Newton. To Gabe the *drugged* world was the unreal one."

She worked her arms through the sweater sleeves and popped her head through the neck-hole. "And besides, he's convinced he's on to something. He believes he's encountered Old Brythonic, which is supposed to have been lost forever. To him that's further evidence that his time travel is genuine."

Eric snorted. "All he's done is extrapolate from the modern Welsh. He's taken some poems and legends that got mixed up in his head and jerked them around a little. They're the cadence of his dreams, not Old Welsh or Old Brythonic or whatever."

"Well, which came first, the chicken or the egg? Take some of the earliest Welsh poets that we know of, like Taliesin and Aneirin. From around 500 AD. They're right on the edge of modern Welsh but their stories are probably older. From the Proto-Brythonic world. So if you start hearing the legends of Taliesin in your head, in a language that's not Taliesin's, are you merely extrapolating Taliesin in some phony way of your own devising, or are you hearing the original, the Old Brythonic from which Taliesin borrowed?"

The sun had thrown a honey wedge across the oak floorboards where Eric's socks lay twisted. He stooped gingerly to grab them, ran his hand through the sun shaft, sat on the edge of the bed. "You realize you're defending all this, when before you insisted it was crap."

"Yes, it's crap to us. I'm just trying to give you an insight into where Gabe is coming from. Isn't that what you wanted?"

"No, sure, you're right. It's very helpful. But it's grinding him down, isn't it? This insistence on living in two worlds? It's making his own survival just that much harder."

"I suppose it is. And he's tired of it, I know. It worries me."

She stood up, clearing and brushing the sheets with a windmill spread of her arms. "But I'm not his partner anymore. Not anyone's. I made that decision. It's a good one. For me. What Gabe does is his business."

By the time Gabe rolled from under the footbridge it was bright mid-afternoon. More than a day had passed. He was so stiff he had to massage his legs before standing and he was weak from lack of food. The stream was high and running fast, tossing light off its surface like so many crooked knives. He was soaked through and covered with mud. Kneeling near the bank he got the worst of the mud off his shoes, washed his hands and daubed his face, undid his pony-tail and shook out his chestnut hair, then dried it with a towel from his day-pack. In his pack, too, he found some mints of the sort restaurants keep beside registers, and a mini-packet of salt. He devoured the mints first, then broke the salt open in his palm and licked it away with his tongue.

On his way to the Four Lakes he moved slowly, stumbled a bit at times, shielded his eyes with his hand to ease his ferocious headache. Stepping off a curb he was nearly run down by a Blazer or Bronco, he couldn't tell which, whose occupants cursed him loudly. Chills washed his insides; he burned with fever. But none of it shook his conviction, his belief that he'd gotten back. The core was a beacon in the center of his brain that matched up with the flame. It only remained to go forward.

Leo, who was standing alone at the counter, looked shocked when he saw him. He motioned Gabe to the back. A lone table of customers joked and giggled, twirled straws in glasses, scraped their chairs in closer as he passed.

"Where on God's green earth have you been?" Leo croaked when they finally reached the kitchen. "You were better off bein' punched in the nose than lookin' the way you do now. Do you know the shit that's been flyin'?"

Gabe watched him through squinted eyes.

"Everyone's havin' fits, includin' the goddamn police. They're lookin' for you now."

"I know."

"You *know*? What kinda answer is that? Look, somebody's pegged you as a *child molester*, if that penetrates at all. Your best friends think you're a pervert, including my own daughter, and *you're* playin' hide and seek?"

Gabe watched him in silence for a bit, absorbing all he said. "It's all going to be okay. I finally made it back."

"Made it back? What the hell does that mean? And don't start talkin' in code or mumblin' any of your gibberish. I need some goddamn answers."

"That *is* the answer, Leo. I needed to get back. I don't know how else to say it. Now I'm ready to talk to the police."

Leo searched for hair on the top of his shiny head, smoothing his palm over baldness as though it were wavy locks. "You amaze me. You really do. How selfish are you gonna get? Don't you know there's people who care about you? Who've been lookin' for you for days? Your own brother was here this mornin'. And your old sweetheart, what's-her-name."

"Pat."

"Yeah, Pat. Even she's been around."

"I know. I'm seeing her next. That's where I'm headed. The police can talk to me there."

"You're damn right they can talk to you. You've got a helluva lot of explainin' to do. And not just to them. The whole thing's way out of hand. Where's your damn common sense, for chrissake?"

Gabe had raised his hands, was ringing both ends of his mustache simultaneously. "That's never been my strong suit."

Shaking his head, Leo dropped his voice to a disgusted half-whisper. "Jesus H. Christ. If you ain't the freakin' limit. Well, for God's sake get outta those clothes as soon as possible. You want a dry jacket or somethin'? Food? How 'bout some coffee?" He sighed. "You look like Death eatin' crackers."

The refrigerator hummed beside them in the silence that followed. Gabe took a step toward the back door. "Thanks anyway. I'll take care of things at Pat's."

"Then how 'bout a lift?"

"Really, no. It's not that far. I, ah, need to unbend my legs."

Leo again shook his head, looking Gabe up and down as if examining a Martian. "Unbelievable. 'Needed to get back.' What did you need to get back for?"

"I had to get back to go forward. Everything matches up."

"Oh, brilliant. That's terrific. That fills me in completely. Yessir, now I'm right up to speed. Well, don't let me keep you from your rounds. I know you're a busy guy."

Gabe pulled off his glasses with a grip through the one empty rim and focused his reddened eyes. "I'm sorry I got you upset. Got everyone upset. It was something I had to do."

For the first time Leo softened. "Yeah, yeah, I understand." He looked down at the door-jamb. "You're on a different wave-length. Sorry I got so excited. It'll all come out in the wash."

The refrigerator stopped humming and laughter drifted back from the customers up front. Gabe unbolted the back door and stepped down into the alley.

"And Gabe," yelled Leo with a parting shot. "Call me if you need me, will ya?"

Gabe threw up his hand in an awkward salute and vanished into the sunlight.

The phone was ringing in her office. Barefooted and still half dressed, Pat glided down the hall, pranced across a rug, snatched up the receiver.

"Hi, is Gabe there?" The voice was husky and abrupt.

"Ah, no. No one by that name lives here."

"Pat?"

"Yes?"

"This is Leo Vigren. Gabe told me he'd be at your place."

"Oh, hi Leo. No, he's not *here*. We're still trying to locate him."

She heard Leo moan. "Jesus Christ. He told me yesterday he was headed to your place. He was lookin' like hell, from sleepin' out and all. Damn him anyway! He said he was headed straight there. I tried to call you last night."

"Oh, well," she soothed. "I did have my phone off for a while. What else did he say to you?"

"Very damn little. Apologized a bit. Said somethin' about how he 'finally made it back' and 'everything matched up'. Nonsense like that."

A little chill touched Pat's spine. "'Everything matches up'?"

"Yeah, that was it. Something like that." He cleared his throat. "The usual gibberish I get from him."

There was silence while Pat collected her thoughts. "Okay Leo, listen. Gabe's brother Eric is in town..."

"Yeah I met him."

"Well, Eric and I are going to look harder today. I've got one or two ideas where Gabe might be. I'll get back to you this evening, or sooner if we find him."

"Well if you've got some leads I wish you'd tell the police. I'd like to clear this up. It's a bogus charge but the longer it goes on, well... I wonder if he's not back at my daughter's place. In that damn garage..."

Pat struggled to project assurance. "But that's all locked up tight. His brother was there yesterday."

"Nothin's locked tight with Gabe around. He mighta just slipped by there to pick somethin' up, then fallen asleep or whatever..."

Her voice grew faintly shrill. "Look, Leo, I've got to run. Thanks very much for calling. I'll get back to you soon."

"Yeah, all right Pat. Sure thing."

Pat bounded for the bedroom.

"Get your shoes on."

"They're on. Who was that?"

She grabbed her purple jeans off the chair and stuffed her long legs into them. "Leo Vigren. Gabe was supposed to come here last night and didn't. He's at the garage. I know it."

"Why would he go there? That woman is on the war-path."

"I'll explain on the way."

The Civic coughed to life twice, then sputtered and died each time.

"We'll take my car," said Pat impatiently.

"No, hold on, it'll start. But what the hell's going on?"

The morning had turned gray and raw and Pat felt chilled all over. "Well, first of all, there's something I haven't told you. Gabe swore me to secrecy but I suppose it doesn't matter. It's all nuts anyway."

She cupped her hands, blew on them for warmth. "This time-travel thing of his. It's tied to an apparatus, the device that distills his potions."

"Oh, his DROP, or whatever?" Eric turned the key but again the Civic fizzled.

"Yes. He makes that stuff from this very complex gizmo that he's constructed from bits and pieces. And the whole thing is an analogue. Every little piece of that distillery corresponds to the Welsh translations that he's put down in his notebooks. You know, the voices that he hears, what he calls his 'verbal signposts'. It's extremely elaborate. Each voice signpost is given a number that relates to some tiny part or section of his distillery gizmo."

"But that's ridiculous!"

"Yes, I suppose. But he's obsessed with it. Nothing goes on the device that isn't numbered and recorded and matched up with the voice fragments in his notes. And he's adding things constantly."

Eric pumped the accelerator. "So the making of his potion is almost like a mechanical and chemical reflection of his trip back in time?"

"Well, yes, that's one way of putting it. " She blew harder on her hands. "But the important thing is, the gizmo is also his map. He uses each fragment of its composition, every millimeter of its construction, to help guide him through the Tunnel. He fixes an image of its workings firmly in his brain, like an engineer might visualize a machine in three dimensions by, say, memorizing blueprints. That way when he travels the Tunnel and hears the voices, he can somehow check where he is."

The engine choked and sputtered and finally caught hold. "Christ! It's like he imagines he *himself* is being distilled! A tiny drop, coursing through the tubes!"

She managed a thin smile. "I never thought of it that way. But it gets weirder. The gizmo corresponds not only to numbers but to Welsh and Old Brythonic letters in his phonetic alphabet. So the first couple

of letters of the first word in each phrase that he hears—like, well, 'thr'
or 'ord'—he writes them down, and links them to a number and place
on the gizmo. It's like a giant acrostic that cross-references the trip, so
he's got multiple map co-ordinates at all times."

They thrummed down to Williamson under ochre-leaved maples.

"Pat, the whole thing is bonkers."

She grinned wanly. "Well, yes. But the thing is, he's been trying
to 'get back' like this for years and has never really made it. I finally
decided that he didn't *want* to get back, to what he imagines is the
start. That it was all just an excuse for him to get lost, to withdraw
more and more from the world and our lives together. I figured it would
just get more complex, the gizmo would get bigger and stranger and his
notebooks more voluminous, until he was completely gone and they
just locked him away for good. That's really when I called it quits."

Eric frowned and wiped some moisture off the windshield with his
palm. "Well, he *did* tell me in Evanston he thought he was 'very close',
but I didn't know what he meant..."

"He's been saying that for ages. There's a core or a flame or
something that he believes is at the beginning. Where his family,
your family, comes from. He'd know he was there, he's always told
me, because at that point 'everything matches up.' Then he'll have
experienced the entire history of who he is, and he'll be able to 'go
forward', whatever that means."

"What *does* it mean?"

Her fingers drummed on her purple jeans. "I don't know. He never
explained and I never expected to find out. Maybe some final utopian
state of mind, when he'll be completely crackers. The thing about
the distillery is, he can't go forward without it. That's its ultimate
purpose. As a final guide or vehicle. A sort of moon module that needs
to get off the surface and re-dock him before he can return. To 'go
forward' he's got to do this whole crazy course in reverse. It's just too
complicated without it. Even for him. And the only gizmo he's got is
in that garage."

They were gliding past the park now, with its little swollen stream
and thick-planked wooden footbridge.

"So you think he really *is* almost back?"

"No 'almost' about it. Leo spoke to him yesterday. He said Gabe
told him, 'everything matches up'."

⌒

There is a place where he gets down between the huts and follows
a little trail through the sedges, the broomsage and the rushes. Dew-
honey sprinkles his naked legs, mist rimes his hair. He finds a tiny
skiff and sits among the reeds. When he stares back at the oak trees he

can see that dawn is near, has pinked the dark behind, edged the sooty crowns. Then the fog-wisps gather and disperse, slowly at first, licking upward, flimsy whitened tongues. The lake-smoke rises, undoes its silver ribbons, sucks away like breath. A bruise colors in to the east, a heron croaks, daylight drips on the highest slopes, seeps mead through the thatch of hills.

Here is the bright powdered dust of those two lands he has wandered, high and low, loud and soft, wet and dry, crag and marsh. Up and down he has slid, night and day and forever, between the light and shadow. Below is the sludge-tide and halting step of the hunter. Here one leaves no footprints. There is no before and after. No memory of deeds. Only the quaking marsh mud, the black slime of moods, the pulse of reed and rush, the web-kick of the frogs. When the rain stops all is whiteness, the dark wind clamors in the willows and spreads the spume of night. Roots drown, there is no rescue for complexity, the meadowsweet goes pale.

Farther up there is color and a drier road. The currant leaves in autumn, red and shining like apples, spill their light on the copper sedges and strum their shadows on silt. Still higher is the sun itself, its rays like saplings leafing, its quartz-light stiffening the loam. New days are marked on this ground, the dawnings and sundowns are noted and all the fruits have seasons. Here the time-sap is collected in jars, meanings rise like rivers and their heights are scored on stone. It is a land of stone, and metal, and molten troughs of gold. Sun-ray, dew-drop, eye-spot, each etched in dreams. Sheep come forth on the hillsides, dogs bark, granite breaks the sun. There is ice in all seasons, beasts stoop to their labor, gravestones cake with hoar. On the highest hills there is silence for the dead, wind intones the sadness, men are clever in their use of old bones, children eat with spoons.

Here are battles, wars in heather and peat, screams of all the living, slaughter end to end, land of demon princes, reaped fields of corpses, scythed down like broomsedge, age to age, between the deep and shallow, stiffening the loam. It is in this place that the fight is fought, immeasurably great. The marsh does not keep graves. Neither stones nor mourners. There are no dogs or sheep. There are hoots and croaks and whispers. Men speak to insects, to frogs and fish and trees. There is sound without comprehension, symbols without thought. The wind is deaf and noisy, the rain has wounded strength and bleeds into the stream. There is feeling without touch, hardness without rock, waves beyond the air. Minutes stick in mud, centuries in clay, all is a rattling in stillness, and moths cannot be netted but glide into the shade.

Now the branch is shattered. Head is bloodied, din has ceased, sword is put away. That which eats has eaten, that which leads is lost, its staff a splintered twig. The smoke curls, the tide pulls, all memory is white. The green ice has melted, its core a shaft of light, a glinting ray, a sunspot on his soul. Set one eye upon it, the only eye you own. It takes you like a serpent, enfolds you with its coils, warms you like a flame, chills you like green ice, breathes you like a pumice, drinks you like a slurry, draws you through its veins. Comets crack, and you each feed on the dust, the hunter and the hunted, predator and prey. You glow like molten ingots, smoke like morning marshes, rise like wisps of cloud-wrack, embrace like son and father, the forward curl in time.

> honnos terr ywas
> honn der yw

Eric was first up the driveway, under the big golden maple. Pat followed close behind. They found Gabe's picks in the key-holes—a half-round in the padlock, a feeler in the knob—and the side-door not quite closed. Eric knocked on the peeling panel, had called Gabe's name two times, and was just shoving open the warp-wooded door when Pat tapped his shoulder and gestured toward the street, where car doors had slammed and Mars-lights flashed red and blue. Leo was striding the drive, his jowls flushed with intensity, trailed by officers Moody and Couch, whose holsters and radios jounced at their sides though they steadied them as they jogged. Eric and Pat pushed inside.

The garage was deep in shadow but for the bay of flat autumn light that washed back from the window. Gabe was hanging in its muted glow, his khaki coat still on, his legs neatly paired and free above the concrete, his neck in a noose of nylon cord suspended from a beam.

Both of them rushed forward, Eric clutching his brother's thighs and Pat grabbing the nearby chair to force it beneath Gabe's feet. Three shadows twisted in the doorway. Leo arrived with his pen-knife out, snatched the chair from Pat, then stepped up, breathing heavily, and sliced the nylon through. Futilely at first, Moody and Crouch ordered everyone back, until both jostled forward and pushed Eric off, clutched Gabe high and low, eased him to the floor. The powerful Moody pumped Gabe's chest, crushed down on his diaphragm in violent rhythmic bursts, hands overlapped, boiled corn-beef back of neck illumined from the panes behind. Crouch got her radio cackling and called up a rescue vehicle. Static simmered and popped, grimness gripped the watchers, Moody pumped and snorted while slowly, like a shy bee closing on a garden, an ambulance wail materialized from the fiction of its first frail murmur.

Chapter 15

THE DARK A-1 SAUCE bottle sat empty on her desk, its shoulders jeweled by a patch of glare from the reading lamp nearby. Pat had the curled sheets before her, was busy unbending meanings from the scribbled Celtic phrases. Beside her on the couch, Eric was sorting the contents of a drawer that they'd brought up from the basement.

"The Welsh is no problem," said Pat, pecking at her keyboard. "But if I had his phonetic alphabet I might make sense of this last bit. It's not Welsh. And I don't think it's his Brythonic."

"Well, this stuff won't help much." Eric tossed down a fist full of paper. "It's mostly old magazine and journal articles he clipped. Plus a bunch of IOUs people have signed off on."

"That's all right. I've worked out most of the rest."

The bottle had come to their hands from the grasp of little Adam, who had burst away from his mother as she watched the loading of the ambulance. Arms akimbo, he'd bolted under the maple, scuffed a channel of leaves in an addled, moth-like flight down the drive to the garage's side-door, and briefly buzzed inside. The adults had gathered near the street in varying states of numbness: Lisa smearing tears below her shades, mouth set with grimness; Leo an ashen, flounder-flesh pale, arms folded on his chest, Eric and Pat barking questions and preparing to follow in the Civic.

Adam had finished his roundtrip flight, was breaking toward a landing, cargo in hand, beside a gesticulating Eric, when Officer Crouch turned suddenly and knocked Adam off his feet. He made an ass-first landing on the curb while neatly shielding his treasure, winced broadly, and popped to his feet at Eric's side, poking him with the bottle.

Eric responded distractedly and tried to steer him toward the lawn.

Adam poked again and held his ground.

Finally Eric looked down.

"It's a message in a bottle," Adam whispered. "For you."

Ambulance doors swung shut, globe lights swirled, figures congealed near the curb and quickly broke apart. Eric shot a glance at Lisa absorbed in her private shock and staring down the street, then stared down the street himself, pretended non-chalance, quickly snatched the bottle.

Gabe had been D.O.A., and a bell-jar of officialdom quickly lowered on the case. His body was whisked to the morgue, the gargage was at once re-locked and cordoned off with police tape, and inquiries met mostly silence. A blurb appeared in the paper:

MAN FOUND DEAD IN EAST SIDE GARAGE

The body of a man believed to have hung himself was found in the East Side garage apartment where he lived, Madison police revealed. Gabriel Dent, 48, was found Friday morning, hanging from a nylon cord. The body was discovered by his brother.

Eric had phoned Jackie, both in L.A. and Kenilworth, and left messages on machines. None were returned. He called his boss at the paper and explained why he'd be delayed. He checked on Glenda's condition but told her nothing, and put off seeing her in person till he'd cleared things up in Madison. With Pat he planned a service and, to give them both some space, took a motel room in town. She became cooler, business-like. They met once or twice in her office to focus on the contents of the message.

"Okay, here's what I've got. The first part is set up in stanzas, like a poem."

Pat pushed aside Gabe's scribbled sheets, picked out a page from her printer and read aloud to Eric.

"An oak tree grows between two lakes

Shadowing sky and valley
If I mistake not
Its limbs are those of her swain.
An oak tree grows in the high glade
Neither rain nor heat can pierce it
Nine score years of fierceness has it weathered
Its crown is that of her swain.
An oak tree grows beneath the slope
Their joining was not delayed
If I mistake not
That night they slept entwined."

"What the hell does that mean?" said Eric brusquely, squirming on the couch.

Pat cleared her throat. "Don't know. Sounds like some old Welsh verse. That's the first page. The second translates as: "Let us by our magic and our enchantment make a wife for him out of flowers. And then they took the flowers of the oak trees, and the flowers of the broomsedge, and the flowers of the meadowsweet, and with those made by enchantment the first match and the last, the maiden and the swain. And she was settled by a valley, between two lakes, where an oak tree did grow. And the swain came, and he set his mind on the maiden, and loved her."

With one hand Eric stroked his chin; with the other he clawed at his elbow. Standing abruptly as she finished, he stepped over to the window. "The poor bastard. Why did I have such a wacko brother?"

Pat had turned off the printer and was busy collecting her notes, slamming books closed and shutting open drawers. "Stop being so callous. You ought to be proud he left you something so personal. I think it's very lovely."

He kept his back to the room. "Yeah. Lovely. But what does it mean?"

"Does it have to mean something?"

"No, not really. But you'd think if someone snuffs himself and bothers to leave a note, it would make some sort of sense."

She was swirling behind him now, tidying up the couch. "Well, maybe it means there's hope. Maybe it's a kind of prayer."

"Hah! You know what I think of *that!*"

She turned in sudden anger. "Christ, Eric, he's *dead!* Allow yourself some tenderness and for once forget your cynicism!"

"I *am* tender. That's what cynics *are.* Tender bastards with a need to build tough armor."

"I'm not talking about *your* bloody needs and *your* pain and suffering. Forget *you* for two seconds. I'm talking about having some faith in what your brother stood for in the end. You lack faith."

He stayed at the window, staring hard at the night.

"Undoubtedly. I won't even fly in airplanes. But I'll never believe in prayer. Things happen or they don't," he said sullenly. "Did I ever tell you my life-boat theory about prayer? Well, there's ten people adrift in a lifeboat and they're all good at prayer. For days, each one prays like hell that they'll be rescued. But slowly they start to die. Some of those that pray the hardest die first. Finally just one is left and he's rescued. Everyone wants to know, 'How did you survive?' 'I prayed all the time for rescue,' he replies. 'It's a miracle!', everyone shouts. 'A miracle!' Of course, nine of them prayed their guts out and died. But no one heard *their* story. The praying was a 90 percent failure but hailed as a 100 percent success." He turned to face her.

"I'm not talking about *that* kind of prayer," Pat said wearily, sitting down on the couch. "I don't mean formal religious prayer or praying to change events. Prayer more in the sense of, well... a hopeful incantation or something. A kind of whispering to the will. Preparing oneself. Maybe allowing oneself to see. We mumble *those* kinds of prayers all the time. Somewhere inside our heads."

Eric sighed. "I'm sorry. I suppose I'm being a shit."

As if talking to someone else she gazed toward the hallway and gestured obliquely. "It doesn't matter. We're both still upset. But you see things differently than I do. That's pretty clear."

She rose again, suddenly full of focus. "Listen, about the service. I thought we could scatter the ashes at this place he liked to visit. Over by the lake."

"That's perfect. Just the thing. He loved watery places."

Pat stepped to her computer and picked up the translation. "Oh, and there's this last bit at the bottom of his message. 'Honn der yw,' which is Welsh for 'now it is ended.' That's easy. But I still can't make heads or tails of this final part. I mean, look at this—'An ur-ma mi wel porth nev a-ger-yz, pella ni olav mwy vel reg col-yz.' Or something... I can't even pronounce it. It'll need a lot of work."

He stood beside her, staring down at the lettering. "Good God. I don't know how you manage. Any of it. It all looks like Chinese to me."

"Not at all! It's our own lovely alphabet," she said with affection. "Don't the letters please you? They reproduce sounds. Phoneticize something. A spoken tongue, never meant to be written. It's not Irish or Welsh. But something Celtic, I'm sure."

The service was scheduled for late afternoon. Eric picked up the ashes around one. Pat had taken the whole day off, spending time in the Celtic archives of the University library. When Eric phoned around four she made a proud announcement.

"It's *Cornish*," she said with satisfied excitement. "A Celtic language that's been dead for two hundred years. Gabe puzzled it out into letters. Where he *heard* it I can't guess."

"Swell. But does that means it's past recovery?"

"No, not at all. Using the internet I tapped some library links and found a plausible word key. I think I've pieced it together. It even works out as a rhyming couplet. 'I see the gates of the new land open wide, and my lamenting I now leave aside .'"

Eric was silent.

"Eric?"

"Well I'll be damned," he finally managed. "He's making some sense after all. It's his breakthrough message."

"His what?"

"Oh, just one of his theories. Listen, let's use it for the service this evening."

"My thoughts exactly," she enthused. "Are we back on the same wavelength?"

"I couldn't say. You know I've got no faith."

"Oh, you hard case! By the way, the Vigrens will be here at five. Treat me right and I'll have you all back for dinner. I've made lasagne."

The day had been bright and windy and the sun was near the treetops, filling the little park by the lake with streamers of light and shadow. Leo and Laura were there, and—much to Eric's surprise—Lisa, Todd, and Adam. And a stocky fellow from Waunakee named Sam, who briefly had been Gabe's partner in the days when they both fixed bicycles. There were others Pat could have asked but she decided to keep things intimate. She led them all to the lakeshore, explaining as they walked how Gabe loved misty mornings and would come down to watch the fog lift.

Wind blew sharp off the water; Pat feared it would fling the ashes back. Adam thought of the stream and small bridge behind them and spoke up full of excitement. They agreed that would be better. Retreating along the gold-barred grass, hair and clothing wind-whipped, they were silent and reflective. They gathered atop the wooden planks, leaned on the slender railing while Leo, then Pat, then Eric, uttered some self-conscious words.

Pat wrapped things up with a passable stab at Cornish, intoning down-wind toward the bright dropping sun: "An urma mi wel porth nev ageryz, pella ni olav mwy vel reg colyz," then finishing in English, "I see the gates of the new land open wide, and my lamenting I now lay aside." When she dipped the tiny urn toward the stream, the pumice of freed ash ignited in the light, glowed for an instant like star-dust, then was beaten toward the bank by a gust, to congeal in a slurry of mud.

"Oh, Pat, it's missed the water!" moaned a teary Lisa. "Adam, go down and help it out. Spread it with a stick or something."

"Never mind," ordered Eric as Adam started to scurry. "It's just fine where it is. The next rain will take it."

Lisa said she was cold. As they straggled off the bridge Pat asked them back for lasagne, but Sam passed, as did Rod and Lisa, who herded a fractious Adam toward their green Taurus wagon. Leo and Laura accepted, made awkward small talk in the kitchen while the oak tree out the window, enlivened by dusk and wind, bounced shadows through the yard. They didn't drink the wine and excused themselves after apple torte, which they ate with the air of the condemned. Pat laughed it off when they'd left and began clearing dishes.

"It's strange," she said, grabbing Eric's dessert plate as he raised his mug of coffee. "The reaction of people to death."

"Very. Love's even worse."

"If it even exists," she countered, flashing her lemur eyes.

"You're mocking me."

"*Me?* Certainly not. Mockery is for cynics."

"Cut it out."

She was standing at the sink, apron tied at her back. He talked to its pink and white strings.

"No, I believe love exists," he continued. "What we call love. It's just a very complex illusion."

"Very."

"Look, let me do those dishes, Pat." He rose and walked to the sink.

"Never mind, I've got them."

He grabbed up a dish towel and began drying plates. "I suppose I do see love as a trap. Even the sweetness of a kiss is a kind of chemical snare."

"Oh, *especially* a kiss."

"You're mocking me again."

She turned her head to the side. "Who's mocking? I believe what you're saying. I don't want to get trapped any more than you do. Less, even."

"Well, one *does* get trapped," he blurted. "And it takes a while to get free."

"Believe me, I know the feeling."

"I mean, *myself*, I don't know... But right now, with all this... Gabe, Jackie, my mother..."

"And Mel." She wiped soap bubbles from her slender wrists.

"Did I tell you about Mel?"

"Yes."

"Well, yes, there's Mel, of course..."

"Eric, you don't have to explain. I've been down the road myself. Had my own little wreck. And I just finished the repairs."

"Look, I know I sound like a madman at times..."

"Not at all. You see things very clearly. I've never doubted that. You know, no one sees more clearly than an Eskimo after a blizzard. But there's such a thing as snow-blindness."

A cup slipped from his grasp but he caught it after a juggle. "That's well put. Yes. You know what I often wish? I wish I could avert my eyes..."

She turned off the faucet and dried her hands on a towel. "My God," she said in a weary whisper. "Don't we all."

Eric left two days later after tying up loose ends. The police cleared Gabe from their records when his accuser would not return phone calls. The garage was re-opened and his effects gathered: the distillery, smashed by Gabe at the end, was junked with most of the rest, but Pat allowed his notebooks to be boxed and stored in her basement. Leo had a plaque made—really a thin strip of brass—engraved with Gabe's Cornish couplet and to be fastened to the bridge in the park.

When Eric returned to Evanston Glenda was worse and had been moved to intensive care. Ringed by machines with small colored lights she slipped in and out of consciousness. He tried to explain about Gabe, put it in terms of a move, that Gabe had left Wisconsin and was seeking a life somewhere else. None of it seemed to register. Wurtzburger told him it was all downhill, maybe a matter of weeks. Jackie did not appear.

Back in Philadelphia he found a letter, posted from California:

> Dear Bro',
>   Some explaining is in order. We don't get along in person and maybe that's my fault. I've had a lot to shoulder and am not the Atlas some (like Mom) imagine.
>   About Gabe. I heard of his death from the cops. I was already back in LA and couldn't return due to business. I knew you would take charge.
>   Mom is worse as you may have discovered. Wurtzburger says it won't be long. I've made all the arrangements.
>   I found a buyer for the house and we settle in November. Banker and family. They love the Gothic touches and the greenhouse. Got my price.

About all the rest. I'll lay it out and you can
believe what you want. I've been trying to expand
MMC, into retail coffee bars. A cafe chain, really.
It's a tricky market and I needed capital and backers.
Found a Japanese consortium willing to support us
if we would set up the first three shops in Hawaii
and run them for one year. After that, profit or loss,
they'd take over and expand us to the States on their
own bankroll. They'd buy me out and I'd be retained
as consultant. I needed a quick burst of capital. Also,
their CEO collects art—loves anything English and
early American, fell for Catesby, Lear, Audubon, all of
Mom's favorites. I made him a deal to sweeten the pot
and he really came up flush. I couldn't say no.

Look, you'll get it all back, and then some. We're
just setting up in Honolulu and when the year is
finished my ship comes in. These nips have got it
coming out their kimonos.

I've invested Mom's other assets in a Malibu
ranch—Santa Monica mountains, actually. That's
where I'm writing from now. One of those old movie
spreads, modest really, and a bit run down, but
nice. Great sunsets, and we avoid some taxes and
probate. There's a little adobe guest house you can
stay at when all this dust finally settles. Right now
my Anaheim neighbor, CeCe, is staying there. My
factotum, or whatever. It's got two bedrooms and a
huge kitchen.

I know it sounds weird but hang in there. This'll
work out.

Your Caffeine Queen, Jackie

Eric was tempted to tear it up, but stuck it in a drawer. He didn't
believe a word of it.

⌒

Around Halloween Mel called him. She'd had it with the guy
she'd been seeing, said he was a moron, and had moved back with her
parents. That had gone sour, too, and she'd quit her job as a temp.
Would he care to get back together? He said he'd give it some thought.
Two days later she was sleeping by his side, her belongings, in bags and

boxes mostly, ringing the rooms of his flat. She had a way of laying in bed those first mornings when he was dressing for work. Naked—the sheets covering just her legs, her head turned on the pillow and blue eyes half watching, her pale peach-shaped ass like a beacon, her sculpted white back faintly freckled near the shoulders where it touched her hanging curls—she would pout or playfully smile. He was usually late for work.

Glenda died near Thanksgiving and he got up at dawn, turned the Civic east toward City Avenue, then north to the Schuylkill Expressway, drove the holiday highways west, was delayed in a snowstorm near Cleveland and just made the funeral on time. She was buried at Calvary Cemetery on the south end of Evanston, in a plot next to Walker, where a knoll looks out on the lake. The casket was lowered in a snow squall. Eric and Jackie didn't speak.

When he got back to Philly the quarrels started anew. Mel pressed him about his mother's estate, asked him what his share was; he said he didn't know. She called him a liar and a wimp, told him to fight for his rights. She'd found Jackie's letter and thought it sounded nuts. When he agreed, she attacked him in a rage.

Then one day Mel found Gabe's final message, a copy that Pat had made for Eric.

"What the hell is this?" she'd demanded when he got home.

"It's my brother's final words. A copy. Translated from the Welsh."

"The *Welsh*? Who the hell knows Welsh?"

"His old girlfriend. She figured it out."

"Well, it's *nuts*. Like everything else in your family." She crumpled it in her hand and tossed it toward a basket.

"What the hell are you doing!" he screamed, retrieving it off the floor. "That's very personal!"

"Personal is right! It's a crazy suicide note. I don't want it around. It's, whadayacall... *morbid*."

"Since when do *you* decide such things! You're living in *my* damn apartment. And he's *my* dead brother!"

She pouted and fixed her blue eyes. "Look, I'm trying to get your head straight, all right? You dwell too much on the negative, you know? That's your whole problem. Your whole crazy family."

He stuffed the crumpled sheet in his pocket, slammed out the door, walked in the cold evening air.

⟋

One night the phone rang while Mel was visiting her parents. It was Pat, and they talked a long time. She got to the subject of her job. Her grant writing business was booming and she was busier than was comfortable. Environmental grants, her specialty, were increasing, while other gifts had shrunk.

"Suddenly it seems like I'm the most popular woman in town. Consultant contracts for 'green' grants are up 20 percent," she said cheerily. "I think half of Madison is applying, especially the post-docs and researchers. I can't keep up."

"Expand your staff."

"My staff of one?"

"Yeah. It sounds like you're ready."

"You know, I was thinking that myself. We're on the same wavelength. I *do* know an experienced writer who also has a lot of environmental expertise. That's partly why I called. To get your advice."

Eric's voice went flat. "My advice? Oh. Well. If you're swamped, hire him. Or her. What's the problem?"

Pat paused, then said: "He lacks faith. And he doesn't believe in satisfactory endings."

He swallowed hard. "Ahhh. *That* guy. Yeah, I noticed that about him. Maybe if you ask him to come out for an interview, you can work on it together."

"My thoughts exactly," she whispered, clearing her throat.

"You're going out of town?" questioned Mel. "What's the deal?"

"A job interview. In Chicago."

"*Chicago*? Oh, I *love* Chicago. A journalism post?"

"No, grant writing. You know, helping to write proposals and applications for people seeking money. From foundations and things."

"Oh. Sounds pretty boring."

"And community reporting *isn't*?"

"No, it's just that... a bird in the hand. I mean, don't do anything hasty. You've been at that place for years..."

"I know. That's the point, Mel. I'm restless."

"Well, restless is restless, but it doesn't pay the rent."

"No, it sure doesn't."

The weather was damp and raw and his Civic took three tries to start. He drove east toward City Avenue but instead of turning north he veered southeast, past the bungalows, trash-strewn lots and half-collapsed fences. A light fog was lifting. He was early and took his time, meandered past Bartram's Gardens, rode Lindbergh Boulevard south. Finally he arrived at a marsh that spread for several miles. Tinicum,

the sign said. It was brown in the low winter light, still curling with
wisps of morning fog and hemmed by tangled rushes.

Pulling off on a shoulder next to the water he sat for a few more
minutes. Jets took off and landed at the airport across the way, above a
wall of reeds. He opened the briefcase beside him, got out and walked
to the passenger side, popped the door open there. Remembering
Jackie's comment about fitting a gun in her own valise, he looked at his
lawyer's special and smiled. Finally he grabbed the black hulk inside
it, stepped away from the Civic toward the marsh just below him and,
in one furious motion, heaved the manuscript skyward, out above
the bronzy water. It sailed past some rushes, hit the water like a log,
floated briefly, then slowly sank out of sight. Pausing, he watched the
marsh devour concentric rings, gazed at a few final fog curls whisking
above the sedges.

He still had plenty of time, time to park his car and ride the little
shuttle, maybe buy some good black coffee before boarding his flight
to O'Hare.

The text of this book was set in Trump Mediaeval, a design formulated by Georg Trump for the C.E. Weber foundry of Stuttgart. A modern re-working of the Garalde Oldstyle types associated with Claude Garamond, it is distinguished in part by its robust serifs and clean legibility.